Summer
at the
Hummingbird
Hotel

by
Daisy James

Cover Design by Berni Stevens

Edited by Laura McCallen

ISBN: 978-1-914304-13-2

To my wonderful friend, Elaine Curtis, with whom I shared an amazing holiday in Corfu.

Contents

Chapter One

Taverna Sofia, Ropa Valley, Corfu
Flower: Frilly Pink Bougainvillea

'A fashion shoot on a private yacht?'

'I know, it sounds really glamorous, doesn't it?'

'It's the stuff dreams are made of.' Rachel sighed as she set a cup of rich, dark, Greek coffee down on the table in front of Abbie, instead of the cappuccino she'd ordered when she'd arrived at Sofia's taverna for her first caffeine fix of the day. 'What I don't understand is why they've opted to celebrate its successful completion at a secluded boutique hotel in the Corfu countryside instead of heading to one of the party resorts for a week of riotous fun and frivolity. That's what I would do.'

'I suppose it must be hard work,' Abbie mused.

'What? Spending your days in pampered luxury, modelling stunning outfits from Pierre Fontaine's brand-new spring/summer collection, with someone to do your hair and makeup every morning, and a treasure trove of shoes, handbags and accessories to choose from? Sounds like heaven to me!'

'I suppose it's all relative. Apparently, they've just completed back-to-back assignments in Antigua, Malta, St Tropez, Sardinia, and now Corfu; that's a lot of travel, and a lot of pressure to get things right. Can you imagine if they get something wrong? It's not as though they can just nip back and do it all again because the model wore mismatched jewellery or the wrong shade of lipstick. I was fortunate enough to work on the contract to supply the floral decorations for one of Pierre's catwalk shows before I left FlowerEssence and I can tell you that he's an absolute perfectionist in every aspect of his business. I totally understand why they all need a break.'

'So, come on, tell me who you've got staying at the hotel this time.' Rachel's green eyes shone with excitement as she slid into the chair next to Abbie, completely ignoring the customers at the table next to the bar who had been calling for their bill for the last ten minutes. 'Anyone famous? Kate Moss? Cara Delevingne? Kelly Brook?'

'Sorry, Rach, you can put your autograph book away.' Abbie saw Rachel twist her lips in disappointment so she added, 'But one of the guests is a fashion model – Allyssa Allen – and there's the shoot's photographer, Josh Anderson, and Katie Edwards, Pierre's assistant fashion designer, whom I've met before, briefly. Although, I don't think she'll remember me because I always dealt with Pippa, the fashion house's event manager, who's flying over from the UK with Pierre on Monday for some sort of big announcement.'

'What kind of big announcement?'

'I have no idea; apparently it's a secret.'

'Intriguing!'

Abbie smiled, but her head was spinning with everything she had to do before her VIP guests descended on the Hummingbird Hotel. Not only did she have to ensure that all four luxuriously appointed guest rooms were squeaky clean and dressed with the most pristine linen and sumptuous toiletries, but she also had to oversee the activity schedule and ensure the meals they had planned met with her guests' approval.

'So who's the fourth guest?'

'Brad Goodman, the guy who handles the business side of the fashion house. He's the one who organised the retreat for everyone as a thank you for the successful completion of the photoshoot as well as a much-deserved long weekend of relaxation and downtime where they can recharge their batteries, and engage in a digital detox. I've spoken to him a few times about what kind of retreat he was interested in, and he was very particular about the itinerary. That's why I'm here, actually. I need to have a quick chat with Felix to see if he's finalised his yoga and meditation sessions. Have you seen him this morning?'

Rachel laughed and pointed over the balcony to the olive grove beyond. Abbie followed the direction of her finger and expelled in involuntary splutter of surprise, followed by a giggle.

'Oh my God!'

There was Felix – resplendent in his finest fluorescent pink Spandex shorts with a turquoise and yellow tie-dye tee-shirt – in the process of executing a perfect Reverse Warrior pose on his yoga mat under the shade of one of the taverna's many lemon trees, completely in the zone and oblivious to the fact that he now had an audience.

'Catch you later, Abbie.'

Abbie watched Rachel saunter serenely towards the table of neglected customers, who had sensibly decided to simply sit back and enjoy the ambience while they waited for their check to arrive, receiving a plate of complimentary baclava for their patience. Rachel might not be the most switched-on waitress in the Ropa Valley – and it was often a lottery whether a diner would receive the exact dish they had chosen from the menu – but better a disappointed diner than a distraught dental patient, which would have been a distinct possibility had Rachel followed the path her family had wanted her to take.

Abbie took a sip of her coffee, grimacing at its bitterness, and switched her contemplation to the mesmerising view spread out before her. It was early, and delicate wisps of mist still hung between the grapevines that meandered up and down the hillside as far as the eye could see. Olive, lemon and orange groves added to the random patchwork of greenery, embroidered with squat, white-washed buildings, the occasional turquoise jewel of a swimming pool, and the neat, slender cypress trees pointing towards the cloudless, translucent sky.

She inhaled a long breath, closing her eyes as she relished the waft of perfume from the white jasmine that clung to the eaves of the taverna, mingled with the fragrance of freshly ground coffee and dusty, baked earth.

The whole scene was truly blissful, and she could completely understand why Brad had chosen to book a long weekend in the Corfu countryside rather than at one of the sprawling hotel complexes in a busy tourist resort – if the group needed a calm and restful break after a stressful photoshoot then this was the perfect place for that.

'Hey, Abbie, great to see you!' Felix called out when he finally noticed her presence.

'You, too, Felix. Do you mind if we have a quick chat?'

'No worries.'

Felix abandoned his Kermit green yoga mat and dropped down into the seat next to Abbie, hooking his ankle over his thigh, and stretching his arms above his head, completely at ease with himself and his surroundings. With his pronounced Australian accent, his messy blonde curls – almost but not quite as voluminous as Abbie's own – and his tanned and toned body, the casual onlooker could have been forgiven for wondering where he'd left his surfboard, which made the fact that Felix had been an investment banker in a former life all the more incongruous. No matter how hard she tried, Abbie just couldn't imagine the man lounging in the bamboo chair in front of her sitting behind a desk in a high-rise Sydney office building, wearing a designer suit and counting up the dollars he'd made that day.

'I just want to make sure you've got everything organised for the retreat this weekend.'

Again, Abbie couldn't prevent the coil of anxiety from snaking through her chest and though she knew Felix had noticed, she pushed on anyway; after what had happened the last time she'd had a group of guests to stay at the Hummingbird Hotel – the first since she'd unexpectedly inherited the hotel from her Aunt Liz – she couldn't risk any complications, especially with such VIP guests about to check in.

'Don't worry. As I've told you, everything's sorted.'

'The yoga and meditation sessions?'

'Check.'

'The water aerobics class?'

'Check.'

'What about the tai chi class?'

Felix's blue eyes sparkled. 'Chill, Abbie, it's all in hand, and I have to tell you how excited I am about doing this. My horoscope this morning assured me that it's going to be a resounding success, and that it'll be the first of many. I had a chat with Nikos last night and I've managed to persuade him to at least think about including a few detoxifying smoothies – blueberry and spinach, avocado and mango, and my personal favourite, kale and apple with a knob of fresh ginger – alongside his more gastronomically mainstream Greek and French dishes.'

Abbie knew that when it came to the culinary side of things she couldn't argue, or even attempt any kind of input. She was the world's worst cook, and, until recently, she'd preferred sitting on the sofa with her best friend and flatmate, Emily, binge-watching cookery shows whilst scooping ice-cream from a tub, to getting her hands dirty in the kitchen. But that was before she'd arrived on Corfu after a mortifying mistake had tossed a grenade into her relationship with her now ex-boyfriend, Dan, which had led to her having to leave her job as a florist at FlowerEssence.

It was early days but, courtesy of Nikos Angelopoulos

– owner of the vineyard and winery that bordered the Hummingbird Hotel, and a Le Cordon Bleu-trained culinary guru with a smile that could melt a frozen heart at fifty paces – she now had at least three recipes in her repertoire that she could complete without setting the place on fire.

The thought of Nikos caused her lips to curl upwards. Not only was he tall, dark and movie-star handsome with tufted mahogany hair, come-to-bed eyes, and a toothpaste-ad-ready smile, he had also taught her a valuable lesson: that her happiness lay in her hands, and hers alone, and that no matter how challenging the circumstances, unless she took a leap of faith and reached for her dreams without fear of the consequences, they would never be fulfilled. So that was exactly what she was doing, but it was also one of the reasons why she was feeling so anxious.

'Sorry, Felix, it's just that… well, after what happened last time, with Savannah…'

'I know, that was hilarious! I mean, how many hotel owners can say they inadvertently turned one of their guests' hair bright pink?' Felix saw the look of horror on Abbie's face and swiftly changed tack. 'You know that wasn't your fault, don't you? It had absolutely nothing to do with the Hummingbird Hotel and everything to do with one of her friends wanting to get her own back on Savannah for something it turned out she didn't even do in the first place. People are crazy! Hey, you look stressed out, not to mention that negative vibe you're projecting. Why don't we do a few breathing exercises to calm your nerves and align your chakras?'

'No, thanks, I'm fine.'

'Stress is futile, Abbie; you must look for sanctuary in

nothing but yourself.'

Abbie rolled her eyes at yet another of Felix's pearls of wisdom, but she knew he meant well. 'I know, I know. But Brad Goodman, the guy who's organised the whole weekend, is very – and I mean very – particular about even the minutest of details being perfect. It's like the four-day retreat is some sort of corporate takeover with every "i" having to be dotted and every "t" having to be crossed, with no room for error or deviation from the written masterplan.'

As she spoke, Abbie could feel her anxiety solidifying into a hard nugget of panic. In the last conversation she'd had with Brad – who spoke to her as though she were the CEO of a Footsie 500 company and not the inexperienced proprietor of a boutique hotel who had, so far, only had four guests to stay – she'd had to concentrate really hard to actually understand what he was trying to say with all of his corporate business-speak and the random acronyms he tossed into their conversations for good measure.

'You'll be fine, Abbie, trust me. Although…'

'Although what?'

'Your horoscope this morning did mention that you would be faced with a few challenges this weekend, mainly of the creature variety.'

'What are you talking about?'

After a month on Corfu, she was used to hearing her daily horoscope courtesy of Felix who, since leaving Australia and spending six months in India, had embraced his spiritual – and astrological – side with a vengeance. However, with everything she had on her plate at the moment, she wasn't sure whether she wanted to hear what the director of celestial fate had in store for her over the next few days. Unfortunately, Felix had other ideas.

'Apparently, you're going to have a tussle with one of our animal friends.'

'Oh God!'

'So you might want to steer clear of hircine—'

'Hey Felix, I thought you had a Pilates class over in Corfu Town in thirty minutes?' said Sofia, the taverna's eponymous owner, as she approached their table with the cappuccino Abbie had ordered half an hour ago, along with one of her favourite breakfast omelettes, the aroma of warm melted cheese causing her stomach to growl in anticipation.

'What is it with people today? All this stress messes with my chi, guys!'

'Tell that to the twelve people who've paid in advance for your weekly services as their very own personal exercise guru.'

Felix rolled his eyes at Sofia, then reluctantly unfurled his six-foot-four frame from his chair, gave Abbie a complicated wave with his thumb and pinky finger extended, and strode from the terrace, only to reappear five minutes later on the back of a yellow-and-black Vespa like a scarecrow riding an over-sized bumble bee as he sped off to his appointment.

Abbie took a sip of her frothy coffee, hoping it would help to douse the anxiety that was now rampaging through her body – so much so that her fingers trembled as she placed the cup onto the saucer.

'Are you okay, Abbie?'

Sofia perched on the seat Felix had vacated, her eyes gentle, her face wreathed in concern. As usual, her short, caramel-coloured bob had been immaculately styled and her wide-sleeved crimson kaftan showcased her chunky gold jewellery to perfection. However, her gaze was fixed immovably on Abbie's, and Abbie knew that no amount of false assurances would satisfy Sofia, so she might as well save time and admit what was worrying her.

'I don't think I can do this.'

There, she'd said it, and she immediately felt better.

From the moment she'd met Sofia, Abbie had experienced an immediate connection. She had tried to put her finger on why that was, and the only explanation she had been able to come up with was that she reminded her of her beloved mum; not only because she wore the same perfume, but because she, too, was generous, caring and supportive of not just Abbie but of the whole community, and they were both keepers of secrets.

'What was I thinking? Why didn't I just sell up when I had the chance? All I ever wanted was to buy a little cottage in the country with roses around the door and a small garden where I could grow a few flowers and live a safe, uneventful life under the radar. How have I ended up running a hotel in Corfu? I'm totally not qualified to do any of this, Sofia; it's going to be a complete disaster!'

'Abbie—'

But Abbie was on a roll, unable to stop even if she wanted to.

'And as though running a hotel and offering retreats wasn't enough of a task, I've gone on to compound the challenge by stupidly offering to take on the management of a vineyard! A vineyard! I might be a qualified botanist, but I've never set foot in a vineyard, or a winery. What on earth was I thinking!'

'You're following your passion, Abbie. There's nothing wrong with that, and anyway, you're not running the vineyard alone – you've very sensibly engaged the services of an expert. Thanos used to run one of the most prestigious vineyards in the south of France, so he'll make sure everything is back on track after the mess Nikos and Dimitris have made over the last two years. I'm sure this year's vintage will be as good, if not better, than when Nikos' father and grandfather were in charge. Let's face it, it couldn't be any worse than the wine Nikos produced last year.'

Abbie allowed herself a brief smile. Sofia was right about that at least; Nikos' first attempt at honouring his father's legacy in the wine-making arena had tasted like paraffin with a soupçon of burnt rubber added for good measure.

'But what if I fail? What if the wine is awful, just like Nikos' was? I've used the last of my inheritance paying Thanos' salary for this year, and if things don't work out, not only will Nikos have to sell the winery and the vineyard, but I'll also be forced to sell the hotel. I don't have a back-up plan; no safety net, no… no family to run to for help.'

Her panic continued to spiral. Only a few weeks ago, selling the hotel was exactly what she had intended to do before scooting back to London to pick up the pieces after her life had imploded. However, to her absolute surprise, she'd ended up turning down a very generous offer from a Greek property investor who'd intended to turn the tiny hotel into an all-inclusive holiday complex, which would have had a devastating impact on the local community and businesses in the area, like Sofia's taverna. She couldn't bear for that to happen, so she had to do everything she could to make the hotel, as well as the vineyard and winery, profitable. If only she could rid herself of the bubbles of doubt that constantly simmered just beneath the surface, ready to burst and erode her already fragile self-confidence.

Sofia smiled and reached out to squeeze her hand. 'You have us, Abbie; Nikos, Panos and me, Felix and Rachel, even Dimitris and Thanos. We're all here for you. If we allow the fear of failure to control us, we would never do anything. Just look at what you've achieved already, with the Angelopoulos Garden. Before you worked your magic over there it was a tangled mess, an eyesore, but now it can give the garden at Mon Repos a run for its money. You can do this.'

Abbie laughed at the outrageously false statement.

'I don't think so.'

But her spirits edged up a notch at Sofia's kind words. She had loved every moment she'd spent returning the Angelopoulos winery's garden to its former glory, relished getting up-close-and-personal with a wide variety of exotic plants and flowers that she would never have come across if she'd pursued her former dream of creating a garden in Devon. Her proposal that she and Nikos should switch roles, with Abbie playing to her strengths by managing the vineyard and winery – and ultimately offering tours and tastings to visitors, along with tours of the garden when it was ready – and Nikos indulging his passion for culinary magnificence at the hotel, had been inspired, even if she did say so herself, and every time she pulled on her gardening gloves, she could feel her emotions calm from gallop to trot.

Sofia was right. She had nothing to go home to, so she might as well try and forget the gaping void that still festered deep inside her soul, ignore the unshiftable feeling that something was missing, and get on with pursuing her newly acquired dreams. She had come to Corfu hoping for an answer to the question that had plagued her for as long as she could remember – why her mum and her Aunt Liz had been estranged her whole life. Sofia had provided that answer and Abbie had been shocked to the core to discover that her aunt had eloped with her mum's fiancé. She was devastated on her mum's behalf, and uncomfortable – feeling as though it was disloyal, even – that she'd found herself in the position of inheriting the Hummingbird Hotel from her aunt. How would her mum have felt about that, if she had still been around?

But she wasn't. No one was.

Abbie had never known her father, her boyfriend had ditched her at the first whiff of the word "commitment", and her best friend was in London learning how to be the best pâtissière outside Paris whilst her family of lawyers thought she was treading the boards as an actress who would shortly be nominated for a BAFTA.

'And…' Sofia hesitated.

'And what?'

'As soon as you feel you can face it, I'm happy to help you sort out your aunt's belongings.'

'Thanks, Sofia.'

Abbie left the taverna a few moments later, her head spinning with random thoughts as she made her way down the dusty driveway towards the Hummingbird Hotel, a smile tugging at her lips when its brilliant-white facade came into view, with its signature blue window frames and shutters, and a frill of pink bougainvillea over the front door. It was picture-postcard-perfect.

'Baaa!'

'What the…!'

Abbie glanced down and performed an involuntary double-take.

'Oh my God!'

Standing in front of her, with an indignant expression on its face, was a black-and-white goat whom she had inadvertently, and rudely, interrupted whilst enjoying a mid-day snack on the grass at the side of the road.

'Sorry, I…'

Hang on, was she actually talking to a goat? Had she gone completely crazy? But there was no time to ponder that question any further because a taxi was bouncing down the driveway towards her.

The Hummingbird Hotel's guests had arrived.

Chapter Two

The Hummingbird Hotel, Ropa Valley, Corfu
Flower: Rosa 'New Arrival'

'Hello, everyone, and welcome to the Hummingbird Hotel. I'm Abbie Coleman, the proprietor, and if there's anything I can do to make your stay more comfortable, then please don't hesitate to ask.'

'Hi, Abbie, Brad Goodman. We spoke on the phone.'

Brad strode forward, his palm outstretched, and as Abbie reached out to shake his hand, she couldn't help but grimace at the unexpected strength of his grip. Despite the heat of the day, Pierre Fontaine's business manager had chosen to wear a charcoal-grey suit – albeit one that was immaculately cut and lined with vibrant, rainbow-patterned silk – along with a crisp white shirt with silver cufflinks, and the largest Rolex watch Abbie had ever seen. With his tortoise-shell glasses, neatly barbered hair, and carefully trimmed beard – not to mention the fact that he smelled like a Parisian lady's boudoir – he looked like he'd just stepped out of a meeting with high-flying executives and not from the deck of his boss's seventy-foot yacht.

'Hello, Brad, it's good to meet you, I—'

'So, do you have a hard copy of the agenda for the weekend? I'd like to run my eyes over the finer details just to make absolutely sure we have all our ducks in order and we're both singing from the same song sheet.'

'Oh, yes, of course.'

Abbie rummaged in the files under the check-in desk, heaving a silent sigh of relief when she located the laminated itinerary that she and Nikos had drawn up to include Felix's yoga and water aerobics sessions, as well as the classes in wine-tasting and the art of chocolate-making Nikos had promised to present.

'Here it is, I think you'll find—'

'Great. I see there's a drinks reception at seven on the veranda, so, if you'll show us to our rooms we'll freshen up and get the ball rolling.'

'Yes, of course, this way please.'

Brad grabbed the handle of his sensible, hard-shell suitcase and marched towards the French doors that Abbie had indicated, which led out to the courtyard around which the hotel's luxuriously appointed guest rooms were situated.

'Just ignore him,' giggled the tall, willowy woman who came to stand next to Abbie. 'He's like that with everyone, you get used to him after a while. I'm Allyssa, by the way, and this is Katie, and that, over there, is Josh.'

Allyssa pointed towards the front of the Hummingbird Hotel where Josh stood on the white marble steps, an old-fashioned Leica camera raised to his eye, taking shots of the impressive view over the Ropa Valley. Abbie couldn't blame him – the interior of Corfu was a landscape photographer's paradise.

Unlike Brad, Josh had embraced the fact that the business side of things was now over and he sported a pair of black designer jeans, and a pristine white tee-shirt with his Ray Bans hooked over the neckline. His tan suede jacket had been carelessly discarded on the ground next to his rucksack, and Abbie suspected that, given half the chance, he would have stayed out there all afternoon recording the many changes in the light until the sun sank towards the horizon and sent streaks of apricot and dusky pink floating across the sky.

'Guys! Come on! Let's park our appreciation of our surroundings until we've settled in, shall we?' Brad called out.

'Yes, Sir!' Katie muttered, performing a mock salute behind Brad's back.

Abbie caught the smirk Allyssa and Katie exchanged, and she couldn't help but smile at the irony of the situation. When he'd booked their weekend retreat, Brad had been very clear about the importance of ensuring their time there was tranquil and relaxing, insisting on there being plenty of downtime so the group could recharge their batteries before the arrival of Pierre on Monday, and yet here he was, ordering the group around like they were undertaking some kind of military manoeuvre or team-building exercise. Thankfully, the group seemed to have chosen to simply ignore him and let his strange corporate-speak wash over them; either that or they'd heard his phraseology so often it no longer registered.

'Coming, Brad!'

Allyssa balanced a cute vanity case on top of her yellow-with-white-daisies wheelie suitcase – one of the largest pieces of luggage Abbie had ever seen, more steamer trunk than suitcase – and made her way towards the French doors. Everything about her screamed "fashion model", from her long glossy hair, the colour of liquid sunshine, to her slender-but-not-*too*-slender stature, and her preference for skyscraper stilettos that ensured she towered over everyone else. Her lipstick-red, ankle-length sundress hugged her body to perfection, and yet her makeup was surprisingly understated – but then, with her impressive bone structure, no cosmetic enhancement was needed.

Abbie followed in the wake of her exotic perfume, conscious that her curls were more bird's nest than Sunday best, and feeling like an elephant in hobnailed boots as she crunched across the gravelled courtyard towards the guestrooms, whilst Allyssa glided down the steps like an elegant gazelle.

'Okay, here are your keys.' She handed an old-fashioned brass key attached to an enamelled hummingbird keyring to each of them. 'All the rooms are identical and are accessed from the colonnade over there to your left. I'll see you on the veranda at the rear of the hotel at seven o'clock, and if you need any additional linen or toiletries, please just give me a call and I'll bring them straight over.'

'Thanks, Abbie, I'm starting to feel relaxed already,' said Katie, the last person to accept her key. 'I think I'm going to like it here.'

'I hope so.'

Abbie smiled at Katie, who was the complete opposite to Allyssa; petite, curvy, with wavy, dark-brown hair and intelligent eyes that missed nothing. Unlike the eye-poppingly bold colours Allyssa evidently preferred, Katie's thigh-skimming sundress was a muted peppermint shade, paired with sensible flat sandals and huge, white-framed sunglasses. However, her understated sartorial choices did not extend to her choice of handbag, which was a rich turquoise leather with gold appliqué shells arranged in the shape of a fish and a large seahorse-shaped tassel dangling from the zip.

'Wow, I love your bag,' Abbie said.

'Thanks, it's actually one of mine.'

'You designed that yourself?'

'Yes, and I stitched it by hand. It's one of my passions.' Katie's gaze swept over Abbie's face. 'Hey, have we met before?'

'Yes, we have. I used to work for *FlowerEssence*; my ex, Dan Heyworth, and I supplied the floral decorations and horticultural sculptures for Pierre Fontaine's last catwalk show at the Victorian baths. It was one of the highlights of my life!'

'Ah, I remember now. You're Pippa's friend.'

'Yes, that's me.'

'Those flower arrangements you delivered were *so* original – you're super-talented! And, didn't you win a couple of prestigious awards, too?'

'Oh, I—'

'So how come you're running a hotel in Corfu?'

Abbie felt the muscles in her stomach tighten. She really didn't want to go there, didn't want to relive the nightmare that had taken place at the restaurant at the top of the Walkie Talkie building, didn't want to remember the look of horror on Dan's face when he realised for the first time that – after over a year together – she had wanted their relationship to progress to the next stage. And she certainly didn't want to think about the fact that a mere twelve hours later he had fired her from a job she loved – by text.

'It's a bit of a long story.'

'Say no more; I get it. Okay, I'd better hop in the shower and shimmy into something a little more glamorous. Don't want to mess with Brad's carefully crafted schedule, do we?'

Katie pulled a face and Abbie saw something she couldn't quite put her finger on glisten in her eyes as she hitched her handbag over her shoulder and dragged her Minnie Mouse suitcase – complete with ears and tail – to the room at the far end of the colonnade and disappeared through the door, leaving a faint whiff of sweet flowery perfume lingering in the air behind her.

Abbie allowed herself a sigh of relief that her guests were now safely checked in, then dashed back across the courtyard, past the fountain in the shape of a hummingbird – her aunt's favourite member of the avian fraternity and a reminder of her previous life in California's Napa Valley – and into the hotel's surprisingly hi-tech kitchen, her heart performing a summersault of pleasure at the sight that met her there.

'Hi, Nikos!'

'Hey, Abbie. Was that our guests arriving?'

'Yes, they're all checked in and settling into their

rooms. How're the canapés coming along? Need any help?'

Nikos' dark eyes sparkled and his lips twisted in amusement at her offer.

'Unless you want our esteemed guests' first taste of authentic Greek cuisine to be caramelised halloumi, charred *dolmades*, and burnt *kolokithopita*, I think we should stick to our agreement to play to our strengths, don't you?'

Abbie laughed. 'Absolutely. I'll sort out the cocktails.'

Whilst Nikos put the final touches to the main course of the evening meal that he'd created for their guests from an old family recipe, Abbie gathered the bottles of spirits – gin, vodka, rum, ouzo – prepared the fruit juices – lemon, mango, pomegranate, cranberry, cucumber – and sorted out the red and white wine, which had been produced from grapes grown on the island – just not at the Angelopoulos vineyard. She suspected that Brad and his friends were aficionados of the best vintages available and whilst she had dreams of the Angelopoulos name joining that fêted club at some point in the future, they weren't there yet.

As they fell into a choreographed routine of chopping, slicing, mixing and shaking, Abbie couldn't help sneaking a surreptitious glance at Nikos, so handsome in his white chef's jacket, his espresso-dark hair gelled into tufts, his muscular forearms flexing as he sliced a block of feta cheese into miniature cubes and sprinkled them theatrically on the top of a Greek salad, the waft of his lemony cologne sending tingles of attraction zinging through her veins.

No one could have been more surprised than she was that their initial irritation with each other, and their opposing dreams for their respective futures, could have morphed into a firm friendship and a fledgling business partnership, not to mention the delicious kisses they'd shared amongst the grapevines when she'd decided to stay on in Corfu to run the Hummingbird Hotel and to help Nikos save his family's vineyard and winery from bankruptcy.

Now here she was, standing by his side in a kitchen, something she would have baulked at only a couple of months ago when everything she touched had turned to cinders. Emily had banned her from even switching on the oven after their building had been evacuated only a few weeks after she'd moved in because she'd tried to make toast using the grill when she couldn't work out how to use the toaster. It was early days, but with Nikos as her tutor, she was expanding her repertoire from scorched coffee to a passable baklava.

But Nikos had done more than show her that cooking could be, if not enjoyable, at least edible. He was the reason she'd found the confidence to take a step towards fulfilling a long-held dream – creating her own garden and opening it to the public, just as her mum had done in Devon before she died. The project was already taking shape, and she hoped that, when it was finished, her mum would be proud of what she had achieved. Now all she had to do was learn everything there was to know about viticulture and oenology from Thanos. Then she could relax, safe in the knowledge that she had accomplished what she had promised Nikos she would do whilst he handled the catering side of the hotel's business – something he could do with his eyes closed, but which clearly brought him a great deal of joy, too.

'Okay, try this.'

Nikos held out a spoon of garlicky tomato sauce for

her to try. She leaned forward, closing her eyes and allowing the bouquet of flavours to crash across her tongue – rich, thick, flavourful with a zingy acidic kick.

'*Nóstimo*!'

To Abbie's surprise, when she opened her eyes, Nikos had taken a step closer, his mouth inches from hers, his warm breath tickling her cheek and sending spasms of desire shooting out to her extremities. Goosebumps rippled across her forearms and every nerve in her body screamed "kiss me!".

Seconds later that was exactly what he did; his lips soft and gentle on hers as he snaked his arm around her waist and pulled her close, so close she could feel his heart beating through his chef's whites, his cologne sending her senses into overdrive. When they finally pulled apart, Abbie felt a little breathless, her cheeks glowing from the desire that whipped through her veins, delighted at her good fortune to be standing there, alongside Nikos, as they prepared to wow their guests with a sumptuous dinner and amazing cocktails.

'Why don't you go and grab a shower while I finish up here?'

'Thanks, I will, and thank you for everything you've done this afternoon.'

'No thanks required; this is what I love to do. Cooking is my passion, *and* because of you I'm getting to fulfil one of my dreams – to be the head chef in my own restaurant!'

'Well, it's hardly a restaurant, and I'm not sure about the calibre of your sous chef!'

'Burnt baklava is the new baked Alaska!'

Abbie laughed as she removed her apron – cream linen embroidered with a jaunty blue-and-green hummingbird motif, which her aunt had handed out to guests who took part in one of the hotel's week-long cookery retreats – and hung it carefully on the hook by the door.

She rushed up the stairs to her room and jumped in the shower, enjoying the feel of the cool water washing away the cares and the tensions of the day. She couldn't believe how much her life had changed over the last six weeks; from escaping the heartbreak of rejection, and being forced to leave a job she had loved, to the surprise inheritance of a boutique hotel in Corfu. Most astonishingly of all, though, was that instead of putting the place on the market and high-tailing it back to London, she had actually found the courage to take a leap of faith and open the Hummingbird Hotel's doors to guests, and the person she had to thank for its success – well, sort-of success – was Nikos Angelopoulos.

After making a valiant attempt to smooth down her wayward curls with a dollop of coconut oil, she selected the most glamorous dress in her sparse closet – a yellow-and-white sundress she'd borrowed from Emily – added a slick of mascara and nude lip gloss, and a pair of pearl earrings, and she was ready to entertain her guests.

Chapter Three

The Veranda at the Hummingbird Hotel
Flower: Goat's Rue

'Hey, Abbie, you look fabulous!' Allyssa smiled as she stepped onto the veranda in an outfit fit for the red carpet at the Oscars – a bronze, pleated silk column with gold chain belt, matching gladiator sandals, and huge gold disc earrings – her hair tumbling over one shoulder in a neat wave, and shimmering metallic eye makeup with lashings of thick mascara. She looked like an Egyptian princess.

'Thanks, Allyssa, so do you. Can I get you a cocktail?'

'Oh, yes please. Could I have a Cosmopolitan?'

'Of course.'

'And can I get a beer, please? I'm not a huge fan of cocktails,' said Josh, appearing at Allyssa's side, his hair neatly coiffed, his jawline newly shaved. He smelled of a mixture of crushed rosemary and charred wood shavings, an aroma Abbie wasn't sure she liked. Inevitably, he'd brought his faithful Leica with him and was already leaning over the balcony, taking snaps of the mini-vineyard her aunt had planted a decade earlier to remind her of her late husband, Greg, and what she'd left behind in California.

'Coming right up.'

Abbie returned to the kitchen where Nikos had changed out of his chef's jacket and into a pale pink linen shirt that accentuated his Mediterranean features perfectly, and a pair of buttock-hugging black jeans. Her heart gave another delicious jolt of attraction when his eyes met hers with a smile.

'Want me to sort out the beers?'

'Yes, please, and the music, if you don't mind?'

To the soft strains of bouzouki music, along with the ever-present concerto of the cicadas, she returned to the veranda where Katie had now joined Allyssa and Josh, sporting a pair of smart white shorts, a diaphanous, emerald-green blouse, and a cute cream leather evening bag embroidered with peacock feathers – clearly another of her own designs. Her sweet, girly perfume mingled with Allyssa's more sophisticated Miss Dior and Josh's strange woody concoction to create a blend that could have given a French perfumery a run for its money.

'Where's Brad? He's usually the first to arrive when there's drinks on offer.'

'It's not quite seven o'clock yet.' Katie smirked, glancing at her slender silver watch. 'Don't forget, punctuality is next to godliness in Brad's business and social etiquette manual!'

Again, Abbie noticed a slight twist of the lips as Katie spoke about Brad and her curiosity was piqued.

Something was clearly not quite right between the two of them and she wondered what was going on.

'You know, when we left the marina in Corfu Town earlier, I actually saw him with a camera,' Josh mused, stroking his precious Leica like it was a beloved pet. 'I wouldn't have put Brad down as the creative type; it's usually all facts and figures and spreadsheets with him. I wonder what he—'

'Evening, everybody,' boomed the man himself as he strode confidently onto the veranda, his palm outstretched towards Nikos. 'Brad Goodman, Pierre Fontaine's business manager, you must be Nikos Angelopoulos. It's a pleasure to meet you.'

Abbie was delighted to see the surprise on Nikos' face when he, too, was subjected to one of Brad's vice-like handshakes, but, unlike Abbie, he rallied well.

'Good to meet you too, Brad. Welcome to Corfu.'

Abbie took in Brad's carefully executed designer stubble, his immaculately ironed Paul Smith shirt, smart navy-blue shorts, polished Gucci loafers, and the gold Rolex that hung so ostentatiously from his wrist. She would have had no trouble picking him out as the corporate guy at the fashion house, even *before* he opened his mouth.

'Can I get you a cocktail, Brad, or would you prefer a beer or a glass of wine?'

'A beer would be great, thanks.'

Abbie handed a cold beer to Brad, and Nikos placed a laden platter of canapés onto the huge wooden table which, in daytime, provided the most panoramic view of the whole of the Ropa Valley, but now that the sun had set was washed with a soft amber glow from the storm lanterns dotted along the veranda and the garlands of fairy lights twisted around the branches of the olive and lemon trees beyond.

'By the way, Allyssa, I've spoken to Pierre and he's confirmed that he and Pippa will be flying in on Monday around midday. Our publicity photoshoot will take place at two p.m. precisely, in the gardens of the Corfu Palace Hotel, after which Pierre's organised an evening of elegant and sophisticated celebration, so all of us need to be ready to leave by eleven o'clock at the latest on Monday morning.'

'I still don't understand why I have to be involved,' said Katie, sipping at her Screwdriver, her forehead creased in irritation. 'I really wanted to fly home today – I haven't seen my friends for six weeks – and Pierre knows that I'm more of a behind-the-camera kind of a girl.'

'Yes, me too,' laughed Josh, waving his camera in the air as evidence. 'Why does Pierre want all four of us—'

'And Pippa,' Allyssa added.

'—and Pippa, to be involved in the photoshoot?'

'It's for the website, and the blog,' said Brad. 'We're planning to do a monthly article on the separate facets of the business to celebrate everyone who's been involved in bringing this season's collection to life – the designers, the models, the photographers, the runway organisers, the marketing guru. The fashion house is more than just a place of work, or a mere building where beautiful clothes are created, we're a family, and Pierre wants to recognise that. I promise you that it will be a much more casual affair than the shoots of the last six weeks.'

'But I still don't—'

'Don't worry, Katie, I'll give you a few tips,' Allyssa offered, as she accepted another cocktail from Abbie with a smile.

Katie glanced at Josh for support, but he simply shrugged his shoulders. 'I'm actually looking forward to it. It'll be interesting, not to mention educational, to see how it feels to be on the "other side" for a change. You know, I did offer to do the shoot for Pierre but he insisted that he had a photographer all lined up. I don't know whether to be upset or grateful.'

'Be grateful; it's going to be lots of fun,' said Allyssa. 'But I agree with Katie, I don't see why we couldn't have flown home today, then come back with Pierre and Pippa on Monday morning, that way I could have spent some quality time with Xavier, and—'

'Okay, everyone, it's seven o'clock on the nose,' said Brad, ignoring Allyssa's gripe, and reaching for another bottle of beer from the bucket of ice Nikos had brought out onto the veranda. 'Shall we eat?'

'Oh, yes, of course,' said Abbie, flustered after hearing that neither Katie nor Allyssa actually wanted to be there at the Hummingbird Hotel that weekend, and that Brad, in effect, had bribed them with the all-expenses paid retreat so that they would stay on the island until the photoshoot on Monday afternoon. She suspected that he knew that if he allowed them to fly home, Allyssa, at least, might not come back, and that would throw his best laid plans into disarray and he couldn't, and wouldn't, allow that to happen. She was now more determined than ever to deliver a relaxing, yet fun-packed and enjoyable weekend, so that they didn't regret their decision to stay, even though they'd had no choice.

'Please, everyone, take a seat at the table, Nikos and I will bring out the food.'

The meal was delicious; after a selection of mouth-watering appetisers, the home-made moussaka and Greek salad disappeared in a flash, to much acclaim. The wine flowed, the atmosphere was convivial, and the conversation encompassed a myriad of subjects until the coffee and brandy was served and talk turned to the Pierre Fontaine Fashion House and the incident that had jettisoned the business into the upper echelons of the fashion industry the previous year.

'Like I keep telling you, there's no such thing as bad publicity; that event was a game-changer for us.'

'But not for Lexie!' snapped Katie, glaring at Brad.

'Pierre offered her her job back – several times.'

'That's not the point! He fired her – in front of everyone – for something that wasn't her fault. If he'd taken the time to at least investigate what had happened, then he would have realised that it was the lighting technician who switched that bucket of confetti for ice-cold water and destroyed his *pièce de résistance* wedding gown and floral headdress, not Lexie. Pippa told me how devastated and mortified she was.'

'But no one could have predicted the images would go viral! You can't *pay* for that kind of advertising and brand exposure.'

'I still think—'

'Okay, guys, I think we should make a move,' Allyssa interrupted, clearly keen to avoid a full-blown argument between Brad and Katie so early in the proceedings. 'Abbie, remind me what's on the agenda tomorrow.'

'Our very own fitness guru, Felix Morgan, will be leading a yoga class at ten o'clock over on the pool terrace, and then in the afternoon Nikos is presenting his chocolate-making course.'

'Mmm, I'm really looking forward to that,' said Katie. 'I'm a confirmed chocoholic! Not looking forward to the yoga session so much, though. I might sit that one out.'

'No rain checks!' Brad snapped, pouring himself another brandy before lighting a big, fat cigar, the smoke curling into the air like a silvery corkscrew. 'Everyone will be on the terrace at ten a.m. sharp, or they'll have me to answer to.'

Katie was about to launch into another argument, but caught Josh's eye and thought better of it, so instead she pushed herself out of her chair and turned to face Allyssa.

'Come on, Allyssa, I'll walk you back to your room.'

Allyssa giggled, her cheeks rosy from the meal – although Abbie couldn't help but notice that she'd had little more than a few slices of cucumber and tomatoes with a splodge of tzatziki which she'd washed down with more than her fair share of cocktails. When she stood up, she swayed dangerously to her left, forcing Josh to jump from his seat and grab her elbow, and with Katie taking the other, they managed to guide her from the veranda towards the courtyard and their guest rooms.

'Goodnight!' Abbie said.

'*Kalinychta*!' Nikos added.

'Ten a.m. sharp, guys!' Brad called after them.

'Are you going to join them?' asked Abbie, watching Brad produce a perfect smoke ring.

'I never sleep longer than five hours a night – and I *never* partake in the Mediterranean habit of a siesta. Snooze and you lose, is my motto.'

'I'll make a fresh cafetière, then.'

Abbie left Brad and Nikos discussing a mutual friend, Jean-Jacques Gasnier, who Nikos had worked with at a Michelin-starred restaurant in Paris, and went to the kitchen to finish wiping down the counters and prepare the coffee. When she returned to the veranda, to her surprise, she saw that Nikos was alone, relaxing in his chair as he finished the last of his red wine whilst being serenaded by the ubiquitous chirp of the cicadas. She sank down onto the seat next to him, kicked off her shoes, and smiled.

'I think that went quite well, don't—'

'Arrr… gh! Arrr…gh! Arrr…gh!'

Abbie exchanged a glance of alarm with Nikos and together they sprinted from the veranda to the courtyard where they found Brad standing next to the fountain, staring at the door to his guest room, an expression of supreme panic on his face.

'What's wrong? What's happened?' asked Abbie.

'There's a… there's a…'

'Brad? What are you shouting about?' said Josh, appearing at his guest room door in just a pair of shorts, and yet with his beloved camera still in his hand, as though it would protect him from a multitude of potential evils.

'In there! In there!' Brad pointed to his room.

Nikos took charge and strode into Brad's guest room.

'What's going on?' said Allyssa, emerging onto the colonnade in an elegant peach peignoir, her hair twisted into huge sponge rollers and a silk eye-mask dangling around her neck. 'Was that you screaming, Brad?'

'I wasn't screaming, I was exclaiming in shock,' Brad mumbled, his cheeks colouring at his out-of-character reaction.

'What was a shock?' asked Katie, joining the furore.

'This!' Nikos laughed.

Everyone turned to look at Nikos who had emerged from Brad's room holding onto the goat that Abbie had bumped into on the driveway earlier that day, who now, instead of grass, was munching on a pair of Brad's paisley boxer shorts.

'Oh my God!' Allyssa and Katie giggled in unison.

Abbie groaned; she assumed Brad must have left his patio door open and the goat had spotted what she had thought was a tasty treat and decided to explore. She watched in mortification as Brad snatched his underwear from the disgruntled animal, and dashed back into his room, returning moments later, his jaw loose in disbelief, as he stared at the jacket he'd been wearing when he arrived at the hotel, its rainbow-coloured lining now shredded into pieces.

Chapter Four

The Swimming Pool at the Hummingbird Hotel
Flower: Red Geraniums

The next morning, Abbie sat on the balcony overlooking the valley as the sun peeked its head above the horizon, but as spectacular as the view was, it couldn't calm her rampaging thoughts. While she had apologised profusely to Brad for the "goat fiasco", *and* offered to pay for a replacement jacket – which she suspected would probably cost more than the profit she made on the whole weekend retreat – what had worried her more was that Brad had been adamant that he'd not left the patio doors in his guest room open.

Which could only mean one thing.

Someone else must have opened them because, whilst she didn't know much about Greek goats – or any other nationality of goats, for that matter – she *did* know that they couldn't open doors. Oh God, why couldn't things go according to plan for once? She didn't have much experience as the owner of a boutique hotel, but she could hazard a guess that in the whole ten years her Aunt Liz had lived at the Hummingbird Hotel she had never had to deal with an attack of goats with a penchant for men's underwear.

What she needed to do now was speak to Josh, who had taken an inordinate amount of pleasure in photographing the incident for posterity, and ask him, no, plead with him, not to post any of the images on social media. Otherwise she suspected her stay in Corfu would be over before it had begun, which in turn would mean so was her career as a viticulturist and would-be wine maker.

Admittedly, the way she felt at the moment, there was something to be said for tossing her belongings into a suitcase and slinking off back to London, or Devon, where life would be simpler and she wouldn't have to continue performing the role of naïve hotel proprietor in the Greek version of *Fawlty Towers*, but she couldn't bear the thought of letting down Nikos, or Sofia, or Felix; all of whom held great hopes that the success of the hotel would boost the local economy, as well as their respective businesses.

And, if she was right and someone *had* targeted Brad, it could only be one of three people. It wasn't beyond the realms of possibility that he had irritated one of them so much over the last six weeks that they'd decided, now that the business side of the shoot was over, it was the ideal opportunity to get their own back on him.

Top of her list of suspects had to be Katie. She'd heard their snippy exchanges, seen the glances and glares Katie had cast in his direction when she thought he wasn't looking; there was clearly something going on between them, and while she really would have liked to brush the whole incident under the carpet and forget it had ever happened, she knew she couldn't do that.

So, instead of spending a few pleasant hours working in the Angelopoulos Garden, she would have to find a moment – preferably *after* the yoga session, because she had no intention of repeating that sojourn of torture – to talk to Katie, and to ask her if she knew anything about the goat incident. Then she, and Nikos, could get on with the business of restoring the Hummingbird Hotel's reputation for providing a restful refuge, a place where guests could come for a little peace and serenity.

'Hey, Abbie,' called Felix, breaking into Abbie's reverie. 'Don't suppose there's any chance of one of those coffees before I start the yoga class? And maybe you can fill me in on the "animal antics" gossip from last night?'

'Oh God, how did you know about that? And don't tell me it was written in the stars!'

'The grapevine is alive and well in Ropa Valley.' Felix laughed as he dropped into the bamboo chair opposite Abbie, running his fingers through his tousled curls so that they stood on end like a blonde halo.

'Who told you?'

'Nikos did when he called by the taverna first thing this morning on his way over to Corfu Town to collect the ingredients for this afternoon's chocolate-making session. And guess what? He said I could join in if I liked – which I do.'

Felix's eyes sparkled with boyish excitement and Abbie's heart softened as she popped into the kitchen to make his coffee. Like her, Felix was an escapee from heartbreak, having unfathomably been left standing at the altar by his wife-to-be who had decided – mistakenly, as it had turned out – that life would be better with his best friend. Carlie had seen the error of her ways, and only a few weeks ago had contacted Felix to suggest that they try again, but, after careful consideration, Felix had gently rejected her proposal, not wanting to return to a life ruled by numbers and spreadsheets instead of astrological predictions.

'One Americano.'

Abbie placed the mug of coffee on the table in front of Felix and watched as he took a sip, smacking his lips with delight. She also took in his outfit for the first time.

'Oh my God, Felix!'

'What?'

She stared at the turquoise leopard-print cycling shorts that clung to the contours of his thighs like a second skin, which he'd paired with a baggy orange tee-shirt with cut-off sleeves that ensured his impressive biceps were on show in all of their glory. Before she had the chance to ask whether what he was wearing was standard yoga attire, Felix had steered the conversation onto his favourite subject.

'So, I read your horoscope this morning.'

'Do I want to know?'

'We can't change our destiny, Abbie.'

She rolled her eyes at him. 'Of *course* we can, Felix.'

But he chose to ignore her comment and instead launched into the details of what the director of fate had in store for her that day, which she hoped would include a quick chat with Katie, a swift admission of guilt, and a promise that there would be no more bizarre shenanigans to disrupt the smooth running of the Hummingbird Hotel's first wellbeing retreat. Of course, it wasn't anything like that.

'Today, Gemini's destiny is governed by Uranus, the planet of unpredictability, but what is clear is that you will enjoy a smooth, dark, and tastebud-tingling experience that ends in a big, celebratory splash.'

She couldn't help but laugh. 'We're doing a chocolate-making course this afternoon! Come on, let's get the show on the road.'

Abbie cringed; that was just the sort of thing that Brad would say. Maybe he was rubbing off on her; although, the way things were going, she could do a lot worse than engage a few of his techniques to ensure the Hummingbird Hotel remained a luxury boutique hotel rather than a comedy club where farmyard animals were allowed to roam free and snack on unsuspecting guests' clothing.

'Hey, Abbie, any chance of a coffee?' Katie asked as she joined them on the balcony.

'Of course, espresso, cappuccino, latte, or Americano?'

'Double espresso, please,' said Katie, rubbing her temples with her fingertips.

'Hangover?' asked Felix.

'What was your first clue?' Katie grinned and Abbie was relieved to see she had decided to attend Felix's yoga session after all, and had dressed for the part in a pair of stretchy black leggings and a pretty floral tee-shirt with ruffles around the sleeves, her hair tied into a high ponytail.

'Then allow me to assist.'

Felix jumped from his chair and jogged into the kitchen; Abbie was surprised he couldn't feel their gaze scorching into his back, as she and Katie took a few moments to appreciate his impressive physique – enhanced by the figure-hugging properties of Lycra – from the rear.

'Wow, loving those cycling shorts!' Katie giggled. 'I'm pleased I changed my mind about having a lie-in. I'm sure an hour or so of gentle exercise will replenish the creative coffers just as much as catching up on six weeks' worth of lost sleep.'

'Are you working on a new handbag design at the moment?'

'I am.' Katie's eyes sparkled as the conversation moved on to something that was clearly close to her heart. 'I've got so many ideas bouncing around my brain, not just for the designs but for the materials and the accessories. I'm determined to use only natural or recycled products, like bamboo, raffia, wool and cork, even car seat belts and fabric made from plastic bottles. I don't just want them to be sustainable and ecologically friendly, but gorgeous and practical, too. And it won't only be handbags and shoulder bags, but also clutch bags and crossbody bags, backpacks and travel bags, wallets and purses. I love every minute I get to spend on every aspect of the venture – in my own time, of course – but I've been so busy with everything that's going on with photoshoot that I've had to put what Brad calls my "pet project" on the back burner.'

A cloud floated across Katie's expression, and Abbie remembered her intention to use whatever opportunity she got to have a chat with her about the goat incident, and this was the perfect time. Anxiety swirled, and her self-confidence demons taunted her, but she inhaled a deep breath.

'Katie, I—'

'Okay, try this!' Felix said, handing Katie a glass of what Abbie could only describe as green sludge. She was horrified when he dashed back to the kitchen to bring her one, too.

'Erm, what exactly is it?' Katie asked hesitantly.

'Kale, avocado, and watercress, with a handful of pineapple chunks from the freezer and a dash of lime juice – from a lime I've picked fresh from the tree over there – and a few cashew nuts for a protein boost! It's bursting with vitamin C and will chase away your hangover in a flash! What are you waiting for?'

Abbie exchanged a glance with Katie, struggling to keep the look of disgust from her face, but she didn't want to offend Felix, especially before he delivered his yoga class to her guests – for which he was charging only half of his usual fee – so she braced herself and took a sip. Fortunately, Katie wasn't so squeamish; she held her nose and downed the smoothie in one.

'Delicious!'

Felix beamed like a Cheshire Cat. 'I have lots of other recipes; all of them vegan, all of them healthy, nutritious and lip-smackingly scrumptious. I could do you a spinach, mint and blueberry one – that one livens up the tastebuds after a night of overindulgence. I also do a mean twist on the—'

'Hey, what are you all doing hanging out here?' called Josh, appearing on the veranda in a pair of football shorts and the white cotton tee-shirt he'd arrived in the previous day, his honey-blonde hair neatly combed into a quiff. His arrival was accompanied by a waft of his strange cologne and Abbie wrinkled her nose – her olfactory senses were certainly being assaulted this morning! 'It's nine fifty-two. You have eight minutes to get over to the pool terrace if you don't want to incur the wrath of our esteemed retreat warrior!'

Katie rolled her eyes, but she immediately pushed herself up from her seat to do as she was bid.

'Hey, Felix, I actually feel amazing! Thank you.'

'No worries.'

Felix grabbed his over-sized sports bag and lolloped off towards the terrace, allowing Abbie the opportunity to pour her smoothie into one of the blue ceramic plant pots at the end of the veranda.

'See you later. Have fun,' she called after them.

Katie and Josh paused in their path and spun round to face her in comedic unison.

'Oh, no, no, no. You're not getting away with that.' Katie strode towards Abbie, linked her arm through hers and started to guide her in Felix's wake. Josh joined in by taking the other arm and she was all-but frogmarched through the courtyard to the swimming pool terrace. 'If I have to partake in a yoga class, then so do you.'

'But I have to service the rooms, and organise lunch, and—'

'Call it customer relations,' said Josh, grabbing his camera to take a photograph of her face. 'And remember what Brad said last night? No rain checks!'

Abbie wanted to continue to argue her case, vociferously. She had never been a fan of exercise, even more so in a group setting, preferring to join Emily on the sofa to watch more willing enthusiasts being put through their paces on-line or on YouTube – one of

Emily's favourite past-times. She could recite the moves *theoretically* but when it came to performing them in real life, she baulked. Felix had already dragged her into joining one yoga session and she had ended up in a breathless, sweaty mess, and had vowed never to repeat the traumatic event ever again if she could help it.

However, on the flip side, she also had no wish to upset Brad any more than he already was.

'Okay, but I need to go and get changed.'

She dashed up the stairs to her room, pulled on an old tee-shirt and leggings, slipped her feet into a pair of blue canvas trainers, then headed to the swimming pool where Felix had already set up his luminous green yoga mats in a circle and was running through a warm-up routine with his four students. She scooted onto the mat next to Allyssa, cringing when she realised why Katie had decided to leave that one free – Allyssa looked like she was born to model yoga attire to its maximum effect, sporting a gorgeous pair of pale pink yoga leggings and a matching cropped vest that showed off her trim and toned body to perfection.

Brad, to Abbie's surprise, also looked at ease on his yoga mat, in a pair of heather-grey yoga shorts and complementary tee-shirt. Without his thick, tortoise-shell glasses and ostentatious Rolex, he looked less corporate, more normal. Until, of course, he opened his mouth.

'Punctuality is a skill worth pursuing if you hope to run a successful enterprise here.'

'It's better to be late than to arrive unprepared,' said Felix, causing Brad to gape in surprise. 'Okay, guys, that's the warm-up done. Shall we get started?'

'Yes!' Allyssa and Brad chorused, whilst Katie exchanged

a grimace with Abbie, causing her to giggle, which she disguised by dropping down onto her mat and trying to force her body into a mediocre attempt at a Crescent Lunge pose.

'The Crescent Lunge pose is perfect to counteract the negative effects of a sedentary lifestyle; it lengthens and tones the arms, legs, hips and feet, and strengthens the muscles in the bottom. Keep that back leg straight, and your front foot flat on your mat between your hands. Okay, good, you're all doing really well, so let's move on to one of my favourites.' Abbie thought she saw a glint of mischief in Felix's eyes and groaned. 'This one's called the *Pawanmuktasana* pose, or, to give it another name, the wind-relieving pose.'

'I need this after that smoothie I downed earlier!' Katie whispered to Abbie.

'So, lie on your back, tuck your knees into your chest, like this, inhale a long, slow, measured breath, exhale a long, slow, measured breath, holding your knees with your hands. Now, slowly lower and straighten your right leg whilst holding your left, hold, inhale a long, slow, measured breath, exhale a long slow measured breath, and return. Now the left leg.'

As the class continued over the next hour, Abbie could feel perspiration trickling down her temples and between her breasts, her face glowing with heat, her muscles screaming their objection to the unfamiliar attempt at exercise so early in the morning. She glanced at Katie and saw she also sported a bright red face, her tee-shirt drenched in perspiration as she concentrated on following Felix's instructions to the letter – or it could just have been that she was trying hard not to release the excess of wind as promised. In contrast, Allyssa, and Brad, were completely in the zone, performing perfect poses and barely breaking a sweat as they carried out the routines.

'Great job, guys. Let's finish with the *Shavasana* pose, shall we? It's an important one for relieving anxiety and promoting muscle relaxation which, after all, is why we're all here. So, lie on your back and let all your muscles relax. Shut out all extraneous distractions, and clear your mind by focussing only on your breathing.'

Abbie thought this might be her favourite yoga pose. After a few seconds, she found herself relaxing, her anxieties of the last day or so seeping from her body to be replaced by a feeling of calm. The cicadas continued with their never-ending song, the silvery leaves of the olive tree rustled in the light breeze, and the fragrance from the red and white geraniums dotted around the terrace – with a top-note of chlorine from the swimming pool – soothed her senses as she breathed deeply, as Felix had instructed.

'Okay, guys, that's it for this session. Tomorrow we'll do a water aerobics class.'

'Yay! I love water aerobics,' Allyssa declared, leaping up from her mat as fresh as a daisy. 'Thanks, Felix, that was amazing. I feel totally energised and ready to tackle anything.'

'Speak for yourself,' Katie muttered, wiping her face with one of the Hummingbird Hotel towels Abbie had handed out to everyone. 'I'm going for a shower and a lie-down.'

'Me too!' said Josh, following in Katie's wake.

'What time's lunch?' asked Allyssa, a question Abbie had never thought she'd hear coming from Allyssa's lips.

'One o'clock!' Brad barked before Abbie could reply. 'On

the veranda; it's on your itinerary.'

However, nothing could spoil Allyssa's serene mood. She simply smiled at Brad and floated off towards her guest room, her pony tail swinging in her wake like a pendulum.

'Is everything in hand for the chocolate-making session?' asked Brad.

'Yes, Nikos will be here at three o'clock.'

'Great. If you'll excuse me, I have a few emails to catch up on.'

Abbie noticed that Brad was unable to meet her eyes and groaned inwardly; he was clearly still annoyed about the previous evening's incident. She didn't blame him; she would be upset too if a Greek goat had munched on her favourite designer jacket. She watched him disappear through the stone archway that led from the swimming pool terrace to the courtyard and the guestrooms beyond, then heaved a sigh of relief that, thankfully, the first of the wellbeing sessions had gone off without a hitch.

Chapter Five

The Kitchen at the Hummingbird Hotel
Flower: Pink Hibiscus

After waving off Felix with a promise to save him a space at Nikos' chocolate-making session, Abbie spent the next two hours sweeping the pathways, removing weeds and dry leaves, and wiping down the sunbeds and the tables and chairs around the pool. When she saw Josh appear with his beach towel under his arm and showing off a pair of voluminous purple trunks, she nipped over to service his guest room, changing the linens and replenishing the bathroom toiletries, allowing herself a satisfied smile as the aroma of fresh lemons invaded her nostrils.

A few moments later, she heard Katie and Allyssa follow suit and quickly made up their rooms, too, adding vases of fresh flowers she'd sourced from the garden. She'd thoroughly enjoyed the task of fashioning a fragrant bouquet from whatever was to hand, just as she'd done when she worked at *FlowerEssence*. A nip of regret invaded her chest; whilst she loved growing flowers, shrubs and plants, she had also adored designing original and quirky arrangements using a myriad of horticultural products, and she missed being able to do that – although she didn't miss the competitions and awards Dan had insisted that they entered to boost the business's profile and attract celebrities and VIPs to their list of clientele.

She briefly wondered how Dan was getting on, whether he had engaged another florist to assist him with the creative side of things, whether any of their customers had asked where she was, and why she was no longer available for consultations and advice on all of their floral requirements. She also wondered whether he had replaced her in other areas of his life. She quickly shoved that last painful thought to the back of her mind. It had been almost two months since they'd split, and she knew they would have to talk at some point, but she had tried many times before she'd left for Corfu, and a few times since arriving on the island, and he hadn't returned any of her calls, nor had he responded to her emails.

She sauntered to the kitchen, pausing to break off a couple of stems of pink hibiscus to use as a table centrepiece, and made a start on preparing lunch; fortunately, not a difficult task as Nikos had, with his habitual forethought, prepared a selection of Greek meze the day before – black and green olives, *dakos*, *keftedakia*, grilled octopus, *tiropites*, hummus, tzatziki – covered everything in clingfilm, and stored it in the fridge. All she had to do was unpack the box of honey-soaked pastries he had bought from his friend Loukas' bakery in Corfu

Town, make a few jugs of home-made lemonade using the lemons from the garden, and lunch was ready.

'Mmm, they look am-az-ing!' Katie declared, when she saw the plate of Greek pastries, doused in confectioner's sugar, her eyes sparkling with delight. 'I love pastries, and cakes, cupcakes, biscuits, cookies, donuts, eclairs, macarons… Well, you get the idea.'

'I do, and I agree. Wait until you taste the baclava! It's to die for.'

'I always say that food is one of the great joys of life. Why do you think I agreed to do this crazy photoshoot project in the first place? I've never been so exhausted in my whole life. Six a.m. starts, no coffee or lunch breaks, and only wrapping up when the light finally disappears. And, despite being Pierre's assistant fashion designer, I've also had to step into the role of Allyssa's makeup artist, hair stylist, and jewellery advisor, as well as Josh's photography goffer. Do you know, he even asked me to source him a glass paperweight the other day while we were working in a tiny harbour in the north of Sardinia? Completely and utterly crazy!'

Abbie laughed at the expression of indignation on Katie's face, although she didn't blame her. No wonder she was exhausted and wanted to go back home to London so she could indulge in a weekend of lie-ins and afternoon siestas, rather than early morning yoga work-outs and cookery courses.

'So, the compensation for all that hard work has been getting to sample the various local cuisines. If there's one thing Brad's good at, it's locating a decent restaurant; I've had black angelhair fritters in Antigua, pastizzi in Malta, bouillabaisse in St Tropez, and a delicious *zuppa gallurese* in

Sardinia, and now I'm really looking forward to sampling home-made chocolate goodies this afternoon.'

'I bet it was fun, though, being part of a fashion shoot on a yacht!'

'It might sound glamorous, but really it's not. It's lots of hassle and stress, and pressure to get every single, tiny detail right. Pierre sent me to supervise the outfits – which I love, of course. I mean, being a fashion designer has been my dream since I could hold a pair of scissors and a pencil, and I know how fortunate I am to be working for such a celebrated French designer, but it grates a bit when I end up being a glorified wardrobe assistant. Anyway, it's in the bag now, or should that be "in the can"?'

Abbie glanced at her watch, an uptick of anxiety niggling at her chest – twelve fifty-eight – two minutes to lunchtime. She had no intention of inviting criticism from Brad, so she handed Katie the jug of lemonade, grabbed the platter of meze and the plate of sticky, honey-and-nut pastries and hustled out to the veranda, placing the food on the table just as Brad, Allyssa and Josh appeared from the courtyard and Felix arrived from the direction of the front steps to join them for lunch. She exhaled a sigh; yet another opportunity to ask Katie about the goat incident had passed her by. She would make a rubbish private investigator!

The group fell on the food as though they hadn't eaten for days – even Allyssa indulged in a few olives and a couple of courgette balls – and everyone was very complimentary about her home-made lemonade.

'Hey, Felix, why don't you make one of your smoothies for everyone?' said Katie.

'Really?' Felix grinned with delight. 'Okay!'

Felix disappeared into the kitchen, and within minutes Abbie heard the buzz of the blender and the tinkle of glasses being placed on a tray before he returned, an unexpected flash of apprehension in his eyes.

'So, what's actually in this?' asked Josh, peering into his glass.

'I call it my tropical paradise smoothie. It has: mango, papaya, Greek yoghurt, honey and a squeeze of fresh lime, all whizzed up and dressed with a sprinkle of chopped mint and fresh basil leaves. It's packed full of iron, antioxidants, vitamins A and C, and it's a great source of fibre, which, I'm happy to tell you, aids digestion.'

'Sounds wonderful.' Katie smirked, having noticed the twist of distaste appearing at Brad's lips. She reached for one of the glasses and handed it to him, a challenge written across her face. 'Brad, why don't you be the first to tell us what you think?'

'Oh, yes, okay. Step out of your comfort zone and you'll soar, right?'

Abbie was surprised that Brad had decided to take the route of least resistance for a change. She watched him take a sip of the tropical paradise smoothie, his expression changing as he met Felix's hopeful gaze, before finishing it off in one gulp and smacking his lips.

'Delicious, and my five-a-day taken care of in one swoop. What's not to like?'

'Wow! Felix, this is truly wonderful!' Allyssa exclaimed after taking a long draught, the most Abbie had seen her consume in one go. 'Hey, would you mind if I use your recipe in my book? I'll give you full credit, of course.'

'Your book?'

Abbie saw Katie roll her eyes; it was clearly a topic Allyssa had spoken about before.

'Yes.' She beamed, excitement oozing from every pore. 'I'm just about to sign a contract with a "Big Five" publisher for a "healthy eating, healthy living" lifestyle and cookery book. I've had such a ball doing all the research, and I'd love to include a chapter on the health benefits of smoothies like this one.'

'I'd love that!' Felix grinned, clearly thrilled by Allyssa's offer. 'I've actually got a few more recipes up my sleeve if you want to try them, too?'

'Absolutely. It's always been important to me to promote balanced eating habits; by all means follow a fat-free, sugar-free, gluten-free or low carb diet, as long as you supplement that with lots of fresh, natural ingredients that can be delicious as well as good for the body *and* our mental wellbeing. In our industry, you have to be "body conscious", but that doesn't mean you can't enjoy the occasional treat. Pierre has long been an advocate of using models with a wide variety of body shapes to showcase his designs in photoshoots and on the catwalk, and I want to emulate his example. I'm having so much fun collaborating with nutritionists and food photographers, and my agent says that if the book does well, there's even the possibility of a TV show! Xavier thinks I'd make a great cookery show presenter. Do you mind if I take a few photographs, Felix?' asked Allyssa, already lining up her mobile phone. 'Just to send to my agent?'

'Not at all. Go for it.'

'See how Allyssa asked permission before she took a

picture?' Katie muttered, holding Brad's gaze for a few long seconds, unaware that Abbie had stepped forward to offer her a refill and had overheard the strange comment.

What was going on?

'Allyssa's got over half a million followers on her Instagram account,' Josh volunteered to Abbie, also raising his camera to his eye and taking a few snaps. 'Her book is going to fly off the shelves! I hope her agent got her a decent advance.'

'You should have asked me to do the negotiations for you,' Brad said to Allyssa, helping himself to a beer from the bucket of ice that Abbie had left next to the lunch table, knocking off the top and taking a slurp. 'There's not much I don't know about the art of persuasion when it comes to closing a deal. What do your publishers have planned for your launch? If you want, I could run a few ideas up the flag pole with them?'

'I'm not sure about the precise details yet,' Allyssa said carefully.

'Well, the offer's on the table if you want to take it up later. Okay, I'm off to check my emails before our afternoon's flirtation with all-things cocoa-related. Now there's one dopamine-inducing activity I can heartily recommend!'

'I think I might join you,' said Josh. 'It's so hot!'

'Come on, Katie, let's grab our swimsuits!' Allyssa said.

Abbie watched them disappear to their rooms, then made swift work of tidying away the lunch detritus, washing up the crockery and silverware and wiping down the countertops ready for the chocolate-making class. Leaving Felix to finish the drying up, she collected a pile of fluffy white beach towels, embroidered with the Hummingbird Hotel's distinctive logo, and delivered them poolside while Allyssa, Katie and Josh were playing a game of water tag.

Brad, still in his business-like navy-blue shorts and pale lemon polo shirt from earlier, was perched on a sunbed only inches away from the edge of the pool, calling out increasingly forceful instructions to the swimmers like a pushy water-sports coach; all he needed was a whistle around his neck and the image would be complete. Fortunately, his colleagues were having too much fun to take any notice of him.

'I'll just leave these towels here.' Abbie smiled, placing them onto one of the sunbeds where Katie had left what was clearly another of her quirky designs – this one a huge, canvas beach bag with wide pastel stripes and what looked like appliqué circus tents – pausing to watch Josh snag hold of Katie from behind and dunk her under the water, howling with laughter as Katie, in turn, powered through the pool, her jaw tight with determination to get her own back.

'Argh! Stop splashing!' cried Allyssa, wading into the shallow end and hauling herself out of the water, her long, slender limbs glistening in the sunshine as she helped herself to one of the fresh towels. 'I love swimming, but I hate getting my hair wet.'

Abbie took in her elegant crimson swimsuit, cut high on the hip and fastened at the neck with a gorgeous diamanté clasp; it was more like something you'd wear whilst reclining on the deck of a yacht moored in the marina at St Tropez, and she wondered whether it was one of the pieces Allyssa had modelled for the photoshoot, especially when she proceeded to cover it with a diaphanous, ankle-length kaftan, embroidered with silver seashells, and plonk a wide-brimmed, floppy sunhat on her head to guard against the ageing properties of the fierce afternoon sun. Even on holiday she looked like she was about to launch down a Pierre Fontaine runway, but then, Abbie supposed, she *was* a fashion model; she probably had to be Instagram-ready at all times just in case a random paparazzo was lurking in the bushes, hoping to snap her in mismatched swimwear. Heaven forbid!

Abbie looked down at her own outfit – white Capri pants, blue and white striped tee-shirt, and a pair of her favourite almost-white Vans – and cringed. She really should make the time to go on a shopping spree. When she'd flown out to Corfu, she had only intended to stay for ten days; long enough to meet with her Aunt Liz's lawyer, Alex Stephanopoulos, sign the paperwork for him to handle the administration of her estate, and to put the hotel on the market.

So, beyond a few tee-shirts, a couple of pair of shorts, and Emily's yellow-and-white sundress, her wardrobe choices were limited. In fact, she didn't actually own a swimsuit or a bikini, or many summer clothes. In the last three years, and more recently whilst she and Dan had been together, the only holiday she'd had was a weekend trip to Amsterdam to visit the flower markets, which had not required a selection of glamorous outfits. She wondered whether Rachel, or Sofia, would be up for a trip to Corfu Town to show her the best places to buy a few essential items. Sadly, her budget would not stretch to Allyssa's extensive wardrobe.

'Here, guys, catch!'

Brad picked up a frisbee from a wooden box Abbie had painted in the Hummingbird Hotel's signature colours, and tossed it into the pool, laughing when both Josh and Katie paused, exchanged a glance, then made a beeline for it, pushing each other out of the way, until Katie reached it first, holding it into the air in triumph.

'Don't be a spoilsport, Brad! Come and join us! The water's amazing!' Josh called out.

'I'm working on my tan!'

And then it happened, the event unfolding almost as though in slow motion.

Brad returned to his sunbed, which was where he'd left it – a few inches from the deep end of the pool – and, for a reason Abbie couldn't fathom, when he dropped down onto the towel he'd draped over its top, the legs nearest the pool collapsed, sending him tumbling into the water with a vociferous exclamation of surprise and a very loud splash.

Several seconds of shocked silence ensued, then Abbie dashed forward to grab one of the beach towels and rushed to the side of the pool, her stomach churning painfully as she waited for Brad to swim to the steps and haul himself out of the water. Allyssa joined her a few seconds later to offer him a second towel, whilst trying to staunch a fit of the giggles.

'Oh my God! That was hilarious!'

'Hey, Brad, when I said you should join us, I assumed you would change into your swimming shorts first! Isn't that a Ralph Lauren shirt? And aren't those Gucci loafers? Oh, and did you have your Rolex on?' Josh asked.

'It's waterproof up to one thousand metres!' Brad

snapped, as he briskly towel-dried his hair, his face glowing scarlet and showcasing a kaleidoscope of emotions; clearly only just managing to cling onto his temper by his fingernails.

'I'm so sorry, Brad, I have no idea—'

'It's not your fault, Abbie,' Josh interrupted, having followed Brad out of the pool. 'My six-year-old nephew does that all the time. Everyone knows what happens when you sit on the edge of a sunbed, it's just an absolute travesty that we got to witness the biggest bellyflop of the decade and I didn't have my camera rolling!'

Brad opened his mouth to retaliate, but thought better of it. He dropped his towel onto the sunbed Allyssa had recently vacated, grabbed his mobile phone, which fortunately had escaped the debacle, and checked the time.

'Okay, okay, the comedy show's over. I suggest we all go and get changed. The chocolate-making course starts in twenty minutes.'

And with that he marched from the terrace, through the stone archway that led to the courtyard and disappeared with everyone staring, slack-jawed, in his wake.

'Hey, everyone, why's Brad got a face like thunder?' asked Nikos, materialising a few seconds later sporting a pale lilac linen shirt, its cuffs turned back to reveal a complementary stripe, and his hands stuffed into the pockets of a pair of cream knee-length shorts. He looked the epitome of cool, calm and collected.

'So would you if you'd taken an unscheduled dip in the pool, fully clothed!' Katie smirked.

'What?'

Nikos' gaze switched from Katie – who had climbed from the water and was in the process of wrapping one of the beach towels around her waist – to the swimming pool where Brad's towel was floating on the surface like a discarded life raft, along with the red frisbee.

'Never mind, I'll tell you about it later,' Abbie muttered, her heartrate at last returning to bordering on normal, despite the cauldron of suspicion that was spinning through her veins as the full implications of what had happened to Brad started to dawn on her. 'Brad's right, guys – the chocolate-making course does start in a few minutes. Why don't you all go and get changed and Nikos and I will tidy up here.'

'Come on, Katie, I need you to help me with my hair. Josh, will you get the bags?'

Allyssa grabbed her over-sized sun hat, hooked her arm through Katie's, and together they made their way from the terrace, chattering away, giggling about Brad's undignified swimming pool debut, whilst Josh was left to collect up their beach bags and stumble in their wake.

'What's going on?' Nikos asked once they were gone.

Abbie provided him with the short version and, as she expected, he burst into laughter.

'It couldn't have happened to a nicer guy.'

'Nikos—'

'Perhaps now he'll realise that he's supposed to be on holiday, not on a corporate team-building exercise.'

'But—'

'Look, Abbie, a dip in the pool never hurt anyone.'

'That's not what I mean.'

Nikos' expression changed. 'What do you mean?'

Abbie strode to the far side of the terrace where a small wooden hut painted in the ubiquitous white and blue colours of the hotel was situated, removed a long wooden pole, and used it to steer the towel towards the edge of the pool, then knelt down to try and drag it out of the water.

'Here, let me help you.'

Together they returned the towel and frisbee to dry land and Abbie went over to inspect the front legs of Brad's sunbed.

'Oh no!'

Her stomach performed a somersault of dismay.

'What?'

'Look.'

Nikos knelt down next to her and scrutinised the area she was pointing to – the sunbed hadn't simply collapsed because of the uneven distribution of Brad's weight, but because one of its legs had broken.

'Should we tell Brad?'

'What good would that do?' Nikos said, still on his knees as he continued to inspect the area where the legs had snapped. 'I think it's better for everyone if he thinks it was an accident.'

'It *was* an accident!'

'I'm not so sure,' said Nikos, pushing himself up to standing.

'What do you mean?'

Abbie could feel tears begin to smart at the corners of her eyes, but she inhaled a breath and forced herself to douse her mounting panic; this was no time to indulge in a festival of weeping.

'I can't be absolutely sure, but it looks like…'

'Like what?'

'Like the leg might have been damaged.'

'Damaged?'

'Like I said, I can't be certain.'

'But… but…'

Abbie's knees wobbled and she dropped down onto one of the other sunbeds.

'Who would do such a thing?'

And then the incident with the goat streaked through her mind and she stared, like a gobsmacked goldfish, at Nikos.

'I don't know, but don't worry, if someone did do this, I intend to find out.'

To Abbie's astonishment, Nikos grinned.

'What?'

'Life's never boring with you around, Abbie Coleman. When I left Paris, I thought I was leaving all the excitement behind for a dull and tedious life in the idyllic, but sedate countryside where I grew up, managing a vineyard that did not inspire the same passion as it had in my father and brother. And that might very well have been the case if you hadn't tumbled into my path, with your crazy curls and penchant for attracting chaos.'

'I—'

'Come on, unless you want to upset Brad even further, we'd better get the chocolate-making course under way.'

Abbie reluctantly shelved the onslaught of questions that were bombarding her. Someone was clearly targeting Brad, intent on embarrassing him for some reason, and she was now more determined than ever to speak to Katie and put a stop to the crazy Corfu capers before they got out of hand.

Chapter Six

The Kitchen at the Hummingbird Hotel
Flower: Dahlia 'Chocolate Sundae'

'Okay, guys, grab an apron from the hook over there, and then take a place at the bench in front of a set of ingredients and we'll embark on our crème de la crème chocolate-making experience.'

Cheerful conversation ricocheted around the kitchen as the group, including a very animated Felix, selected Hummingbird Hotel aprons, embroidered with a colourful depiction of hotel's namesake, and tied the strings, dashing back to the counter to nab the best place – which for Allyssa was next to Nikos who looked so handsome in his chef's whites, the collar cracked open to reveal a tantalising glimpse of dark chest hair.

'So, before we create a delicious gooey chocolate fudge–'

'Yum!' Katie interjected.

'We will indulge in a brief chocolate-tasting session.

Chocolate has many subtle flavours, which depend on where the original cacao beans are grown. The climate, the altitude, and the soil all have an impact on the final taste, and it's not just nature; the production process matters, too. So, how a grower harvests, dries, roasts and conches the cacao pods, all affect the final product and so the true chocolate connoisseur will check the origin of their cacao bean carefully.'

'Where do cacao trees grow?' asked Josh, peering into the container next to Nikos that was filled with a variety of foil-wrapped chocolate bars.

'Mainly in hot, humid climates around the equator. My personal favourite is a bean that is produced on the slopes of Gran Piton on the south coast of St Lucia. Okay, first I want you to taste this chocolate.' Nikos handed round two squares each of the chocolate that had been wrapped in a bronze-coloured foil. 'As you probably can tell, this is milk chocolate. See how shiny it looks – there should be no white blooming on the surface – and listen to the sound when I break off a square; it's a quiet, dull snap, telling us the chocolate is soft, and will melt easily. Next, we inhale the aroma; notice the rich, sugary-sweet smell, maybe it's a little waxy as it's low in cacao butter content.'

'Mmm, it smells amazing!' said Abbie.

'I'm more interested in tasting it!' said Katie, almost drooling.

Nikos laughed. 'Okay, now we can taste. Allow the chocolate to melt a little on your tongue, then inhale, try to isolate each flavour as you chew, then when you swallow, remember the sweet afternote.'

'Absolutely delicious.'

'We rarely use this type of chocolate to cook with as it's so easy to overheat and difficult to temper properly. Okay, now we'll move on to the next – this time, we taste a dark chocolate, one with at least forty percent cocoa.' Nikos passed round squares of a darker chocolate taken from a bar wrapped in silver foil. 'Notice how the snap was more discernible, the surface of the chocolate smoother, and how it doesn't melt so quickly in the hands? When we taste, we use slightly different tastebuds in a different part of the mouth, and the flavour is more intense, more chocolatey, less sugary.'

'I much prefer this one,' said Josh, chewing slowly like a seasoned expert.

'Okay, and finally, we taste the king of chocolates, in my opinion at least; the dark chocolate from St Lucia.' Nikos removed the final bar of chocolate, enveloped in shiny gold foil, with something approaching reverence. 'Listen to the sharp snap when I break off the pieces, that's an indication of a high percentage of cocoa solids, up to one hundred percent, and a lower level of added sugar. See how it doesn't melt when handled? Smell the deep, bitter chocolate aroma, and when we taste, notice the distinct nutty undertones.'

'Sounds like we're tasting wine, not chocolate,' said Brad, following Nikos' instructions to the letter, unlike Katie and Allyssa, who were really just scoffing the chocolate and waiting for the next.

'It is similar, especially when we are tasting the more expensive varieties.'

'Well, I prefer the second one; this last one is too bitter for me,' said Katie, reaching out to help herself to another two squares of the second chocolate.

'Okay, shall we start baking?'

'Yes!' the group chorused.

Abbie helped Nikos to hand round a selection of bowls into which he'd weighed the ingredients needed to create his gooey chocolate fudge.

'First we mix our butter, condensed milk and vanilla extract, like this.'

Everyone watched as Nikos beat together the three ingredients and then followed suit. Then he moved on to demonstrate the technique of melting the chocolate in a bowl over a pan of water so that it didn't burn.

'We are using the second chocolate you tasted for this recipe, which for some is very sweet – too sweet, sometimes – but it complements perfectly our rich, dark Greek coffee. Now we pour this melted chocolate into the butter mixture, beat once again, then add eight hundred grams of sifted icing sugar. See how it comes to a soft, dough-like texture?'

Abbie looked around the kitchen, trying not to giggle when she saw everyone wiping their foreheads as though they'd been working over a hot stove all day, creating Michelin-starred masterpieces for a dining room full of discerning diners. Allyssa had a smudge of chocolate on her left temple – as though she was modelling a new range of edible cosmetics – whilst Katie's cheeks bulged from dipping her hand into the chocolate bar container when Nikos wasn't looking.

To her surprise, Felix, and of course Brad, had produced an almost perfect pliable fudge which they were now pressing into a paper-lined tray ready for the freezer. She, however, wasn't so proficient, and for some reason her chocolate had turned into a grainy lump of gloop.

'How are you getting on?' asked Nikos.

'Well, if we're creating sludge, instead of fudge, I think I'm doing okay.'

'You've overheated your chocolate. Here, let me show you.'

Abbie knew that the kitchen was hot, but the temperature edged up a notch when Nikos threaded his arms around her waist and guided her in preparing a new bowl of perfectly melted chocolate to add to her butter mixture. She could feel her cheeks glowing, her breath quickening as her heart pounded out a symphony of desire. With a concerted effort she pulled herself together before she was teased by the rest of the group for having one-to-one instruction.

'Shall we move on to our next recipe?' Nikos asked.

'Yes, please, I adore truffles!' Allyssa said enthusiastically.

'Really?' Katie gaped at Allyssa.

'A girl can treat herself every once in a while,' Allyssa retorted, slight colour appearing in her cheeks.

'Okay, so a little history lesson first. Truffles were invented in 1895 in the small town of Chambéry in south west France, by chef Louis Dufour, who combined melted chocolate with cream and created what we now call ganache. He rolled it into perfect bite-sized balls, coated each one in cocoa powder, and voilà! The most delectable morsel of chocolatey bliss!'

'I prefer the kind of truffles that are snuffled out of the ground by highly-trained pigs,' Brad remarked, inspecting the plate of decorated truffles Nikos had handed round for everyone to inspect before they got started on making their own. 'Especially in omelettes. *Délicieux*!'

Nikos laughed. 'I have to agree with you, and it is thought that the sweet variety of truffles were named as such because of their resemblance to the exquisite earthly-brown mushroom. Today we will be making our truffles the traditional way, with the very best dark chocolate and the richest of fresh cream, and it is for this reason, in France especially, that the truffles must be eaten straight away – they have a short shelf-life.'

Nikos handed round a new set of bowls filled with finely chopped dark chocolate, thick fresh cream, vanilla extract, and cocoa powder.

'Of course, truffles can be made with additional flavourings, such as orange, mint, espresso, Grand Marnier, rum, or with chopped nuts, dried fruit, or perhaps a sprinkle of chilli. We could dip them in white or milk chocolate, or even colourful candy melts and roll them in sprinkles, but today we will stick to the traditional method. So, first we melt the chocolate, as we did for the fudge, and *warm* the cream. Never boil it.' Nikos glanced at Abbie, a mischievous smile tugging at his lips. 'Then we combine the two, with a drop of our flavouring, and leave it to cool, preferably overnight, which is why I made a batch yesterday. Okay, let's get rolling!'

'Yay!' Katie grinned.

'Sprinkle a little cocoa powder on your hands, then take a tablespoon, scoop out the ganache and roll it between your palms, like this, but not for too long; we mustn't allow the ganache to melt.'

There then followed ten minutes of noisy hilarity as everyone created a variety of misshaped balls, ranging from the size of a sprout, to a golf ball, to a cricket ball –

Josh – the trays filling up until all the ganache had disappeared and Nikos placed them in the fridge.

'Now for our final recipe, which I think may surprise you.'

'Is it a Death by Chocolate cake?' asked Katie, her eyes shining.

'No.'

'Is it chocolate soufflé? I *lerrve* chocolate soufflé!' said Allyssa.

'No, it's chilli and chocolate moussaka.'

'What?' said Brad, his nose wrinkling.

Nikos laughed. 'Wait until you taste it.'

As the group watched on, with practised expertise Nikos proceeded to demonstrate his unique recipe that featured all the ingredients expected of a traditional moussaka, except the meat sauce was infused with a generous portion of his favourite bitter chocolate, which Abbie had to admit gave it amazing depth and complexity.

'For the vegetarians amongst us, the recipe can be amended by using a selection of wild mushrooms – porcini, chanterelle, shiitake, trompette, field or button – adding the same amount of grated chocolate for a rich harmony of flavours that even the carnivores will love.'

'I'll take your word for it,' Josh muttered, staring at the vegetarian moussaka Nikos had made earlier as though it contained poisoned berries.

'And for a twist on the truffles you've just made, maybe think about adding things like feta and chopped thyme, or beetroot and crushed walnut, or caramelised figs with a dash of Cointreau. Nothing is off limits when it comes to culinary experimentation; either your dinner guest will love what you create or they won't; it's simply a matter of taste, and everyone's palate varies. Okay, shall we taste our fudge now?'

'Yes, please!' Felix grinned, striding to the fridge to help Nikos remove the first of their chocolate-making projects and place them on the marble island unit where Nikos took a sharp knife and deftly cut his slab of fudge into sixteen pieces.

'Mmm, they all look mouth-watering,' said Brad, genuinely enthusiastic about what he'd created, rolling his eyes when Katie cut her gooey chocolate fudge into nine much larger pieces, and shoved one of them into her mouth, groaning in delight as the sugary sweetness hit her tastebuds.

'Scrumptious! Truly scrumptious! I'm definitely making this at home.'

When everyone had devoured their chocolatey creations, Nikos called them to order one last time, waiting for the general hubbub of animated conversation to quieten before speaking. Abbie could tell from the broad smile on his face how happy he was to be doing what he was most passionate about; he was a natural in front of an audience, delivering clear instructions, praise where it was justified, assistance where it was needed. She wondered where he had learned his presentation skills, and then recalled something Emily had said about him having a YouTube channel and made a note to seek it out when she next had a spare moment.

'And finally, in my humble opinion, the best use of chocolate of all – a chocolate Martini!' Nikos said with a flourish.

'Yay! No argument there!' agreed Allyssa.

Nikos handed a cocktail glass, silver shaker and a pastry brush to each of them, and placed a bowl of melted chocolate in the middle of the counter. 'First, we coat the inside of our glass with a layer of chocolate, like this, then we chill it in the fridge while we prepare our delicious cocktail.'

'I don't think you're supposed to eat the melted chocolate, Katie!' Brad scolded.

'Oops, sorry!'

'Okay, now we mix the Martini. You can tweak the ingredients to your personal taste, but we will use vodka, chocolate syrup, coffee liqueur and a dash of Irish cream, then add a handful of ice, and shake, shake, shake until the outside of our shakers are cold.'

There followed a great deal of excitement as each of them created their own version of the perfect chocolate Martini, shaken, not stirred, then poured the resulting mixture into their chocolate-coated cocktail glasses.

'And we finish with a sprinkle of shaved chocolate or dusting of cocoa powder.'

'Mmm, I don't know about you, but mine is absolutely delicious!' said Josh, running the tip of his tongue along his lower lip to collect every last morsel of chocolate.

'Let's enjoy them on the veranda,' said Brad, removing his Hummingbird Hotel apron and making his way outside, his cocktail glass held aloft as he turned back to address the group. 'Then we need to head to our rooms to change into our evening attire. We don't want to be late for Pierre's friend, Jean-Luc, especially as he's flying in on his helicopter from his villa in Zakynthos just so he can take us out to dinner at his favourite restaurant.'

'Wow, it must be amazing to own your own helicopter,'

sighed Allyssa, following Brad out to the veranda, with Josh, Nikos and Felix in her wake, each carrying their cocktail as though it was the elixir of life.

Katie remained with Abbie in the kitchen, mixing a second chocolate Martini even more proficiently than Nikos had, and Abbie knew she couldn't allow the opportunity to have a chat with her to escape a third time. The future of the hotel was important to her, which meant so was the happiness of each and every one of her guests, even those who were irritating and infuriating.

She couldn't let personal disagreements, or personality clashes, between guests impact on their enjoyment of their stay at the Hummingbird Hotel, especially as she suspected Brad was the sort of person who would feel it was his civic duty to write a well-crafted, no holds barred review when he returned home. The thought of the headline "Greek Goat Munched My Undergarments" spurred her on, despite her rampaging nerves.

'Katie? Do you think I could have a quick word?'

Chapter Seven

The Lobby at the Hummingbird Hotel
Flower: Clematis 'Dark Secret'

Katie met Abbie's eyes, her smile slipping slightly from her lips when she saw Abbie's uncharacteristically serious expression.

'Sure. What's going on?'

'I've… I've noticed a bit of tension between you and Brad since you arrived. I just want to make sure everything's okay.' Abbie smiled, her confidence ticking up a notch now that she had actually broached the subject. 'This weekend is supposed to be a wellbeing retreat, and I really want you, and everyone else, to have a restful and relaxing time while you're here, and when you're around Brad you seem to be uncomfortable, jumpy, on edge.'

'Everything's fine, completely fine.'

Katie took a sip of her chocolate Martini, but Abbie knew from her body language and the way she avoided her gaze that she wasn't telling the truth, and what was more, Katie knew that she knew. Then something burst into her brain like a runaway express train, and her heart skipped a beat.

No, surely not!

She met Katie's gaze and, when Katie read the enquiry there, she gasped in horror.

'Oh my God, no! No, Abbie, you're completely wrong; there's absolutely nothing, nothing at all, going on between me and Brad. Okay, so we're both single – unfortunately – but he's definitely not my type, no way. In fact, he's the complete opposite to me; Brad Goodman is an absolute…'

Katie paused, her cheeks glowing crimson with the fierce indignation with which she had denied Abbie's unspoken suggestion, and a splash of guilt invaded Abbie's chest.

'I'm sorry, Katie, I didn't mean to—'

'But you're right, there *is* something going on between us, but it's as far away from a romantic dalliance in the sun as you can get. I detest him! He's a complete and utter…'

Kate stopped again to take a few deep breaths and rein in her temper, reaching out to replenish her Martini glass for the third time, and snatching up one of the truffles. Then, after glancing over her shoulder to check that Brad and the rest of the group were happily enjoying their cocktails and cold beers whilst chatting away on the veranda, she hooked her arm through her sequin-bedecked handbag and strode from the kitchen to the hotel's lobby where Abbie's aunt had thoughtfully arranged several squashy white sofas; an oasis of peace where guests could linger awhile out of the blazing heat of the sun, and the perfect place to have a heart-to-heart.

Abbie picked up a coffee and followed in Katie's wake, her thoughts ricocheting around her brain as she tried to fathom what was going on between Katie and Brad. She was grateful that Katie had decided to confide in her as it meant she was one step closer to ensuring that no more embarrassing incidents would befall Brad, and the Hummingbird Hotel's reputation for serenity and calm would remain intact.

Katie selected the sofa furthest away from the entrance to the kitchen, hidden behind a white-washed column and a blue ceramic pot containing an ornamental palm, and sunk into its embrace with a ragged sigh. Abbie placed her coffee cup on the glass table in front of them, piled high with the glossy homes and interiors magazines her Aunt Liz had adored, and perched on the edge of one of the cane chairs.

'Katie?'

'I'm sorry, Abbie, I didn't mean to spoil everyone's enjoyment. Heaven knows, we all need this break, but when I saw what Brad was doing, I just, well…'

'You just what?'

'It's complicated.'

'My mum always used to tell me that the best way to deal with complicated situations was to start at the beginning and not stop until I got to the end.'

Katie stared at Abbie, and Abbie could almost see the cogs turning in her brain as she wrestled with whether to confide in her. To her relief, a few moments later, she saw Katie's shoulders sag as she exhaled a long sigh of capitulation and finally met her gaze, her chin raised in determination.

'Okay, so, yesterday, after we'd finally disembarked from Pierre's yacht, we all went to this amazing pavement café in Corfu Town overlooking what looked like a cricket pitch, and Brad ordered several bottles of Champagne – Dom Perignon, would you believe – to celebrate the end of the shoot whilst we waited for the taxi to arrive and drive us over here. We sat in the sun, on this amazing colonnade, laughing about the things that had happened over the last six weeks, what our favourite bits were, what we planned to do first when we got back home, relaxing for the first time for over a month and having a great time together.'

Katie paused to take a sip of her cocktail before continuing, her eyes fixed on a vibrant watercolour of a hummingbird in flight, one of many pictures of the colourful bird that Abbie's aunt had scattered around the walls of the hotel.

'I remember Allyssa pressing Brad quite forcefully about why Pierre had chosen just us four to enjoy a long weekend break at his expense. Don't get me wrong, it's very generous of him, and I'm grateful, but why us? Why not Suzie, or Carlton, or Martha, or Andy? They all worked on the shoot, too. And why hasn't Pierre, and Pippa, flown out here to join us for the weekend, instead of coming over on Monday – for one night!'

'Well, there *are* only four guest rooms here,' Abbie reminded Katie, but she knew she wasn't listening.

'Anyway, we finished every drop of the delicious Champagne, and I thought Brad had disappeared to pay the bill, but when he'd been gone for over twenty minutes, I decided to see if everything was okay.' Katie's jaw tightened, her sharp eyes narrowed, and a dark cloud floated across her face. 'Only he wasn't paying the bill, was he?'

Abbie stared at Katie, completely nonplussed. She had no idea where their conversation was going but she had no intention of interrupting her until the whole story had been disclosed, so she simply sat back in her chair and waited, hoping she would get to the point soon.

'Guess what I caught him doing? I can hardly believe it, even now.'

Again, Katie paused, and this time Abbie couldn't help herself.

'What was he doing?'

'Taking photographs of us.'

'Ok… ay.'

'From behind a bush, like some kind of crazy paparazzo! Well, when I say "us", of course I mean Allyssa. Why on earth would Brad want to take covert photographs of me and Josh? Now that *would* be crazy!'

Katie took another sip of her Martini, her temper calmed. Her red cheeks had returned to normal, yet her eyes were filled with indignation and annoyance as she recalled the incident and tried to work out what was going on. Abbie's brain was working overtime, too.

'So is that why you made that comment earlier, about Allyssa asking for Felix's permission before she photographed his smoothie?'

'Yes, it is. You know, what I don't understand is why he didn't just stand in front of us and take a few random photographs of us all, together and individually. None of us would have thought anything of that, but he didn't do that.

It's creepy, and totally unacceptable behaviour.' Katie's eyes flashed.

'Did you speak to him about it?'

'Of course I did. I wasn't going to let him get away with something like that.'

'What did he say?'

Katie's lips twisted into a humourless smile. 'Well, he was shocked when he realised that I'd rumbled him, I can tell you. At first, he tried to deny it, but he knew I'd seen him, so then he gave me some kind of garbled excuse about wanting a photograph of the cricket pitch for a friend at home. I wasn't buying that one either, because when I asked him to show me the photographs he'd taken, he refused.'

Katie had now finished her Martini and started to twist a strand of her hair between her fingers.

'There's something going on, I know there is, because when I told him I was going to tell Allyssa what he'd been doing, he…'

'He what?'

'He… well, he threatened me.'

'Threatened you? What did he say?'

A flicker of something Abbie couldn't identify flashed across Katie's face, and she suddenly looked uncomfortable, clearly starting to regret how much she had confided in Abbie. She plastered on a false smile and jumped up from the sofa.

'Hey! Look at the time! I need to make a start on getting ready or we'll be late for dinner.'

Abbie's heart began to pound against her ribcage as she realised that she hadn't even mentioned the reason she had wanted to talk to Katie in the first place. Now, with everything she'd heard over the last ten minutes, she was even more certain than ever that Katie was the one responsible for the goat incident, which meant she was within touching distance of tying up the issue and being able to relax for the rest of the retreat, safe in the knowledge that there would be no more Brad-targeted frolics.

'Katie, before you go, do you mind if I ask you something?'

She knew from the expression in Katie's eyes that she would rather Abbie didn't ask her *any* questions, that she would love to refuse but that politeness prevented her from doing so.

'Of course.'

'Did you… was it you who let the goat into Brad's room yesterday?'

Katie stared at her in bewilderment, then burst out laughing.

'What? No way, absolutely not, but, you know, if I had thought of it, I definitely would have done something like that. In fact, do you hire Gertie the Goat's services out by the hour? The look on Brad's face when he saw his precious boxer shorts in her mouth was absolutely priceless. Hey, I've just thought of something!' Katie's eyes sparkled with mischief as her previously downcast mood elevated to almost joyous. 'Josh took loads of photographs, didn't he?'

Abbie groaned; she knew exactly what was coming.

'It's perfect, absolutely perfect! If he won't tell me what's going on, or why he's taken to hiding in a bush taking secret photographs of everyone without their permission, then I might just have to splash a few of those "goatie snaps" across my Instagram page!'

'Okay, please don't do that, Katie.'

Katie met Abbie's eyes, serious for a moment. 'You don't think that was an accident?'

'Well, Brad *was* adamant he didn't leave his patio doors open.'

'True, true, but even super-efficient Brad can be wrong sometimes, don't you think? However, if you're looking for someone who might want to upset him by playing a bit of a practical joke, then I suggest you have a chat with Josh.'

'With Josh? Why?'

'Because when we were in Sardinia last week, he and Brad had a blazing row. I only heard the last bit of it, but it was something to do with money, and I've never heard Josh so furious. He's usually really laid back; nothing upsets him, unless it has something to do with his beloved cameras, *and* he was supposed to be joining us all for dinner at this fabulous Michelin-starred restaurant in Cagliari, but he never showed up, so he was obviously still angry with him. Perhaps Josh thought that Brad deserved a surprise visit from one of our little goat friends to get his own back on him. Okay, must dash, catch you later.'

Katie hooked up her handbag and skipped off towards her guest room, leaving Abbie staring after her, wishing fervently that she hadn't interfered in the first place. Not only was she no nearer to finding out who could have targeted Brad – if indeed he was being targeted at all – but she now needed to talk to Josh about not handing the goat photographs over to Katie as well as try to find out what he and Brad had argued about.

Why did running a small boutique hotel in the glorious Corfu countryside have to be so complicated?

Chapter Eight

The Gardens at the Kassiopia Estate, Corfu
Flower: Purple Honesty (Lunaria Annua)

Twenty minutes later, Abbie stood on the marble steps at the front of the hotel waving the group off for their glamorous Saturday night dinner with Pierre's friend in Corfu Town. As the taxi disappeared from view, leaving only a cloud of dust in its wake, she allowed a long sigh to escape from her lips.

Why had she thought she could glide into her aunt's shoes and simply take over where she left off? She had no experience whatsoever of running a hospitality business, even one as small as the Hummingbird Hotel. So many questions tumbled through her brain that she would have loved to have asked her; not just about the ins and outs of managing a boutique hotel in the Greek countryside, but also the reasons behind the shocking elopement with her sister's fiancé and the inevitable estrangement that followed. One lesson she wished she had known earlier was "do not, under any circumstances, interfere in your guests' personal lives". Her conversation with Katie had only made things worse, and instead of being able to draw a line under the goat and sunbed incident she now had even more conundrums to wrestle with.

She gazed at the hillside opposite the hotel, taking in the kaleidoscope of colours from the silvery green foliage of the olive groves and the emerald frill of the grape vines to the honey-hue of the buildings and the random splash of cerise from the bougainvillea. No matter what happened, she knew she would never grow tired of the view, and as her lips stretched into a smile at the sound of a lone bee collecting that day's quota of nectar, a welcome blanket of calm descended.

'Hey, Abbie, what are you doing out here?'

She turned to see Nikos, so handsome in his buttock-hugging jeans and smart lemon-coloured shirt, his hair immaculately teased into neat spikes with a smidgeon of gel, and her heart ballooned at his presence. Her current worries paled into insignificance when she thought of what he had been through over the last two years; losing his father and brother at the same time, and in such tragic circumstances, must have been devastating. Not only that but it had meant he'd had to leave his life in Paris, and a job he had clearly loved, to continue their legacy at the Angelopoulos vineyard – something, by his own admission, he was singularly unequipped to do – and yet he had done it without complaint or objection. She could learn a great deal from him.

'I've just spoken to Katie.'

'Great. Have you ironed everything out?'

'Not exactly.'

'What do you mean?'

Abbie provided him with the shortened version of their conversation, seeing his forehead crease when she got to the bit about Brad's clandestine photographic exploits, and his row with Josh.

'So, the plot thickens.'

Abbie dropped down onto the top step, resting her elbows on her knees and chin in her palms. A sudden wave of despondency threatened to engulf her as she tried to battle the self-confidence demons that had begun to circle, whispering their spiteful mantra that she wasn't strong enough to do this, or anything else, on her own. She knew her issues stemmed from the loss of her beloved mum, leaving her with no one – no parents, no relatives, no extended family – to catch her should she fall. It was an unsettling sensation, like being at sea, searching for a safe harbour. She had thought she'd found it, briefly, when she was with Dan, but that had ended, too, and she was alone again.

'I'm a completely useless hotelier. My aunt would be horrified if she could see what a mess I've made of things here. I don't know for sure, but I can hazard a guess that she never had a guest complain about a goat munching their underwear!'

Nikos took a seat beside Abbie and laced his fingers through hers, his expression serious.

'I think you underestimate what you've achieved since you arrived here. The Hummingbird Hotel is an amazing place; filled with peace and tranquillity as well as laughter and exhilaration. You've already delivered a successful hen weekend for Savannah and her friends – didn't she sing your praises in the review she left on the website? – and bookings are starting to increase already, especially for the retreats you've got planned. Liz wouldn't have been horrified; she would have been proud.'

Nikos gave Abbie's hand a squeeze of reassurance and softened his voice.

'You've got to give yourself a break, Abbie. You are an extremely competent hotelier, a welcoming retreat host, an accomplished gardener, a talented florist, *and* an improving sous chef. If anyone had told you a few months ago that you would be doing any of these things – and in Corfu – what would you have said?'

Abbie laughed. 'That they were crazy!'

'Self-belief evades us all at some point in our lives, but we have to face our challenges with determination and the certainty that, even if we fail, we will have at least learnt something that will strengthen our chances of success next time. We must celebrate our talents and hone our abilities, for doubt erodes our confidence more than failure ever will.' Nikos dragged his thoughts back from some faraway place to hold her gaze. 'And if you don't know how to do something – like I didn't know how to be a vineyard owner, or a wine maker – you know what you do?'

'What?'

'You fake it. That's my approach.'

'Really?' She smiled.

'Absolutely, but I've learned that you can only do that for a short time, preferably whilst you're doing everything you can to learn the ropes from those who are experts in their field. That's where I went wrong, and where you can benefit from my mistakes. I have complete faith in Thanos to teach you, me and Dimitris everything he knows about viticulture, and I just know that the winery's fortunes will be turned around, if not this season, then next year. We have a choice; wallow in the past, or lift our chins and embrace the future.'

'Thanks, Nikos. I couldn't do any of this without your help.'

'I'm sure you could, but you don't need to.'

Nikos jumped up and held out his hand.

'Come on, I've got a trip planned.'

'Where to?'

'It's a surprise, and don't worry, you'll love it, I promise you.'

'Okay.'

Nikos pointed to the small wooden shed, painted in the Hummingbird Hotel's signature blue and white colours where, a few days after she'd arrived, Abbie had stumbled upon her aunt's ancient bicycle. Surely he wasn't expecting her to cycle? The sun's rays were lengthening, and whilst she could perhaps enjoy a ride to the local town for a drink or for dinner, there was no way she could cycle back along the serpentine Greek roads in the dark, especially after a glass or two of wine. Fortunately, when she arrived at the rear of the shed, she saw Felix's bumble bee-esque Vespa.

'Ah.' She laughed with relief.

'Hop on.'

'Okay.'

She climbed on behind Nikos and wrapped her arms around his waist, closing her eyes to relish the waft of his citrussy cologne as they set off down the driveway, the breeze whipping her curls into the air, her spirits lifting further out of the doldrums with every metre they covered. While Nikos steered around the twists and turns of the narrow coast road, Abbie took the opportunity to drink in the scenery; the tiny villages and hamlets with just a few houses, the coves and beachside tavernas along the narrow strips of beach to their right.

By the time they arrived at their destination, dusk was well into its second act and the sun had disappeared behind Mount Pantokrator, the highest peak in Corfu, delivering a welcome respite from the heat of the day. Nikos slowed down to navigate the steep hill that led to a rocky headland offering the most spectacular view across the sparkling sapphire sea, all the way to Albania in the distance, and parked the Vespa beneath a majestic wild pear tree.

'This way.'

Nikos strode towards a wooden gate, hidden from view by a cluster of verdant foliage, and pushed it open with a flourish, and when Abbie stepped into the garden beyond, she gasped. Everywhere she looked there was botanical beauty; olive trees, strawberry trees, pomegranate trees, carob trees, and arrow-straight cypresses, with winding limestone pathways weaving their way through grasses, chamomile, irises, and purple honesty, sending puffs of fragrance into the air as she walked past.

Every corner she turned delivered a jaw-droppingly magnificent vista; a courtyard here, a stone terrace there, a pergola providing shade for a dalliance to appreciate the almost magical landscape, every glimpse set against the backdrop of the deep blue of the Ionian Sea.

'What is this place?'

'It's the Kassiopia Estate; designed by an architect who trained with Norman Foster. I went to school with one of the gardeners here, Andreas, who actually dated my sister for a few months, but that didn't stop us from being friends.' Nikos laughed, taking her hand to lead her along a narrow walkway that led to a smart decking area overlooking a pebble beach where two upholstered sunloungers were stationed in the perfect position for their users to take advantage of the view. 'I called him this afternoon, and, as a favour, he agreed to arrange for us to spend an hour alone in the garden.'

'Oh, Nikos, that's…'

To Abbie's surprise she experienced an uptick of emotion. She sunk down onto one of the sunloungers, and stared out at the undulating sea, watching the sky morph from pale blue to apricot, dusky pink, pale lilac, the colours reflecting in the elegant plunge pool at their feet. As she continued to sit, awed by the natural beauty spread out in front of her, smiling at the ever-present symphony of the cicadas, a mantle of serenity wrapped its tendrils around her body, and all of her worries about the Hummingbird Hotel's guests faded into insignificance.

'Thank you for doing this, Nikos. Just being here has reaffirmed my love of all-things botanical; I can see the blue and white agapanthus and the purple honesty in a gorgeous bouquet, those irises in a stylish wreath, those cyclamen in a wrought-iron planter, and wow, look at the orchids! I love orchids! In fact, the pink butterfly orchid was my mum's absolute favourite plant and I've been trying to source one for the winery's garden without any luck.'

Abbie could feel her passion for floral design burst from the hiding place she'd relegated it to after her fall-out with Dan, and for the first time since she'd left London, her heart broken, acutely embarrassed at the way their relationship had ended in full view of all of their family and friends, she realised that the sharp sting that episode engendered had diminished considerably.

'I knew you would love it here.' Nikos grinned, delighted at her reaction as he took a seat next to her, his lips twisting slightly at the proximity of the pool. 'Sofia told me that you won several prestigious awards for your designs when you were working at the florists' shop in London.'

'Yes, I did.'

'That must have been very gratifying.'

'It was, I suppose, but it wasn't just me; the awards, the prizes, they were a team effort…'

Abbie paused and she couldn't help but smile as an image of Emily shaking her head at her in annoyance floated across her mind's eye, insisting that the accolades were in recognition of *her* creative genius, and for the way *she* utilised a wide range of flowers, plants, shrubs and foliage to create eye-catching floral arrangements and architecture.

Even now, she could hear the cry of her confidence demons telling her to hang back and to let Dan take credit for her talent, to enjoy the limelight. But what was wrong with that? They'd been a couple, and she had loved seeing the smile on his face when he walked onto the various stages to accept a trophy, or a certificate, or a rosette, and what was more, Dan loved all the attention, the applause, the congratulatory handshakes, and she did not.

'So why did you leave?'

'I didn't leave, I was fired.'

'You were fired! After winning all those awards?'

'Well, "fired" might be too strong a word, "let go" would probably be more accurate – in both senses of the word.'

'What do you mean?'

Abbie's heart began to race. This was the perfect opportunity, and setting, for her to talk to Nikos about Dan; something she had wanted to do for a while but just hadn't found the right time. She had tried not to think about that night at the Sky Garden restaurant and the subsequent implosion of life as she'd known it, but she knew that wasn't a very healthy way of dealing with her relationship breakdown. She had to accept what had happened, take responsibility – for she was the one to blame, after all – and concentrate on the future instead of raking over the past until she was looking at her sanity in the rear-view mirror. Part of doing that was talking about what had happened.

'I used to work alongside my boyfriend, Dan, who owned the boutique – *FlowerEssence* – so that meant he was my boss as well as my partner. His parents bought the business for him, so, when we broke up… well, he thought it would be best for both of us if I moved on and found something else.'

'That must have been difficult.'

'It was. I adored my job, well, the design side of things, at least. I even enjoyed getting up at four a.m. to go to the flower market when Dan couldn't be bothered. I miss the friends I made there, and I regret not having had the chance to say goodbye to them.'

A surprise whoosh of sadness ambushed her for the loss of her previous life, a life that would have been so different if it were not for a quirk of fate that had meant she had caught a glimpse of Dan through the window of Tiffany's and stupidly thought that meant he was choosing an engagement ring for her.

'I know how you feel,' Nikos murmured.

'You do?'

She turned to see that Nikos' gaze was fixed on the point in the distance where the sea met the darkening sky, his jaw clenched, his hands bunched into tight fists, and a surge of compassion flooded her veins. What she had been through with Dan was nothing to what Nikos had endured when his father and brother had died in a sailing accident, and even now, two years later, she'd seen first-hand that he still harboured a deep-seated fear of the water.

'When I got the call about the accident, I dropped everything in Paris and flew straight over here to support my mother and sister. I didn't go back to France for several months, and only then to resign my position at the restaurant so I could take over full-time at the vineyard and the winery. For me, that decision required no consideration. I had no choice. I couldn't expect my mother to manage the winery, and anyway she'd already decided to move to Athens to live with Helena and her grandchildren.'

'I'm so sorry, Nikos.'

Silence descended, save for the gentle splash of the water in the plunge pool, and out of nowhere, a thought occurred to Abbie. Nikos had done so much for her since she'd arrived in Corfu, teaching her to cook without judgement of her sub-par culinary skills, allowing her to renovate the winery's garden to her own specifications, gifting her the opportunity to learn from an expert about viticulture, as well as gently urging her to work on banishing her confidence monsters to the dark crevices where they belonged, so it was time she repaid his support, but she knew she had to tread carefully.

She pushed herself up from her seat, kicked off her shoes, and sat on the edge of the tiny plunge pool, savouring the delicious coolness of the water between her toes and the way the light from the solar lanterns dotted around the garden danced on the rippling surface.

'I think our hour is up.'

The slight wobble in Nikos' voice caused Abbie's heart to perform a summersault of sympathy, and yet she wanted to do this. When her mum had passed away, she had struggled for weeks to even take one step into the garden she had tended so lovingly at her Devonshire cottage, knowing that every flower, every leaf, every shrub would remind her of her loss and add to her grief.

Only when her mum's best friend, Barbara, had taken her gently by the hand and walked the gravelled pathways with her, had she realised that the garden could be a place of solace. In that moment, she experienced a flash of self-insight – that was exactly what she was doing now by avoiding dealing with her aunt's personal possessions, still there in her bedroom at the hotel, just as she had left them, but she pushed that fact aside for the moment to concentrate on the present.

'Nikos, why don't you come and sit beside me; the water is wonderful.'

'I don't—'

Abbie smiled at him and reached up for his hand. She saw the hesitation, the vacillation between wanting to run away and hide, and yet also wanting to show her that he could at least do this simple act. Time seemed to grind to a halt as Nikos wrestled with his own terrible demons, his fear of water since his father and brother's accident threatening to overwhelm him to such an extent that he seemed to be frozen to the spot. Abbie took pity on him, stood up, laced her fingers through his and slowly, gently, guided him to the water's edge of the pool.

'Take your shoes off,' she whispered.

As though in a trance, his eyes fixed on the water's surface, Nikos did as she asked, and she coaxed him downwards until they were sitting side by side, their toes in the water, watching the ripples undulate as they moved their feet backwards and forwards. Abbie had no idea how long they sat there, or what caused her to do what she did next, but it was as though some external force was at play, directing her actions like she was performing a role in a film. She released her grasp on Nikos' hand and slipped into the pool, exhaling a sigh of pleasure as the cool water caressed her skin like silk.

'Abbie, I—'

She had no intention of forcing Nikos to do anything he didn't feel completely comfortable with. In fact, the fact he had actually sat on the edge of the pool at all was sufficient progress for one evening, and yet, she saw a flicker of determination flash across his eyes. To her absolute amazement and delight, she watched as Nikos slipped into the water to join her, all the while holding her gaze until he reached her side, pulled her gently towards him, removed a tendril of damp hair from her cheek and tucked it behind her ear. Then he kissed her, and kissed her again, and again, and again.

A maelstrom of emotions tumbled through Abbie's body, her heart beating so violently that she was sure Nikos could feel it through her flimsy tee-shirt. Desire zoomed through her veins and sparkled out to her fingertips as the water rippled rhythmically around them, and she lost herself in his ardent embrace, breathless when she eventually pulled from his arms, a smile on her lips as she bobbed in the pool beside him.

'Are you okay?'

'Never better!'

Nikos grinned and Abbie's heart soared as once again he threaded his arm around her waist and drew her close, his breath tickling at the tip of her earlobe and sending a kaleidoscope of sensations cascading through her body, which reached a crescendo when again, his soft lips met hers. She wished she could have stayed there all night, wrapped in Nikos' embrace, but to her embarrassment, her stomach had other ideas and gave a loud rumble of objection at its neglect.

Nikos laughed. 'Come on, we'd better get out of here before Andreas finds us.' He hauled himself quickly from the water, then turned to offer Abbie his hand and pulled her from the pool, too, before running his fingers through his hair to reinstate the cute spikes.

'Nikos, I—'

But Nikos placed his finger on her lips to stop her from

talking, from dissecting the meaning of what had just happened, the giant step forward he had just taken to conquering his fears, and she had to respect that. Nevertheless, she was so proud of him, and once again he had, maybe unwittingly, taught her another lesson; to have the courage to take a leap of faith into the unknown, because until you did that you had no idea what you were actually capable of. And she didn't have to do it alone, there were people around to help her. Okay, not family, but good friends who would help her to achieve her goals, and wouldn't judge her if she failed.

'Come on, let's go grab some food. I know a great little taverna just around the corner, run by an old school friend that serves the best souvlaki in the whole of Corfu.'

Together, they dashed from the garden, hopped onto the Vespa, and within minutes they were sitting at a secluded table on the balcony of Taverna Yannis with a bottle of wine from the neighbouring island of Kefalonia, enjoying freshly baked bread, a huge Greek salad, and as promised, the most delicious chicken souvlaki Abbie had ever tasted.

When she couldn't manage another mouthful, Abbie sat back in her chair, exhaled a long, satisfied breath, and sent up a missive of thanks to the director of fate who had decided to send her to this little corner of paradise and ensured that her path crossed with a man as amazing as Nikos Angelopoulos.

Chapter Nine

The Balcony at Taverna Sofia.
Flower: Fragrant White Jasmine

The next morning, Abbie woke to the uplifting sound of the dawn chorus, something she had missed whilst living in London where she was invariably roused from her slumber by the roar of commuter traffic and the blaring horns of impatient drivers. As usual, shafts of sunlight sliced through the shutters, highlighting the dust bunnies dancing a jig on her bedside cabinet. With a burst of energy, she jumped out of bed, grabbed a towel, and stepped into the shower, running an extra-generous dollop of conditioner through her hair in the faint hope that it would make it look less like she'd stuck her fingers in an electric socket.

As she pulled on a pair of white shorts and turquoise tee-shirt, memories of the previous evening, of Nikos kissing her in the plunge pool at the Kassiopia Estate, floated through her mind and delicious slivers of attraction curled through her body. However, what really caused her heart to soar was the fact that, with her encouragement, he had taken a first step towards dealing with his fear of water. And yet, her euphoria was short-lived because she knew that meant it was now her turn to face the issue she had been avoiding since arriving in Corfu – sorting out her Aunt Liz's personal possessions.

Abbie stepped onto the landing and paused outside the room her aunt had used as her private space before she had passed away at the beginning of the year. Apart from a brief glance, Abbie had avoided going in there, making excuse after excuse to not have to face the task of packing up the items her aunt had loved – even now, there seemed to be an invisible force preventing her from opening the door and just getting on with it.

Instead of discovering her family's secrets for herself, Sofia had provided her with the bare facts; that her aunt had eloped with her mum's fiancé, and that had been the catalyst for the sisters' estrangement. She didn't know any of the details, apart from the fact that Liz had left with Greg to live in California. She didn't know why she'd moved to Corfu to run a hotel, or why they'd never been able to find a way to bridge the rift and move forward to forgiveness, a situation that had meant Abbie had never had the chance to know her aunt, even after her mum had died. She had been disappointed when she'd visited her aunt's lawyer in Corfu Town to be told that, other than the will leaving her the Hummingbird Hotel and a small financial legacy, there had been no letter or any other document to explain why she'd done so.

Abbie continued to stare at the door, her heart

pounding, causing her breath to come in shallow spurts. Maybe there was something amongst her aunt's belongings that would tell her the full story; a diary, a journal, that letter she had been hoping for, and yet far from being excited by the prospect of at last understanding the most traumatic event in her family's past, she was scared of what she might find, and it was much easier to put it off for another day – one where she didn't have four guests to look after.

She skipped down the stairs into the kitchen and began preparing breakfast; an assortment of pastries she'd sourced from the local bakery along with home-made yoghurt, a pot of local honey, and a huge platter of fresh fruit – melon, strawberries, figs, mangoes, pineapple. She set out the Hummingbird Hotel's logoed cups and saucers so her guests could help themselves to the coffee from the hi-tech machine, which looked like something from the International Space Station, when they eventually surfaced from their rooms. She then grabbed her satchel and sauntered down the driveway to Sofia's taverna.

'Hey, Rachel, can I get a cappuccino, please?'

'Sure.'

To Abbie's surprise, Rachel didn't greet her with her usual smile, or linger for a chat. Instead, she headed straight for the bar where Kostas – the taverna's handsome barman – had been conspicuous by his absence for the last two weeks, and began to prepare Abbie's coffee; another break from the norm as she invariably made several detours before fulfilling any customers' order, although Abbie wasn't surprised when she got an espresso, which, when she saw the distress on Rachel's face, she decided to accept with good grace.

'Rachel? What's wrong?'

'I—'

Rachel hesitated for a second, and then dropped down into the seat next to Abbie, tossed her long, copper-coloured hair over her shoulder, and inhaled a breath. But when she opened her mouth, no words ensued. As Abbie waited for her to gather her thoughts, her friend's whole body seemed to crumple, and her eyes filled with tears.

'Rachel?'

'It's Kostas,' said Rachel, her voice strained with emotion.

'What's happened? Is he okay?'

'Sofia's just told me that he's handed in his notice.'

'But why?'

'Because… because he's got a job at another restaurant… in Kefalonia, and…' Rachel paused and met Abbie's gaze, struggling to deliver her next sentence. 'And he's announced his engagement.'

'Oh, Rachel, I'm so sorry.'

Abbie reached out and drew Rachel into her arms, holding her until her friend's tears abated. She knew that Kostas had been one of the reasons Rachel had stayed on in Corfu after spending the previous summer there, post-graduation, to pursue her love of painting and to escape her family's expectation that she would join their dental practice and spend the rest of her life staring into patients' mouths.

'Are you okay?'

Rachel nodded, drying her eyes on a serviette from the pocket of her apron.

'It's such a shock. I had no idea—'

'Hey, guys! Want to know what our celestial gods have

in store for us today?' Felix chirped, materialising before them in the most outrageous outfit yet – an all-in-one Spandex bodysuit in fluorescent green that left very little to the imagination.

'Oh my God, Felix! You can't wear that.' Abbie gasped, although she was relieved to see that his appearance had cheered Rachel up immeasurably, and she was now making an unsuccessful attempt to disguise her giggling.

'This? Why not?'

'Because you look like a Kermit's more… more… muscular cousin.'

'I'll take that as a compliment.' Felix beamed, glancing down at his outrageously eye-popping attire before pulling up a chair next to Rachel. 'Okay, so, Abbie first. I've read your horoscope, and today you will be frolicking in the water like a sea nymph before revelling in the nectar of the gods, with a side order of arboreal splendour.'

Abbie laughed. 'Felix, you know there's a water aerobics class at the hotel this morning – you're leading it! And we have a vineyard tour and wine-tasting session at the winery this afternoon.'

Felix, however, ignored Abbie's eye roll and turned to face Rachel, taking her hand into his, his expression more serious than usual.

'And Rach.'

'Yes?' She smirked, exchanging a glance with Abbie.

'You are going to receive the most amazing offer of your life so far!'

Rachel's smile melted from her lips.

'I don't think so, Felix.'

'Trust me! I can't wait to share your joy because…'

'Because what?'

'Well, because *my* horoscope says I should spend the day alone, meditating and aligning my chakras, otherwise disaster will befall all those around me.'

'Well, that bit's true, at least.'

'What do you mean?' Felix's eyes sharpened as he stared at Rachel.

'Disaster has already "befallen" someone close to you.'

'Who?'

Rachel shook her head, once again overcome with emotion, so Abbie stepped in to explain.

'Kostas has announced his engagement.'

Felix stared at Rachel for a beat before reaching out to lace his fingers gently through hers. 'I know you might not want to hear this right now, but there's someone special waiting for you where you least expect it.'

'Where exactly?' asked Rachel, unable to prevent a smile from tugging at her lips despite her despondency.

'Amongst the magnificence of nature.'

Now it was Rachel's turn to roll her eyes. Shaking her head, she leaned forward to deposit a kiss on his cheek before jumping from her seat to serve the table of customers who had been trying to catch her attention for the last few minutes.

'Amongst the magnificence of nature? Really?' asked Abbie, raising her eyebrows at Felix.

'Time will prove me right. There was something about an opera, too, or it could have been an aria, or a concerto, or maybe it was a rock concert, but I didn't want to confuse her any further.'

'Wise.' Abbie checked her watch. 'Okay, I'd better get back to the hotel. I'll see you on the pool terrace in thirty minutes for your aerobics class. Oh, and Felix?'

'Yes?'

'Do you think you could throw on a tee-shirt?'

'Lavender or saffron?'

'Your choice.'

'Your wish is my command!'

'Thank you.'

Abbie finished her espresso and all-but jogged back to the hotel. When she checked the kitchen, she was relieved to see that every crumb of the breakfast she had left had vanished and her guests were lounging in the courtyard, sipping coffees and admiring the mesmerising view.

'Hi, everyone! How was dinner last night?'

'Absolutely amazing!' declared Katie, the only one not shielding her eyes behind a pair of sunglasses. 'Pierre's friend is a really interesting guy, and the food was delicious, but I think this lot might have indulged in a few too many ouzos.'

'That stuff's lethal,' Allyssa muttered, massaging her temples with her fingertips. Despite her obvious hangover, she still looked like she was about to step onto the catwalk in her gem-encrusted sandals and her scarlet wrap-around sundress with matching bandana that held her hair away from her expertly made-up face. 'I'm never drinking again.'

'Well, no one forced you to sample every cocktail on the menu,' said Brad, tossing back the last of his rich, dark Greek coffee before jumping from his seat with a burst of energy that caused Allyssa to grimace. 'Okay, guys, it's nine fifty-five; time for our water aerobics session, which I'm sure will provide the perfect antidote to a Corfiot hangover. Come on, punctuality is the foundation of success!'

'Ergh,' Josh groaned, but he still grabbed his camera and joined Brad.

'Come on, Ally, an hour in the pool will do us good,' said Katie, extending her hand to pull Allyssa up from her chair, the collection of silver bangles jangling around her wrist as she hooked her arm through Allyssa's and guided her to the stone archway and through the jasmine-bedecked pergola that led to the swimming pool.

The heady aroma of the jasmine, coupled with Katie's sweet, floral scent and Allyssa's more exotic oriental perfume, tickled at Abbie's nostrils, and her spirits raised even further when she arrived poolside to see that Felix was already waiting for them to arrive, and although he *was* wearing a tee-shirt – the lavender one – it did little to disguise the contours of his impressive physique.

'Okay, now I'm glad I came!' Katie giggled, her eyes out on stalks as she watched Felix lean forward to fiddle with the sound system until a blast of music finally burst forth from the three speakers that he'd stationed around the swimming pool.

'Me too.' Allyssa grinned, her hangover having miraculously disappeared as she strode over to one of the sunloungers where she proceeded to untie her wrap dress to reveal a gorgeous one-piece swimsuit in a rich raspberry colour, cut high on the hip with one ruffled shoulder strap, her long, colt-like legs seemingly endless as she kicked off her heels, padded towards the pool steps and lowered herself slowly into the water. 'Ah, I feel better already. Come on, Katie, what are you waiting for?'

Katie dropped her over-sized beach bag – woven

from indigo and white raffia in the shape of a sailing boat, complete with attached pirate flag – onto the sunbed next to Allyssa's, and quickly stepped out of her shorts to reveal a pretty pink tankini embroidered with butterflies. She gathered her hair into a high ponytail, secured it with a clip, and waded into the pool, closing her eyes as the cool water washed over her skin.

'Josh! What are you doing?' Allyssa called out.

Abbie watched as Josh made sure his camera was carefully stored beneath his beach towel, then ripped off his polo shirt and jumped into the water, at speed, feet first, causing a huge splash, and Allyssa and Katie to squeal in consternation.

'Oh my God, Josh, stop it! You know I hate getting my hair wet!'

'Sorry, Allyssa, I forgot.'

However, Josh couldn't look any less sorry as he waded through the water to join them in the middle of the pool where they were waiting for Brad to remove his beautifully pressed, peppermint-green linen shirt and smart navy-blue shorts, fold them with practised care, and place them deliberately on the sunlounger furthest away from the pool before, like Allyssa and Katie, lowering himself slowly into the water and turning to face Felix, an expectant look on his face.

'Okay, everyone, welcome to this morning's water aerobics class! It's great to see you all so bright-eyed and bushy-tailed and ready to indulge in an invigorating session in the pool. I can promise you that, by the time you've finished your workout, you'll be zinging with energy and vitality!'

'Hey, Abbie, aren't you joining us?' Katie called.

Abbie made an on-the-spot corporate decision that Brad would be proud of. 'Actually, no, I'm not. I've got a few things to sort out, but I'll see you for lunch on the veranda at one.'

And before they could persuade her otherwise, she hotfooted it from the terrace as Felix cranked up the music and began calling out the warm-up routine, demonstrating the vigorous moves from the side of the pool, and clearly enjoying every moment.

Chapter Ten

The Angelopoulos Vineyard and Winery
Flower: Vibrant Yellow Marigolds

After servicing the rooms and replenishing the towels and toiletries, then scrubbing the kitchen until it sparkled, sweeping the veranda and raking the gravel in the courtyard, Abbie changed into a fresh tee-shirt and made her way to the little wooden shed at the front of the hotel where she liberated her aunt's old bicycle, which, like many other things, her Aunt Liz had painted in the hotel's signature blue colour.

This was what she had been looking forward to since she woke up that morning – spending a couple of hours in the Angelopoulos Garden. She pedalled quickly down the driveway, turned right past the taverna and onto the main road, enjoying the physical exercise, the cool breeze on her cheeks, and the rhythmic chirp of the cicadas, which would always be the backing track to her time on Corfu.

Ten minutes later, she arrived at the impressive forecourt

of the winery. She leaned her bicycle against the wall of the central fountain – fashioned in the shape of an angel – and made her way to the rear of the building, her heart skipping a beat with anticipation as she strode across the terrace towards the garden in which she'd spent nearly every waking hour of the last three weeks.

With Nikos, Dimitris, and Felix's help, she'd worked hard to clear the tangle of overgrown bushes, shrubs, and plants, before spending several enjoyable days and nights in front of the computer designing the layout, the excitement bubbling in her stomach almost too much to bear. She had created six interconnected zones, woven together with a network of limestone footpaths, punctuated by shady nooks and crannies housing wooden and bamboo seating – even a garden swing – the occasional stone statue and carved niche, and a collection of solar fountains she'd found discarded in the corner of a barn.

However, the most exciting part of the project was always going to be the planting and when Nikos had taken her to the local nursery she'd been like a kid in a sweet shop, dashing from one section to the next, exclaiming at the myriad choice of all-things horticultural, especially the orchids whose name, she'd been delighted to discover, was derived from the Greek word for testicles.

She had always adored orchids – the bumble bee orchid, the bird's nest orchid, the burnt-tip orchid, and of course, her mum's personal favourite, the pink butterfly orchid – and was more than a little disappointed when Nikos sought out the owner to enquire about buying one for her, only to be told they were difficult to find.

Undeterred, she had continued her explorations, and if she hadn't been constrained by her ever-dwindling bank balance, she would have splurged on everything that was there. Instead, she took photographs of those shrubs and plants she would like to cultivate in the future when her funds allowed, then threw herself into creating her dream garden – one that was a great deal more exotic than she had dared wish for.

Strolling along the main pathway now, she marvelled at how easy it was to grow things on Corfu. While the island boasted year-round sunshine, it also enjoyed one-hundred-and-twenty-eight days of rain, and the Ropa Valley, in particular, had rich, fertile soil – the perfect combination to produce a vibrant and diverse selection of plants. Of course, the garden was by no means finished yet, and there was still a great deal to do, and lots more plants and flowers she wanted to showcase to potential visitors, but she had made more progress than she had thought possible – it was amazing what you could do when a life-long passion for something took over.

She crouched to remove an errant clump of grass from the middle of the cactus garden she had spent a whole week designing and planting, including not only a host of pretty flowering cacti, but also a swathe of colourful pea gravel and larger-sized stones and rocks to add interest and texture. Satisfied the area was pristine, she meandered through to the herb garden where she'd chosen a mixture of plants – some in the ground, some in terracotta pots – then to what she had to admit was her favourite part of the garden – the wildflower area. It was a place she had filled with colourful flowers and grasses of all shapes and sizes – geraniums, poppies, buttercups, daisies, primroses, cornflowers, and gorgeous vibrant yellow marigolds, with a small area of soil reserved for when she eventually managed to locate her longed-for pink butterfly orchid – anything that would attract bees and butterflies and the indigenous wildlife.

She paused where the path bordered the vineyard and took a moment to appreciate the view. As well as relishing her passion for all-things flower-related, she had been excited to learn everything there was to know about cultivating vines, impatient to hear the secrets from Thanos, her burgeoning interest in the subject like an itch that needed scratching. She was also keen to understand the broader botanical landscape, to expand her knowledge on not just a theoretical basis, but a practical one too, to actually watch the plants grow instead of simply purchasing the end product to sell in Dan's florists' shop.

Abbie sighed; she had so many plans for the garden, and the vineyard, and the olive groves, but running the hotel, welcoming guests, servicing the rooms, organising the retreats, and doing the admin and the promotion, too, meant she had little time to spare.

Then a flash of inspiration burst into her mind.

Why didn't she ask Felix to come on board in a bigger way? He'd already told her that he'd done a variety of odd jobs for her aunt; maintaining the swimming pool, painting the exterior of the hotel, the occasional simple plumbing job. He clearly loved presenting his yoga classes, so could he also be the hotel's assistant manager? Website designer? Goat herder? Smoothie supplier? It sounded like the ideal solution, and with the extra help at the hotel she could spend more time at the vineyard and the garden.

A surge of exhaustion washed over her, and, as the temperature started to climb, she dropped down onto a sun-bleached chair in the shade of a magnolia tree next to a solar fountain made from a set of upturned Greek urns. The only sounds around her were those created by nature; the tinkling of the water, the birds hoping from branch to branch, the bees enjoying a nectar bonanza amongst the petals of the plethora of flowers she'd selected, and, the ubiquitous symphony of the cicadas.

She inhaled a deep breath and closed her eyes, relishing the fragrance of so many different aromas that floated on the scant mid-morning breeze; the baked soil, the sweet fragrance from the garland of honeysuckle entwined around the pergola overhead, which offered much-needed shade from the midday sun, and the faint whiff of lavender and lemon mint from the herb garden.

Abbie smiled. She could never have created something as breath-taking, uplifting, or soul-affirming as this if she'd stuck to her original plan to move from London to a tiny cottage in the Devonshire countryside. As she sat there, she sent up a missive of thanks to the Greek god in charge of her destiny for delivering her to that wonderful place, and she made a mental note not to forget that no matter what kind of obstacles life tossed into your path, if you worked hard enough, dreams could come true. They might not be the same dreams you started out with, but that was okay; dreams didn't stay frozen in isolation but morphed with circumstances, with opportunities, with people who came along to share them with you, and it was the ability to embrace change, to reinvest in yourself and your passions, that truly delivered happiness.

Dreams could change, because it was the *journey* not the destination that mattered.

An image floated into her mind and suddenly there was something she wanted, no, something she needed to do. She removed her phone, selected the most-used number in her contacts list, and waited, crossing her fingers that her call would be answered, her heart filling with joy when her wish was granted.

'Hi Emily, how's things?'

'Oh God, how long have you got?'

'Is everything okay?'

'Well, I knew it had to happen at some point, but I hadn't anticipated that it would be so soon. I thought I'd have until at least the end of the year. I was planning on taking a week off at the beginning of December, before things went crazy with Christmas shows and stuff at the pâtisserie, but, well, best laid plans and all that.'

Abbie could hear the strain in Emily's voice and knew immediately what had happened.

'Your mum?'

'Yes. Would you believe she decided to come down to London to "surprise me"? It's the first time she's done something that hasn't been organised right down to the last five minute unit, and she actually handed over one of her court cases to her assistant so she could treat me to afternoon tea. At first, when I saw her standing on the doorstep, I panicked. I thought something awful must have happened, but she said she just wanted to see me, then proceeded to cross-examine me on which theatre I was working at, which show I was in, what role I was playing, and insisting that she grab a ticket for that evening's performance. Only I wasn't working at the theatre that night, I was working at the pâtisserie, so…'

Abbie heard Emily inhale a deep breath to deliver her next words.

'So I took her for a drink at the wine bar on the corner and told her the truth.'

'What? Everything?'

'Yes, everything. I told her how much I appreciated what she and Dad had done for me, that I had thought I wanted to be an actor and had loved the time I'd spent at drama school, but that the industry just wasn't for me, not long-term anyway – that my heart just wasn't in it, that I didn't feel that scorch of passion that my fellow thespians did.'

'What did she say?'

'She couldn't resist reminding me that she had cautioned me, on several occasions, against a career in the acting profession, that she knew I should have taken her advice and signed up for a degree in law, that I would have made, still would make, a great solicitor or barrister. So imagine her shock when I told her that wasn't what I wanted either; that I had a new dream, something that made my heart sing, especially when I saw a customer's eyes light up at the first taste of one of my raspberry and white chocolate millefeuille, or my lavender-infused macrons, or my blueberry and ginger eclairs, how I'd already learned so much from André, but that what I truly wanted was to go to Paris and take a course in real French pâtisserie from one of the master confectioners there.'

'How did she react?'

'Oh, Abs, it was awful, seeing the confusion on her face,

the bewilderment, the disappointment, then she proceeded to lecture me on how much she and Dad had spent on voice coaches, extra acting classes, uni fees, and told me in no uncertain terms that they weren't going to waste any more of their hard-earned money on another one of my whims, especially not as a baker. That if that was what I wanted to do, then I was on my own, and she grabbed her Ferragamo handbag and stormed out of the bar.'

'Em, I'm so sorry, I really am. I'm sure it was just the shock. When she's back home, and had time to reflect on everything you've told her, I know she'll come round.'

'I'm not so sure. I've already had a very strained conversation with Dad, in between his police station call-outs, about "letting the family down for a second time", how it's about time I grew up and took some responsibility for my future, that chopping and changing my career path would look bad on my CV, would make me look unreliable, or words to that effect. I understand their reaction, I really do. I know Dad was hoping I'd be some kind of judge one day, but the thought of that fills me with horror – I could never sit in judgement on anything, let alone something important enough to be litigated over!'

'So, what are you going to do?'

'I've got a week off at the end of the month, so I might take a trip home to Chelmsford and talk to them when the dust settles, explain to them how I feel, hopefully help them understand that I appreciate everything they've done for me, but I've got to follow the path that makes me happy. You know, I had a dream last night that I bought a decrepit campervan, painted it orange, and drove it around the country selling hand-made pâtisserie, and when I woke up, I had a huge smile on my face. That's where my future lies, not some dusty old courtroom or in a dressing room that smells like sweaty socks. Anyway, enough about me, how's things at the Hummingbird Hotel?'

Abbie hesitated. Emily clearly had enough going on in her life without Abbie adding her own problems to the list.

'Everything is fine, great, really great.'

'So does that mean you've sorted out your aunt's personal stuff?'

Abbie groaned; typical Emily, straight in there with the crucial question, slicing to the core of any problem. She swallowed down on her rising emotions, and forced her voice to remain neutral in the hope of diverting the conversation to a less difficult subject.

'Erm, no, not yet, but I—'

'What are you waiting for? I thought you were desperate to find out more details about what happened after your aunt eloped with your mum's fiancé? If there was nothing at her solicitor's office, and you suspect Sofia was holding something back, then the answers you want could be there, in her papers and documents. Maybe she left a letter for you, or kept a diary or a journal. The only way you'll know is to get in there and take a look.'

Abbie's stomach performed a summersault of anxiety. Emily was right, of course, she was desperate to uncover the mystery of her past, to find the answers to the questions that had been plaguing her for so long so she could, at last, banish the demons that had sapped her confidence all the time she had been living in London, and throughout her relationship with Dan. Whilst the truth of what had happened between her aunt and her mum had hurt, the disorientation she had felt in the "not knowing" had diminished, but it hadn't gone; there were still things she needed to understand, details she needed to know to fill in the gaps before she could totally move on.

But could she?

Even if she found a diary or a journal or a letter amongst her aunt's personal belongings, and even if it provided every tiny detail of her aunt's life after she had eloped and settled in California, how she felt about what she'd done, what had happened when – as Sofia had told her – she had reached out to Abbie's mum only to be gently, but firmly, rebuked, there would still be one huge question, a glowing ember of uncertainty festering deep, deep in her soul. Until she found the courage to deal with that issue, she would never be able to move forward and achieve the elusive sense of belonging she craved.

'Abbie? Are you okay?'

'I'm fine.'

'You don't sound fine.' Emily paused, then a determined note entered her voice. 'Right, I'm coming over to Corfu, and we'll sit down and go through your aunt's things together. We'll pack up her personal items, donate everything we can, then sort through her papers and documents. You don't have to do this on your own, Abs, I'm here for you, and whatever we find, I—'

'No, no, Em, that's really kind of you, so thoughtful, and I really appreciate the offer, but you can't do that. You have to go home to talk to your parents, you have to tell them about your dream to buy a campervan and fill it with delicious French goodies. Please, you have to do that, you have to sit down with them, face-to-face, and help them to understand how you feel. You have to let them ask all the questions, and you have to answer truthfully, and then you have to make your peace with them. I'd give anything to have just one more conversation with Mum, mother to daughter, to tell her that I love her, that whatever happened in the past would never affect the way I felt about her, and that keeping secrets was the route to sadness, not happiness. I can't do that now, but you can.'

'Abs—'

'I'd love you to come over to Corfu, but go see your family first. I promise I'll sort through my aunt's stuff just as soon as the current guests have left. I'll parcel everything up, then I'll paint the room, buy some new bed linen, hang a few pictures and have it ready for when you next have a week off from the theatre and the pâtisserie. Okay?'

'Well, I—'

'Please, Em.'

'Okay, okay, on one condition.'

'What's that?'

'That you scour the island for a gorgeous Greek Adonis with sexy, come-to-bed eyes, great abs, and a penchant for nuclear-fall-out-strength cologne, who will sweep me off my feet and persuade me to stay on in the Corfu sunshine and launch my new business there. Do you know any bakers that fit that description?'

Abbie laughed. 'Actually, I do – Nikos' friend Loukas – but unfortunately he's married.'

'Keep looking, Abs, keep looking.'

'I will. And thanks, Em, you're an amazing friend.'

'Back at'cha, darling.'

Chapter Eleven

The Veranda at the Hummingbird Hotel
Flower: Origanum Laevigatum

It was almost lunchtime when Abbie arrived back at the hotel. She quickly set about organising the various dishes that Nikos had prepared and left in the fridge ready for her to simply uncover and put out on the table in the dappled shade of an ancient olive tree. She prepared a cafetière of coffee and huge jug of lemonade – made with lemons she picked from the tree outside the window – determine to avoid serving any kind of alcohol so as not to interfere with the wine-tasting session that afternoon.

At one o'clock on the dot the group arrived on the veranda, laughing, chatting, and being instructed by Brad on the detailed requirements of the corporate photoshoot the following day – something he seemed to be increasingly obsessing about.

'Okay, so, as well as the group photographs of all six of

us, Carlton has been instructed to ensure we each have an individual portrait taken, so I want you to—'

'I still don't see why Josh and I should—'

'I've already explained this to you, Katie,' Brad sniped, the irritation obvious in his voice as he helped himself to a coffee and took it to the chair that presided over the head of the table – clearly unable to eschew the habits of a lifetime, even while on holiday.

Abbie noticed a steely glint in his eyes as he held Katie's gaze, a clear message being sent to her to drop the argument and accept the situation as it was. She watched Katie draw a breath, determined to continue with her argument, but for some reason she changed her mind and helped herself to a plate of salad and a huge slice of *tiropita* instead, choosing a seat as far away from Brad as possible.

'I'm looking forward to having a good gossip with Pippa when she gets here,' said Allyssa, carefully spooning two slices of cucumber, a couple of tomatoes, and a cube of feta cheese onto her plate and folding her six-foot-two frame into the chair next to Katie.

'Me too. I feel like we've been away from home for *so* long. Apparently, she met a Poldark look-alike when she was at Lexie and Theo's wedding in Cornwall a few weeks ago. I can't wait to hear all about it, *and* to drool over the photographs. I wonder if he has a brother?' Katie mused, picking at her salad disconsolately. 'I never thought I would say this, but I'm sick of dating male models who are only interested in the next best thing in skincare or which celebrity parties they've been invited to this month. I think it's time I started dating a few *real* men.'

'You mean like Josh?' whispered Allyssa, pointing

over the veranda to the mini-vineyard beyond where Josh was crouched amongst the vines' frilly green leaves, pointing his camera at a bunch of fat grapes and attempting to catch an image of a lone bee in flight.

'Dating colleagues is against company policy,' Brad interjected, clearly listening in to their conversation.

'Oh, give it a rest Brad,' Allyssa snapped, rolling her eyes at him.

'Just saying.'

'Hey, Brad, I meant to ask you, did I see you with a pair of binoculars earlier? Have you taken up bird-watching, or perhaps you were indulging in a spot of espionage? I mean, who knows what's going on in the peaceful countryside of Corfu,' Katie said sarcastically.

Just as Abbie feared that the whole lunch break was about to descend into a bout of childish bickering, Felix arrived, this time in a pair of patterned board shorts and a pale aquamarine tee-shirt, its sleeves rolled to display his muscular biceps, his tousled blonde curls gathered into a short ponytail. The only thing that was missing was his surf board and a water bottle advertising a Bondi Beach bar.

'Can I get you a lemonade?' asked Abbie.

'Love one, thanks.'

'Hey Felix, are you going to join us for the wine-tasting this afternoon?' asked Josh, dropping his camera onto the table and helping himself to a plateful of food before plonking himself down in the seat next to Katie.

'I'm not sure,' Felix hedged, raising his eyebrows at Abbie who couldn't help but smile at the eager anticipation she saw in his eyes.

'You're very welcome to come along, if that's okay with

Brad.'

'Sure,' Brad mumbled, more concerned with scrolling through his phone messages.

'Awesome! Count me in! And what about Rachel? Can she tag along, too? It's exactly what she needs to lift her spirits.'

'Great idea,' Abbie agreed as Brad was clearly not listening.

'Talking of delicious beverages,' said Allyssa. 'Do you think you could rustle up another one of your amazing smoothies, Felix? I feel like I deserve one after all that exercise you made us do in the pool earlier!'

'I'd love to!'

Felix almost skipped from the veranda into the kitchen. Abbie followed him to see if he needed any help, and to make sure he didn't use the fruit she had planned for the following day's breakfast.

'What do you have in mind this time?'

'Well, we've done green, so I thought red or orange, depending what you have.'

Felix stuck his head in the huge American-style fridge, scrutinising the contents before moving on to inspect the fruit bowl and the various pots of fresh herbs on the windowsill. After careful consideration, he chose a selection of figs, passionfruit, and mangoes, then, to Abbie's surprise, a beetroot salad she had forgotten to put out on the lunch table, a packet of frozen blueberries from the freezer, and a pot of Greek yoghurt.

'Beetroot? Really?'

Felix ignored her grimace and got to work. Within minutes he had whipped up a couple of his exotic concoctions, added a sprinkle of chopped mint and oregano for additional flavour, poured out six glasses and placed them onto a silver tray, even arranging a couple of hibiscus blossoms for aesthetic effect. Abbie was about to carry them outside when the loud rev of a motorbike engine invaded the peace and she heard the cheerful toot of a horn from the front of the hotel. She exchanged a glance with Felix who simply shrugged his shoulders, and together they left the kitchen and went to investigate.

'Wow, dude, that's completely awesome!' Felix declared, jogging down the marble steps and coming to a stop where Nikos was sitting astride a shiny Harley-Davidson, a broad smile on his face.

'Want a ride?'

'Sure!'

Nikos alighted, handed his helmet to Felix, and went to stand next to Abbie to watch him shoot off down the driveway in a cloud of dust, the powerful engine roaring through the air as he put the bike through its paces.

'Don't worry, I'm babysitting it for a friend who's gone to work in Athens for a week.'

Abbie knew how upset Nikos had been when he'd had to part with his own motorbike the previous month, when it looked like the winery was about to descend into bankruptcy. Seeing the boyish excitement in his eyes now made her heart soar and she resolved that, as soon as the business was making a profit again, she would make sure they invested in another – just perhaps not a Harley-Davidson.

Felix skidded to an abrupt halt in front of them, pulled off the helmet, and shook out his curls, looking every inch a rebel without a cause. Not for the first time did Abbie question his ex-fiancée's sanity in leaving him standing at the altar to run off with his best man. For a reason she couldn't fathom, an image of Emily floated into her thoughts; maybe, instead of the Greek Adonis she had so eloquently requested, Abbie could introduce her to an Australian Adonis instead.

'Come on, I could murder a cold drink,' said Nikos.

Abbie led them up the steps to the lobby, through the kitchen, and out to the veranda where she saw that someone had taken the initiative and brought the tray of Felix's red and orange smoothies outside, and that four of the six glasses were empty. She added a bottle of sparkling water, a fresh cafetière of coffee, and a plate of Greek pastries to the table, all of which were consumed within minutes.

'I'm loving this passionfruit and mango smoothie, Felix. This one's definitely going to feature in my book. Don't forget to send me the recipe, will you? And, would you be up for a few promos on Instagram and TikTok?'

'No worries, happy to help.' Felix beamed.

'Wow, it's so hot! I'm off for another dip in the pool,' said Katie, hooking the handles of yet another of her off-the-wall handbags – this one looked like a fluffy white poodle, complete with red leather collar and engraved name tag – over her arm and heading towards the end of the veranda where she paused and looked back over her shoulder.

'Coming, Allyssa?'

'I think I'll take a siesta before we go over to the winery. What time do we need to be ready, Abbie?'

Abbie opened her mouth to answer but Brad got their

first.

'Four p.m. The taxi's due at three forty-five, so please set your alarm, Allyssa. I don't want you oversleeping, although why you should need to sleep in the middle of the day baffles me.'

Allyssa ignored his snipe and followed Katie from the veranda.

'Was that a Harley-Davidson engine I just heard? I'm not a lover of motorbikes myself, wouldn't swap my Audi for anything, unless it's a Ferrari, of course,' Brad mused, picking up one of the remaining red smoothies and downing it in one. 'What did you say was in this weird goo of yours, Felix?'

'Beetroot, blueberries, banana and a sprinkle of basil.'

Abbie couldn't help but smile when she saw Brad twist his lips slightly; it was exactly the same reaction she'd had, except she wasn't brave enough to even taste it – beetroot was the most disgusting vegetable, in her humble opinion.

'Okay, I've got a hundred-and-one emails to catch up on, so I'll be relaxing by the pool with my laptop if you need me for anything.'

As Abbie watched Brad disappear in the wake of Allyssa and Katie, she wondered why she would need to consult him on anything, but decided not to comment – it was probably something he said to his colleagues all the time.

'Want another spin on the bike, Felix?' Nikos asked.

'Love one, mate!'

Felix strode off towards the kitchen, but Nikos hung back for a moment and caught Abbie's eye, nodding his head in the direction of Josh, whom Abbie hadn't noticed was still sitting at the table, contemplating the view and completely lost in his thoughts.

'What?'

Once again, Nikos repeated his weird head nod, and this time she understood what he meant. She groaned, although she knew he was right, this *was* the perfect time to have a chat with Josh, whilst the other guests were otherwise engaged. Her stomach churned. Oh God, she really didn't want to do this. What possible reason could Josh have for ushering a goat into Brad's suite, or positioning his sunbed in such a way that it tipped him into the swimming pool? The more she thought about it, the more she convinced herself that they were both unfortunate accidents and that Brad, and Nikos, had blown things out of proportion.

Nevertheless, Katie had told her that there was some animosity between Brad and Josh and she knew that if she didn't take the chance to ask him about it whilst they were alone, she would regret it later.

'Hey Josh, can I get you anything else to drink?'

Josh gave a jolt of surprise. 'Oh, sorry, I was miles away. No, thanks, I'm good. Where is everyone?'

'Katie's cooling off in the pool, Allyssa's gone for a snooze to build up her strength for the wine-tasting this afternoon, and Brad's answering emails on the terrace.'

'Right, then I think I'll also hop back to my room and run through a few of these photographs. You know, you're so lucky to live here, Abbie, it's a photographer's paradise. The light is just perfect, not to mention the landscape. I wish I still had my Canon EOS R6; I took some stunning images with that camera. Okay, I—'

'Actually, Josh, before you go, do you mind if I ask you something?'

'Of course not; how can I help?'

Josh paused, his second-favourite camera in hand, his caramel-coloured quiff wilting slightly in the mounting humidity. That afternoon, he had chosen to wear a pair of designer chinos and another of his collared polo shirts – this one a muted peppermint – with leather boat shoes, and his friendly face was open with enquiry, which made Abbie feel awful about what she was about to ask him.

'I don't suppose—'

She paused, feeling the heat flood into her cheeks. However, she knew she had to do this, because if Josh was responsible for either of the incidents, she had to make sure he had nothing else up his sleeve that might have a negative impact on the reputation of the hotel.

'I don't suppose you know how the goat managed to get into Brad's guest room on Friday?'

Josh stared at her, and she could almost hear the cogs in his brain turning as he tried to work out what exactly she was asking him.

'I… no, of course not. Why would you ask me that?'

Abbie cringed inwardly, but despite the confusion she saw in his eyes, she stumbled on. 'It's just that… well, goats can't open doors, and Brad was adamant that he hadn't left his patio doors open… and then there's the sunbed, and Katie said—'

'Katie said what?'

Josh's jawline tightened, his knuckles turning white as he clutched his camera and waited for her to answer his question.

'Katie said that she heard you and Brad having an argument, when you were in Sardinia.' Abbie paused again, wondering whether to continue but decided that, as she had dug her hole, she might as well jump in it. 'About money.'

Colour rushed into Josh's cheeks and his jaw dropped.

'Katie listened to a private conversation?'

'I think it was more that she "accidentally overheard" it.'

'Well, she should keep her nose out of other people's business!'

Josh jumped out of his seat and Abbie thought he was going to storm from the veranda, but he seemed to change his mind, deciding to stay and argue his case instead.

'It's true; Brad and I did exchange a few words about money. Before we left for the photoshoot, I asked Brad if he would pay part of my fee upfront, just so I could cover some of the expenses. You have no idea how much it costs to maintain a fashion shoot lifestyle for six weeks; the luxury hotel rooms, the expensive restaurants, the free-flowing Champagne cocktails, the designer clothes so you don't look like the poor relation.'

Josh exhaled a long, ragged sigh and dropped back into his chair, fiddling with the strap of his camera like it was a string of worry beads.

'I'm not a high-flying executive with an expense account like Brad, or an internationally acclaimed model like Allyssa, or an up-and-coming fashion designer like Katie. I'd already maxed out my credit card, but still, Brad refused my request, which meant unless I could find some cash from *somewhere*, I couldn't do the shoot – that was why I had to sell my Canon.'

Abbie saw the genuine distress in Josh's eyes – as though he'd had to say goodbye to a cherished pet – and she experienced a sharp twinge of sympathy for him.

'So, yes, like Katie said, we did argue in Sardinia last week, just before we were due to eat out at *another* of Brad's favourite Michelin-starred restaurants, which I couldn't possibly afford – not even a glass of water! I asked him again if he would give me an advance on my fee, which I can tell you was really embarrassing, but he told me he had more to worry about than my financial circumstances, and that I had to wait until the shoot was over because there were some "great things on the horizon". I asked him what he meant but he wouldn't budge, so I said a few choice words – which I'm not proud of – and stormed off and ended up eating at this fabulous, family-run pizzeria, which I enjoyed much more because I wasn't worrying about the bill all night. So, there you have it; I'm completely broke, and this will have to be my last shoot for the Pierre Fontaine Fashion House because I doubt Brad will use my services again. But, Abbie, I can assure you that however angry I am with him, I did not, and would not, stoop so low as to feed his underwear to a goat!'

'I'm sorry, Josh, I—'

'If you're looking for a potential culprit, then you need to talk to Allyssa.'

And before Abbie could ask what he meant, Josh had slung his camera around his neck and strode from the veranda, his head held high with indignation. Regret cascaded through her veins that she had caused him such distress. She resolved that, from now on, she would draw a line under what had happened and instead, when Pippa arrived the next day for the photoshoot, she would ask her to have a quiet word with Brad in the hope that she could persuade him not to post a bad review of the Hummingbird Hotel's extra-curricular activities when he got back to London.

Chapter Twelve

The Swimming Pool at the Hummingbird Hotel
Flower: Fuchsia 'Sleepy'

'Where's Brad? The taxi's due any minute,' Abbie said to the group.

'Yes, I thought he'd be standing here on the steps with his clipboard and whistle, ready to do a full roll call,' said Allyssa, looking cool and relaxed in a white, ankle-length sundress with a cut-out midriff, her hair styled in a complicated knot on the top of her head and a huge pair of white-framed sunglasses.

'Last time I saw him he was over by the swimming pool, working on his laptop, I think. In fact, he was so engrossed in what he was doing that he didn't even reply when I told him I was going to take a shower and a snooze.' Katie – who had changed into a mini-dress made from fabric printed with various colourful cocktails and carried a bright pink satchel in the shape of a cocktail glass, complete with cherry – twisted her lips in irritation. 'To be honest, it looked like he was napping. I wish I'd taken a couple of photographs, especially after his sneering remarks about siestas being a waste of life, and all that. I mean, hasn't he heard of power naps? I thought all high-flying executives indulged in a quick forty winks at lunchtime so that they're refreshed and super-alert for an afternoon of ordering people about.'

'Want me to investigate?' offered Josh, avoiding Abbie's eye, clearly uncomfortable after their earlier heart-to-heart.

'No, it's fine, I'll go,' said Abbie.

'I'll come with you,' Nikos said, his tone brooking no objection.

Abbie hurried through the lobby, the heels of her sandals click-clacking on the marble tiles, then crunching as she made her way across the gravelled courtyard and along the colonnade to Brad's guestroom. She raised her hand to knock on the door, then paused.

'What's wrong?' asked Nikos.

'I have an awful feeling about this.'

Nikos smiled. 'An attack of goat zombies?'

'It's not funny, Nikos.'

'Look, he's probably just fallen asleep, like Katie said. He *is* human, after all, despite the evidence to the contrary.'

Abbie smiled, the knot of nerves in her stomach

loosening as it always did when Nikos was around to reassure and bolster her confidence. She had come a long way from the person she had been in London, constantly deferring to Dan and allowing him to take the credit for things she had done. She inhaled a breath and rapped on the door, then took a step back and waited for Brad to answer.

Several seconds passed and when there was no response she knocked again, this time louder.

'Brad? It's Abbie. It's time for the wine-tasting class.'

Still there was no reply, and Abbie exchanged a worried glance with Nikos.

'Do you have a key?' he said.

'Yes, but I'm not sure—'

'What's the alternative? Are you going to leave him here while everyone else goes off to the wine-tasting? What do you think he'll say about that?'

'I… okay.'

Abbie reached into her pocket, took out the master key she kept on her person at all times, and cracked open the door a few inches.

'Brad? Are you okay? Brad?'

She paused for a few seconds again. When there was no response, she took a tentative step forward, with Nikos so close behind her she could feel his breath on the back of her neck. Images of increasingly disastrous scenarios swept through her mind, and her heart hammered out a concerto of trepidation against her ribcage. However, when she finally mustered the courage to walk into the room, she saw that it was empty and that the bed was exactly as she had left it when she'd made it up that morning.

'There's no one here.'

'Shame.' Nikos smirked. 'I would have loved to have seen Brad cowering in the corner over there, having been taken hostage by a gang of ninja goats, pleading for mercy and safe passage to the pool in return for a generous supply of sugar lumps. Or should that be designer boxer shorts?'

'Okay, so if he's not here, and he's not waiting on the front steps, where is he?'

'Didn't Katie say she saw him at the pool?'

Abbie strode from the guest room, waiting impatiently for Nikos to saunter out, and locked the door behind them, testing the handle twice for good measure. She then almost sprinted past the hummingbird fountain and through the pergola to the terrace where she came to an abrupt stop, causing Nikos to bump into her.

'Oops, sorry. Look, I told you there was nothing to worry about – there he is!'

Abbie stared at Brad, whom – bearing in mind the time – she was surprised to see was still reclining on the sunlounger furthest away from the pool, his laptop abandoned on the table next to him, sunglasses covering his eyes, clearly enjoying a spot of sunbathing.

'It seems that even hardworking executives are allowed to indulge in a few moments of relaxation whilst they ponder their next assault on the corporate battlefield,' Nikos said with a grin.

'I think he's asleep,' whispered Abbie, tiptoeing across the terrace towards him.

'Brad?'

'Mmm?' Brad murmured groggily as he turned his head slowly towards Abbie, clearly having just woken up, before he pushed himself into an upright position.

'I just came to tell you that it's almost four o'clock; the taxi will be here soon for the wine-tasting tour, but, of course, it's okay if you'd rather stay—'

'Ergh, my head feels fuzzy. I must have fallen asleep. How did that happen? I never fall asleep in the afternoon, never, and certainly not in a public place!'

The horror on Brad's face was almost comical and Abbie couldn't prevent a smile from tugging at the corner of her lips… until he swung his legs over the side of the sunbed and whipped off his sunglasses so he could rub his eyes.

'Oh my God!' Abbie gasped, her hand flying to her lips.

'What?' said Brad, looking over his shoulder to see what had caused her such consternation. 'What's wrong?'

'I… how long have you been asleep?'

'I'm not sure. Why?'

Brad tried to focus on his Rolex, his eyes squinting against the bright sunlight.

'I don't believe it! That's just not possible. I've been asleep for over an hour!'

'And during the hottest part of the day,' Nikos added.

'Did you… did you use sunscreen?' Abbie asked tentatively.

'No, I was sitting in the shade when I… Why?'

Abbie shot a glance in Nikos' direction and had to look away immediately as he was clearly struggling to not laugh out loud.

'Well, because…'

'Because you look like a scarlet panda,' Nikos blurted, unhelpfully.

'A what?'

'Oh, I'd say it was more like a Mister Tomato Head,' said Katie, who had just joined them and clearly had no intention of sparing Brad's blushes.

'I don't know what you're all—'

'Here's a mirror; take a look for yourself.'

Katie scrambled in her Martini glass-shaped handbag, extracted a lipstick case, opened it to the mirror and handed it to Brad, her hazel eyes alight with unconcealed amusement at the sight of her sunburnt boss. Brad all-but snatched the mirror from her, and when he saw his reflection, his jaw dropped in astonishment at the sight of his lobster-red face, glowing like a Belisha beacon from sitting in the direct sunshine – save for two white circles around his eyes where his sunglasses had been.

'Oh, God, I look—'

'Ridiculous? Silly? Bizarre?' Katie supplied.

'But I don't understand…'

'What bit about "mad dogs and Englishmen", don't you get, Brad? Everyone knows that you have to avoid the midday sun, otherwise you get sunburnt, which, I have to tell you, is *so* ageing.'

Brad was still staring at himself in the mirror, unable to accept what he was seeing, until his eyes widened, his jaw dropped, and a streak of panic flashed across his face.

'Oh no! The photoshoot! It's tomorrow! I can't have my photograph taken looking like this!'

Katie giggled. 'Maybe we should leave it to the professionals then, just like I've been telling you for the last six weeks.'

'No, you don't understand, I have to—'

Brad stopped abruptly, then narrowed his eyes at

Nikos as something dawned on him, and he was clearly about to ask him a question when he was interrupted.

'Hey guys, what are you doing here? The taxi's arrived,' Felix called, appearing at the stone archway that led onto the swimming pool terrace. 'Is everything okay?'

'No, everything is most certainly *not* okay,' Brad declared, tossing Katie's lipstick case back to her and jumping up from his sunbed before striding towards Felix whose face morphed from his usual serene contemplation to nervousness at the expression on Brad's scarlet face and the sharp tone of his voice.

'I *never* fall asleep in the afternoon, never! So do you know what I think?'

'Erm, no, I—'

'That disgusting goo stuff that you made at lunchtime?'

'You mean my smoothies?'

'We'll go with "goo"; what exactly did you put in it?'

'Well, that depends.'

'What on?'

'Which one you had.'

'Brad, do we really need to do this now?' Abbie interjected, her throat dry with anxiety. 'I think you need to go back to your room and bathe your face in cold water while I go and see if Allyssa has some aloe vera in her makeup bag that might soothe the skin and take some of the sting away, and then we can—'

'The red one, I had the red one. In fact, I had two.'

'Okay, so that was beetroot, blueberries, banana and yoghurt with a sprinkle of fresh oregano leaves and a few spices to pep it up a little.'

'Then, it's obvious, isn't it? I must have had some kind of

adverse reaction to one of the ingredients which caused me to fall asleep, and look what happened! This is all your fault; you and your organic, vegan, gluten-free, concoctions!'

Brad's temper was rising, his breath coming in spurts, and Abbie could see that his fists were clenched at his sides as he stared at Felix, who was starting to look distressed.

'Okay, okay,' said Nikos, holding up his hand to interrupt Brad's flow. 'I think we should go with Abbie's suggestion. Brad, when you've had chance to think things through, you'll realise that it's highly unlikely that consuming a couple of Felix's smoothies could have any soporific effect on you, or anyone. We all had them, and none of us have indulged in an ill-advised afternoon nap in the scorching hot sun. If you want my opinion, the most plausible explanation for what happened is that you are exhausted from everything you've been doing over the last six weeks, and, now that it's over and you can relax at last, your body is simply catching up on the lack of sleep. Katie, will you go and ask Allyssa if she does have any lotion that could help?'

'Sure,' said Katie, still grinning as she left the terrace.

'Abbie, can you fetch a glass of iced water for Brad to counteract any potential dehydration, and Brad, maybe you should cool down in a darkened room and take a rain-check on the wine-tasting event this afternoon.'

'No way! I'll see everyone on the steps in ten minutes.'

Brad snatched up his laptop, tucked it under his arm, and strode from the terrace, leaving Abbie, Nikos and Felix staring after him. As soon as he'd disappeared, Felix combed his fingers nervously through his hair and then slumped onto the sunbed Brad had vacated, his head in his hands.

'So, this is what my horoscope meant when it said that if I didn't heed the warning to spend the day meditating, then disaster would befall all those around me.' He groaned. 'I should have known something like this would happen, I should have cancelled the water aerobics session this morning, I shouldn't have stayed for lunch, and I shouldn't have experimented on your guests. Abbie, I'm so sorry. Brad's right, this is all my fault.'

Abbie moved forward so she could place her hand on Felix's shoulder.

'But Felix, how could it be your fault? You know as well as I do that a glass of liquidised fruit does *not* cause the unsuspecting consumer to turn into Rip Van Winkle. This is *not* your fault and Brad knows that; he was just looking for someone to blame apart from himself, although why he's so upset about succumbing to an afternoon snooze is beyond me.'

Nikos sat next to Felix and slung his arm around his shoulder.

'Come on, why don't you head back to the taverna to collect Rachel for the wine-tasting? She must be thinking you've forgotten her. We'll see you over at the winery in twenty minutes, ready for a tour of the vineyard.'

'Okay, no worries.'

Felix leapt from the sunbed, his habitual smile back on his face. He gave Nikos a friendly fist bump, dragged Abbie into his arms for a hug, and disappeared the same way as Brad.

'Nikos, I think we should—'

'Come on, let's park this for the time being and get on with the afternoon's itinerary, just like Brad wants us to do. We can dissect the ramifications of whatever's going on – if anything – later. Okay?'

Abbie smiled, and linked her arm through Nikos', grateful that she had someone like him in her corner to support her through the crazy trials and tribulations of the role of a hotelier, a role that so far had been more comedy and drama than factual documentary of how to run a successful hotel on the Greek island of Corfu. There was no way she would be featuring in any of Brad's corporate management videos any time soon.

'Okay, but dinner's on me,' she said.

'Will you be cooking it?'

'No.'

'Deal.'

Chapter Thirteen

The Angelopoulos Vineyard, Ropa Valley, Corfu
Flower: Rock Rose

Twenty minutes later, the Hummingbird Hotel's guests, along with Abbie, Felix and Rachel stood beside the Angelopoulos winery's magnificent angel fountain, in front of Nikos, and a very nervous Dimitris, ready for the inaugural tour of the family's vineyard and – the part everyone was looking forward to the most – the subsequent wine-tasting session.

'Welcome to the Angelopoulos estate,' said Nikos, the pride in his voice clear for all to hear and looking extremely handsome in a pair of buttock-hugging black jeans and fresh white linen shirt cracked open at the collar to reveal a tantalising glimpse of dark chest hair. 'First of all, allow me to introduce you to our vineyard's assistant manager, Dimitris Laskaris, who will be happy to answer any questions you might have about the grape cultivation and harvesting side of the business.'

Abbie couldn't help but giggle when she saw a look of surprise, followed swiftly by panic, dash across Dimitris' face, watching as he reached for his beloved penknife hanging from a loop on his belt to settle his nerves. She noticed that, in honour of the auspicious occasion, he'd spent a little time on his appearance; his usually ruffled mahogany curls were neatly combed and fixed with a smidgeon of gel, he wore a spotless white tee-shirt, a pair of smart navy-blue shorts – complete with creases down the front – and he had clearly raided the cologne cabinet.

'*Yassas*.'

'Hi, Dimitris!' chorused the gathering, much to his delight.

'After the tour, we'll head over to the winery where we'll be tasting two Angelopoulos wines – one white, one red – as well as several others sourced from wineries around the Ionian islands. Then, before you leave, you're in for a special treat. You will be our very first visitors to enjoy a tour of the recently restored Angelopoulos gardens, designed and planted by Abbie.'

'I didn't know you were a landscape gardener as well as an award-winning florist, Abbie,' said Allyssa. 'That's awesome, I can't wait to see what you've created.'

'Well, I'm—'

'She's a woman of many talents,' said Rachel, reaching out to squeeze Abbie's hand before she could launch into a self-deprecating soliloquy instead of simply thanking Allyssa for her compliment.

'Like Brad; he's a man of many talents, too.' Allyssa laughed, gathering her dress into her hands to avoid the dusty path as they followed Nikos and Dimitris through the huge oak gates that led to the vineyard. 'Business manager, publicity guru, retreat organiser, obsessive time-keeper, and now that I've worked my magic on him, he could be a Hollywood actor. I think that shade of foundation rather suits him; I told him that he should definitely wear it more often to smooth out his blemishes. I think he looks like a younger George Clooney.'

'A circus clown, more like,' Katie muttered.

'Well, I did have to trowel it on. It was the only way to conceal the glowing redness and disguise the white panda eyes, which most certainly is *not* a good look.'

'Yes, but did you have to give him those slug-shaped eyebrows?' Josh asked, joining them as they made their way down the first row of vines, his camera trained on an unsuspecting Brad as he tried to steal a snapshot of his new look, something Brad had forbidden him to do on pain of death before they'd arrived at the winery.

'No.' Allyssa giggled.

'I'm surprised he hasn't insisted you remove them.'

'He doesn't know. I told him I didn't have a mirror.'

'Hilarious!'

'No less than he deserves,' said Katie, darkly.

Abbie noticed that since they'd arrived at the winery Brad had diligently avoided any proximity with Felix, studiously avoiding his eyes and the necessity to speak to him, and, when he thought Felix wasn't looking, sending virtual daggers soaring into his back. Thankfully, he'd strode ahead with Nikos and Dimitris, interrogating them about the business side of the vineyard and winery, asking about their plans for maximising production and expanding their range of wines, before going on to provide them with a multitude of unsolicited ideas for potential marketing ventures to attract as many of the one million tourists who arrive on Corfu every year to the winery as possible.

The rest of the group followed at a more leisurely pace, pausing to inspect the vines, and chatting about a whole host of other subjects ranging from that season's swimwear – Allyssa – to that day's horoscopes – Felix and Katie – until they reached a gravelled area at the end of the first row of vines where Nikos was waiting with Dimitris and Brad to continue in his role as vineyard tour guide.

'So, grapes have been grown on Corfu for more than two and a half thousand years. We are blessed with the perfect Mediterranean climate of hot summers and mild winters, and we have more rain than many other Greek islands, which produces the verdant landscape you see all around you, and plenty of irrigation for the vines. You will note that we are standing on a south facing slope, with a magnificent view of the whole of the Ropa Valley, which ensures we receive maximum sunshine during the day and cool temperatures at night; the perfect combination for maintaining the grapes' acidity levels.'

Nikos paused to look around at his audience, clearly delighted to see he had their full attention.

'Here on the Angelopoulos estate, we cultivate two types of grape; *Kakotrigis*, which gives us a fragrant white wine, and *Petrkoritho*, which yields a dry red wine, both of which we'll be tasting later. We also grow a few *fraoula*, which is a table grape, but has been known to be used in wine production, for personal use, all over the island.

Would you like to try them?'

'Yes, please!' the group chorused.

Before Nikos could move an inch, Dimitris had crouched to carefully remove a bunch of the dark red dessert grapes from the stem of the *fraoula* vine using his beloved penknife, then passed them round to everyone to sample.

'How come I've never met Dimitris before?' murmured Rachel, her eyes trained on the taut curve of his buttocks as he bent to remove a second bunch.

'I know, he's gorgeous, isn't he?' Abbie smiled, happy to see the uptick of interest on Rachel's face, and that she had ditched her usual waitress attire of black trousers and white cotton blouse in favour of a short sundress with spaghetti straps and a pair of silver sandals. She'd also taken the time to add a slick of mascara and apricot lip gloss and to twist her long auburn hair into an elegant up-do, held in place by one of her paintbrushes.

'Well, he certainly doesn't look like a typical viticulturist or wine maker.'

Abbie laughed. 'That's because he's not, he's absolutely not. He's actually one of Nikos' friends from high school, and also one of the reasons why last year's vintage tasted like paint stripper, but, like me, he's determined to learn everything he can about growing the best vines possible from Thanos. To be honest, though, he's not really what I would call a natural; he doesn't have the passion, that all-consuming desire to gather every detail and file it away for future use. That's reserved for his love of music – he'd much rather be belting out a tune in the clubs and bars of Sidari and Kavos.'

'Really?' said Rachel, watching as Dimitris offered Allyssa a grape but, in the process, managing to drop it down the front of her dress. 'Interesting.'

'What do you mean?'

'I'm wondering whether I can persuade Sofia to let me organise a local music night at the taverna, and the star attraction could be the cutest singer in the whole of Corfu.'

'Sounds like a plan.'

Abbie was relieved to see Rachel smiling again and, now that the grape-tasting was over, she left her chatting to Felix about a meditation class he was leading the following week for a coterie of stressed out divorce lawyers who were staying at a five-star resort just outside Corfu Town for what was apparently billed as a digital detox. She suspected there would be some cheating going on; whilst she wasn't glued to her social media accounts, a whole week without her phone would freak her out, which in itself made her sad. Maybe she should join them?

The group were now firing random questions at Dimitris and Nikos, some of which were so outlandish that Abbie couldn't help but giggle when she saw the expressions on their faces. She made a mental note to suggest that the next vineyard tour should be conducted by either herself or Thanos, and that it should focus on the horticultural and botanical aspects of growing wine-worthy grapes rather than how singing different genres of music – rock, country, reggae, opera, rap, pop, blues – enhanced the vines' growth and improved their sugar content.

Whilst Nikos led everyone down an adjacent avenue of vines, back towards the winery for the part of the afternoon everyone was looking forward to, Abbie decided to take a short detour to where the Angelopoulos estate bordered the Hummingbird Hotel's mini-vineyard, separated only by a California-esque white picket fence. She smiled; her aunt had clearly lavished a great deal of love on her vineyard – choosing to plant the same type of vines she and her husband had cultivated at their vineyard in the Napa Valley – instead of creating a garden for the hotel's patrons to enjoy.

The three short rows of Cabernet Sauvignon grapes were flourishing; big fat purple grapes that would be ready to harvest weeks before those on the Angelopoulos estate. A thought jumped into her mind; what if they blended the grapes? After all, wasn't that what she and Nikos had done with the tasks required to run their businesses? She filed that possibility away for the time being and, on a whim, she leaned over the fence to pick one of the grapes and pop it into her mouth, the sweet, tangy juice crashing against her tastebuds and giving her a precursor to what their wine might be like.

Abbie glanced over her shoulder and saw that the group had now left the vineyard and were gathering in the courtyard outside the winery. She was about to dash in their wake, but as she spun round, she caught a glint of something on the ground beneath one of the Hummingbird Hotel's vines.

Was that glass?

If it was, she couldn't leave it there, so she hopped over the low fence, dropped onto her knees and began to scramble in the earth between the branches until she found what she was looking for; a brown glass bottle with a tiny rubber stopper.

How had that got there?

She squinted at the bright yellow label, and recognised it

as the well-known herbal remedy that Emily used when she had trouble sleeping before an opening night, or felt stressed before a particularly taxing audition. She knew it contained only natural ingredients – extracts from herbs, flowers and plants like white chestnut, rock rose, star of Bethlehem, clematis – but when she realised what that meant, her heart crashed against her ribcage, whipping the breath from her lungs.

She now had her answers. Brad's unscheduled afternoon snooze hadn't been an accident, a product of his exhaustion after a long and stressful photoshoot. No, someone had added a few drops of this herbal remedy to his smoothie to prove some kind of point about siestas being a good idea and not a waste of time, or only for sissies, as he constantly professed. An almost overwhelming surge of emotion pulsed through her. Whoever was responsible clearly had no regard for the painful consequences of their actions – Brad's sunburnt face – or who would get the blame – Felix.

And it could only be one of three people. Abbie's stomach churned with trepidation, and she desperately wanted to talk to Nikos, to ask him what she should do, but she also knew that this was her problem and she had to be the one who sorted it out, for Felix's sake, and to protect the reputation of the Hummingbird Hotel. This wasn't the time to hide behind someone else because she didn't have the courage to face difficult issues head-on. The sooner she identified the culprit, the sooner she, and everyone else, could relax and enjoy the last few hours of the weekend.

Okay, so, where to start?

She'd already spoken to Katie and Josh, both of whom had denied any responsibility, although that was before Brad's sunburn incident. She now needed to have a chat with Allyssa. Perhaps this had something to do with Brad spying on her, taking photographs without her knowledge or permission. Maybe she'd found out and wanted to get her own back for his unacceptable behaviour.

Abbie exhaled a long sigh. Whoever was to blame, all she wanted was for them to confess to what they'd done, and to apologise to Brad for the unintended consequences of him falling asleep in the height of the afternoon sun. However, as the wine-tasting session was about to start, she would have to shelve her interrogation for the time being.

She dropped the tiny brown bottle into her pocket and hurried towards the winery.

Chapter Fourteen

The Angelopoulos Winery, Ropa Valley, Corfu
Flower: White Myrtle

When Abbie's eyes finally adjusted to the light, she saw that everyone was crowded around the polished table she and Dimitris had set up in the middle of the winery, staring longingly at the numerous bottles of wine and empty glasses, clearly keen to get to the tasting part as soon as possible. She exchanged a brief smile with Nikos and received a questioning raise of the eyebrows in return. She felt lightheaded, from the heat and exposure to the late afternoon sun, but also because of her recent find, which slumbered in her pocket like a primed grenade. She inhaled a steadying breath, and went to stand next to Rachel and Felix.

'Okay, before we start, I wanted to tell you a little about the history of wine-making in Corfu. It is widely agreed that wine has been produced here since the eighth century BC when Homer, the famous Greek poet, wrote about it in "The

Odyssey", and until the Venetians arrived here, the whole island was covered in vineyards. Sadly, the Venetians preferred olive oil, and so the vines were ripped up and replaced with olive trees which, as you can see, still cover the hillsides all over the island, and the olive oil industry is still more prevalent today than the wine industry.'

'Crazy,' muttered Katie.

'Most wineries here are handed down through families, and we follow a slightly different process of wine-making to that utilised by other wine-producing countries. After harvesting, the grapes are crushed in a large vat and when the juice comes into contact with the yeast on the skins, fermentation begins and the sugars in the juice turn to alcohol, releasing carbon dioxide. In the French method, the juice is quickly separated from the skins, but here in Corfu, we leave everything to ferment for between two and five days, after which the juice is transferred into barrels and left to mature for several months, and then it's bottled and ready to drink.'

'And it's the most delicious wine in the whole of Greece,' added Dimitris, a proud smile on his face. 'But you don't have to take my word for it. What has to be the highest praise for the wine produced on Corfu, is that in the film *For Your Eyes Only*, instead of ordering his usual "vodka Martini, shaken not stirred", James Bond asked for a glass of white wine produced by a winery just down the road from here.'

'Wow, that's an awesome anecdote.' Felix grinned, his eyes shining as he tossed his long curls over his forehead.

'Right, shall we move on to the tasting part of the afternoon?' Nikos asked the group.

'Yes please!'

'Absolutely!'

'At last!' Allyssa muttered. 'I'm parched.'

'So, the first wine we are going to be sampling is an Angelopoulos white, made from the *kakotrigis* grapes you saw in the vineyard earlier.' Nikos waited while Dimitris opened the first bottle with a theatrical flourish, and handed everyone a very generous measure. 'You will note it has a fresh, pale straw colour with a slight tinge of green, and a wonderfully distinct aroma of pear, apple, a hint of pineapple, perhaps. Please take a sip.'

'He said a sip, Allyssa, not a gulp!' Katie giggled, but Nikos fortunately didn't notice.

'What do you taste?'

'I can detect floral notes, perhaps a soupçon of peach?' Brad mused, holding his glass aloft as he swirled his sip around his mouth, his eyes partially closed as he considered the flavour of the wine like a seasoned connoisseur. 'And it has an agreeable harmonious aftertaste.'

'Well, I detect a lemony/lime flavour, with a hint of freshly cut grass and a smidgeon of asparagus,' countered Katie, not to be outdone in the tasting, or hyperbolic language stakes.

'I just think it's delicious,' said Allyssa, finishing off her glass and holding it out to Dimitris to refill.

'You are all correct.' Nikos smiled, clearly delighted that his first audience was immersing itself into the whole sensory experience. 'As a professionally trained chef, it is my firm opinion that wine tastes better with food, and conversely, that food tastes better with wine, so I've prepared a few nibbles to accompany our tastings. For this first wine, I have chosen to pair it with a young goats' cheese made by a farm within a few miles of here.'

Dimitris scooted over to the large American-style fridge in the corner of the winery and produced a wide silver platter of tiny crackers topped with the local goats' cheese and a sprinkle of dill, and handed them round to the group to taste alongside the wine.

'Tell me what you think of the wine, now, please?' Nikos encouraged.

'Wow, that's amazing! I feel like my tastebuds have taken a trip to heaven!' said Katie, clearly surprised by her discovery.

'The wine also works well with shellfish – oysters, prawns, crab – and lightly grilled mackerel, and is particularly good with sushi. Okay, shall we move on to our second wine?'

'Yes, please,' said Allyssa, already eyeing the next set of bottles on the table.

'Okay, so this is also a white wine, produced by a friend of the family who owns a vineyard on Kefalonia. It's made from the *robola* grape, which thrives in the stony soil of the semi-mountainous regions on the island. You will notice that it's a deeper yellow in colour, with a richer, more lemony perfume, and when we taste…' Nikos paused to take a sip from his glass, rolling the wine around his palate which encouraged everyone else to follow suit, even Allyssa. '…we detect a citrussy acidity accompanied by herby tones, and the distinct aniseed character of fennel.'

'So what would you pair this with?' asked Josh, as Dimitris returned to the fridge.

'I would order a red mullet, but it also goes well with poultry dishes – duck, goose, turkey, poussin – and all vegan and vegetarian recipes, as you will see.'

Dimitris was now weaving his way through the group, handing out skewers of grilled chicken, and, as promised, a vegetarian option of tiny cubes of marinated halloumi dotted with dried herbs, and a creamy avocado dip accompanied by triangles of toasted pitta.

'Oh my God, this is delicious!' said Rachel, finishing off one skewer and reaching for another, her cheeks colouring when Dimitris held her gaze for a few seconds longer than necessary.

'I always said that oenophiles will inherit the earth,' Brad mused, as he swirled the wine in his glass like an over-active whirlpool, randomly sticking his nose into the rim and closing his eyes to inhale deeply, letting out a rather disturbing "ahhhh" sound. 'I'm personally more of a red wine fan, though. There's nothing better than a decent Bordeaux.'

'Brad, we're tasting Greek wines,' Katie chastised, rolling her eyes at him.

Abbie couldn't tell if Brad's cheeks coloured at his faux pas, but she saw his eyes flick to where Nikos was busy opening the next set of bottles.

'Okay, shall we move on to our red wines now?' Nikos asked.

Abbie cringed inwardly as she accepted a glass of the Angelopoulos red from Dimitris. She had sampled this wine before – it was Nikos and Dimitris' first attempt at wine production since the untimely passing of Nikos' father and brother and it was not the best example of a full-bodied red wine she'd tasted. She was no expert, but judging by the reactions of those around her, it seemed, sadly, she was right, which made her even more determined to learn everything she could about cultivating the best grapes possible so she could help Nikos to produce a wine worthy of his family's name.

'You will see that this wine has a bright deep red colour, with an aroma of cherries and plums, and a hint of vanilla bean. When we taste, we detect ripe red fruit of strawberries and raspberries, of red currents, perhaps, and a soft tannin aftertaste. I recommend a pairing with a slice of *tiropita* or a rich tomato sauce-laden pizza.'

'Aren't you drinking that?' Allyssa asked when she saw Katie surreptitiously abandon her glass.

Katie flashed a quick glance over her shoulder to where Nikos was removing yet another platter of nibbles from the fridge – this time generous slices of the Greek cheese pie made with feta and filo pastry – and offering them to Brad and Josh, and a very animated Rachel whose cheeks were splashed with pink, before handing her glass over to Allyssa.

'No, I'm not, it's disgusting,' she whispered. 'Tastes like sweaty cardboard.'

'I actually think it has a certain *je ne sais quoi*,' said Allyssa, downing it in one before reaching for a slice of the *tiropita* and cramming it in her mouth. 'Mmm, Nikos is right, it's a match made in heaven.'

Katie stared at Allyssa as though she'd gone crazy. 'Since when did you start eating cheese? I thought it was the Big Bad Wolf of the dairy kingdom, loaded with saturated fat, salt and the hazardous type of cholesterol?'

Allyssa paused in her munching, staring wide-eyed at Katie as she contemplated her response to what was a reasonable question, bearing in mind her adamant adherence to all-things healthy and fat-free since arriving in Corfu.

'I—'

'So, for our next red wine, and our final tasting of the afternoon…'

'Boo!' cried Allyssa, giving a little hiccup, followed by a giggle that caused Katie to gift her with an eye roll.

'…we have a blend – *Petrokorithos*, Cabernet Sauvignon, and Merlot – produced by a vineyard on the mainland that's run by a friend of my mother's who is making great strides in cultivating grapes using environmentally sound practices with limited use of pesticides, herbicides and fertilisers.' Nikos held his glass in the air and tipped it to the side. 'See the deep crimson colour, smell the aromatic perfume of dark red fruits – damsons, blackberries, blackcurrants – enjoy the full-bodied flavour of the glaring tannins, the spice notes of vanilla bean, a hint of green pepper, and the long-lasting aftertaste.'

'Now this is a truly fascinating wine,' said Brad, smacking his lips after draining his glass so he could hold it out for Nikos to refill with the rich, blood-red wine. 'It has great legs, a true indicator of a decent vintage. I can taste a complex combination of tobacco, maybe of eucalyptus, or freshly chopped mint? I don't know about you, but I'd pair this with a big juicy steak.'

'I recommend trying it with a slow-roast shoulder of lamb, minted new potatoes and buttered spinach,' said Nikos, giving a nod to Dimitris who collected the final platter of nibbles and handed them round to their guests. 'But it also works well with *spetzofai*, a spicy sausage dish made with sweet peppers, tomatoes, garlic, a sprinkle of dried oregano, or for a vegetarian dish, we substitute the sausage with grilled eggplant. What do you think?'

'Well, this one is definitely my favourite,' Brad said, helping himself to another glass without asking. He then repeated his "wine aficionado" ritual of swirling the contents, closing his eyes as he inhaled the aroma, then – and only then – proceeding to the tasting part, making a slurping noise as he sucked the wine between his teeth, a gesture that caused Abbie to grimace. However, she was relieved to see that his demeanour was a great deal mellower than when he'd arrived at the vineyard, courtesy of Dimitris' loose wrist when topping up everyone's glasses. Whilst, sartorially at least, Brad looked as polished as usual, in his smart belted trousers and cream linen shirt, when Abbie caught a glimpse of his face, she couldn't help but gasp – the excess of wine had caused his temperature to rise and his theatrical-grade makeup had started sliding southward, revealing the white rings around his eyes. It wasn't a good look and she didn't want to be around when he eventually got to see himself in the mirror.

Katie, Josh, Allyssa and Rachel had now taken a seat at the table with Dimitris, chatting about the best bars and nightclubs in Corfu Town, clearly intending to stay until every last drop of wine had been consumed, and Abbie wondered whether she could grab a moment with Nikos to tell him about her discovery in her aunt's vineyard. However, just as she was about to draw him into a shady corner of the winery on some convoluted pretext, Brad knocked back his “favourite” wine and consulted his Rolex.

‘Time for the garden tour, guys.’

Abbie saw the disappointment flash across Katie and Allyssa’s faces until they remembered it was her dream project they were rejecting, and when they realised that she had seen their reaction, they swiftly switched their expressions to polite interest.

‘It’s okay, guys.’ She laughed. ‘You don’t have to come.’

‘Yes, they do. It’s on the itinerary,’ said Brad, ushering the group out of their chairs.

‘Well, why don’t I refill your glasses and you can bring them along with you?’ offered Nikos, holding one of the bottles of the Angelopoulos white wine in the air.

‘The perfect solution,’ said Katie.

To Abbie’s surprise, Allyssa elected to go with a glass of sparkling water, which she downed quickly so she could replenish it straight away, while everyone else accepted a generous top-up from Nikos, then followed Abbie out of the winery, squinting in the still-bright sunshine as they made their way to the terrace at the rear of the Angelopoulos winery.

‘Wow, what a stunning view!’

Katie was right; from where they stood at the head of the Ropa Valley, whichever way they looked – north, south, east or west – there was a jaw-droppingly beautiful vista, and Abbie wasn’t surprised to see Josh get to work with his camera. Vines wriggled up the hillsides, watched over by battalions of cypress trees and olive groves, and punctuated by the tip of the occasional church spire or topsy-turvy roofline. Time seemed to stand still for a few moments, with only the breath of a breeze tickling at the glossy leaves of the lemon grove to their right, and the cicadas performing their interminable serenade.

Abbie felt a spasm of guilt as she reluctantly broke the spell.

'Okay, everyone, the garden's this way.'

She led them down a flight of stone steps, along a winding pathway bordered by purple and pink alyssum, its sweet honey-dew scent wafting into the air as they brushed past. When she'd first seen the garden, it had been more a mini jungle, overgrown and neglected since Nikos' mother had left to live with his sister in Athens. She couldn't blame Nikos for abandoning the plants and shrubs to their own devices – and it *had* offered a safe haven for bees and insects to thrive – knowing that he'd had to focus all of his time and energy on the business of running the vineyard and winery.

Unlike Nikos, she had relished every moment she'd spent cutting back the unkempt branches of bougainvillea, clematis and honeysuckle, trimming the two metre tall hollyhocks, pruning the leaves of the magnolia, fig and lemon trees. She had also had lots of fun learning about the Greek legends attached to the various plants and shrubs; the myrtle tree, in particular, which was said to have a close association with love and marriage, and therefore found in the wedding bouquets of Corfiot brides.

Of course, her favourite part of the garden was where the flowers grew, and she had resisted the temptation to go overboard by planting only those blooms she could use in her floral arrangements for the lobby at the hotel, and could give Sofia to dress the tables at the taverna. She had been overjoyed when Sofia had suggested she think about using her creative skills to supply other businesses in the area with bouquets and planted pots, and whilst she had to concentrate on the hotel and the vineyard at the moment, it was certainly something on her wish list for the future.

'So, I wanted there to be a variety of zones in the garden; nooks and crannies where a visitor could sit in the sunshine, or in the shade, listen to the trickle of water from a fountain, or enjoy the perfume of a trailing clematis, feast their eyes on a kaleidoscope of colourful petals, or appreciate the beauty of a fruit tree – in this section alone we have orange, lemon, pomegranate, fig, even kumquats! We have many tropical and exotic flowers, too, as well as cactus plants, and a well-stocked herb garden, which you've already been enjoying the benefit of.'

'What do you mean?' asked Katie.

'I used a few sprigs of oregano in the dishes I prepared for your lunch this weekend,' said Nikos, stooping down to pick a few leaves of the fragrant herb. 'You know, in ancient times, oregano was believed to deliver good luck, good health, and joy. And this is thyme, which I used in the *tiropita* that I served earlier with the red wine; it's said to be a source of courage. Women gave it to warriors before they went off to battle, and it was also placed into coffins to ensure safe passage to the afterlife. And of course, you'll all recognise this.'

'It's basil,' said Allyssa.

'Yes, and I used this in the tomato salad you had for lunch yesterday.'

'And I used some of it in my smoothies, too,' Felix added, smiling at his contribution to the presentation, until he realised what he'd said and took a quick step backwards so that he was standing behind Rachel and hidden from Brad's view.

'Okay, perhaps you'd like to explore the garden on your own now? Find your own perfect spot?'

'Great idea,' said Josh, already moving towards the flower-bedecked pergola, his camera held aloft, photographing it from all angles before striding off to take a few snaps of a resplendent yellow broom set against the backdrop a smooth azure of the sky.

'Thirty minutes, that's all,' Brad cautioned. 'We'll meet in front of the angel fountain promptly at six thirty for our taxi. Don't forget we have cocktails on Pierre's yacht at eight, and we don't want to be late. If anyone wants me, I'll be on the terrace, sitting in the shade with a glass of ice-cold water. I think I'm starting to feel a little dehydrated after all that wine.'

The group dispersed, meandering along the serpentine pathways in different directions, some pausing to smell the flowers, some to pick a few stems of the herbs, others to throw a penny into the fountain or find a seat in the shade like Brad.

'You've created something very special here, Abbie,' said Katie, threading a garland of oregano through her hair, clearly having taken what Nikos had said earlier to heart. 'I wish I could stay here forever, soaking up the tranquillity, listening to the hum of the bees, the birds in the trees, the breeze in the leaves.'

'Thanks, Katie, that means a lot.'

Abbie watched her stroll off towards the fountain, where Josh was now lying on the ground trying to get a shot of the falling water from a quirky angle, her ponytail swinging jauntily in her wake.

'Okay, we'd better get back to the taverna if we don't want to incur the wrath of Sofia,' said Rachel, linking her arm through Felix's. 'Will we see you later?'

'Maybe,' said Nikos. 'Abbie's promised to treat me to dinner, but I'm sure we'll call in for a nightcap on the way home.'

'Okay, guys, *ciao*!'

Abbie laughed as she tried to copy Felix's "Hang Ten" wave.

'*Yassou*!'

'*Yassou*!'

'I think that went really well, don't you?' said Nikos, hooking his arm around Abbie's shoulder as they sauntered towards a sun-bleached wooden bench in the shade of mango tree.

Abbie wished she could just sit there, next to Nikos, appreciating the serene ambience, savouring the pleasure the merest whiff of his cologne caused, celebrating the successful completion of their very first wine-tasting and garden tour, but she couldn't. She couldn't ignore the nugget of dread that had taken up residence in her chest, telling her that she couldn't relax until she had unravelled the reasons behind who was targeting Brad, and why.

Chapter Fifteen

The Garden at the Angelopoulos Vineyard and Winery
Flower: Fuchsia 'Swingtime'

'Abbie? What's wrong?'

Abbie sighed, then smiled when she saw the genuine concern in Nikos' eyes. She took a moment to once again send up a missive of thanks to the Greek goddess of destiny for arranging for their paths to cross when they did, even though – at the beginning at least – they hadn't been the best of friends.

'I think we can be certain that Brad's brushes with calamity are no accident.'

'What do you mean?'

In as few words as possible, Abbie filled him in on her vineyard discovery, and to her relief he didn't shoot her hypothesis down in flames – like Dan would have done, telling her she was being ridiculous and blowing everything out of proportion – but looked as shocked by it as she had been.

'So, someone is deliberately targeting Brad?'

'Yes, there's no other explanation, and, of course, it has to be one of his colleagues.'

'Or all of them.'

She stared at him; in all of her permeations of the whys and wherefores, that scenario hadn't occurred to her, and somehow the possibility made her even more anxious.

'Oh God!'

'Okay, let's think this through,' said Nikos, as usual the voice of calm. 'Katie's upset with him because she doesn't want to do the photoshoot, and she saw him photographing Allyssa without her permission, and Josh is annoyed with him because he refused to give him an advance on his fee to cover his expenses. What about Allyssa?'

'I don't know, but I intend to speak to her when I get the chance.'

'No time like the present.'

Nikos pointed through the branches of the mango tree to where Allyssa was sitting alone, scrolling through her phone, no doubt checking her emails and updating her social media accounts.

'Oh, I…'

'Want me to come with you?'

'No, no, I'm fine.'

She would have loved to have accepted Nikos' offer, but she had already decided that as the owner of the hotel where the incidents had taken place, this was her responsibility. There was also the fact that if Allyssa was to blame for tampering with Brad's smoothie, she was more likely to talk to Abbie if she was by herself then if Nikos was with her.

'Thanks, though.'

She reached out to squeeze his hand, and then pushed herself up from the bench and made her way towards the bamboo garden swing that she and Dimitris had spent a whole afternoon securing to the branch of a huge oak tree. It was the perfect shady spot to rest awhile, appreciate the view, and to contemplate life, and it was also the perfect place to have a difficult conversation about Allyssa's relationship with Brad.

'Hey, Allyssa.'

'Oh, hi, Abbie. I have to say, your garden is gorgeous. You are very talented.'

'Thanks.' Abbie removed her straw sunhat and sat on a wooden tree stump opposite Allyssa who, clad as she was in a long white floaty dress, her golden hair released from its up-do and flowing almost to her waist, looked like she was auditioning for the role of woodland nymph invited to cavort amongst the glades and dells with a bunch of Greek fairies and elves. 'My mum was a passionate gardener; she even opened her garden to the public. I wanted to honour her memory by doing the same thing. I know she would have loved it here.'

'I'm sorry for your loss, Abbie. I can't even contemplate what it must be like to lose your mum so young. What about your dad? Did he like gardening, too?'

'Oh, it was just mum and me. I never knew my dad; he left before I was even born, which was why Mum and I were so close, I suppose.'

A few beats of silence ensued as memories swirled.

'My parents divorced when I was eight, and it was hard. My sister and I spent every other weekend with Dad, and it was always awkward. I know it sounds awful, but I was relieved when he remarried and went to live in Alaska with his new wife. I see him once a year now and that's just fine. Mum's currently in Sri Lanka, still trying to "find herself", but she's found some peace, as well as taken up yoga and veganism. She's actually been the driving force behind my healthy living/healthy eating book.'

'It must be really exciting to get a publishing deal.'

'It is, but I haven't signed on the dotted line yet.'

Abbie noticed a flicker of unease flash across Allyssa's face and decided to press her on it.

'So was it the book that made you decide to go vegetarian?'

Allyssa held Abbie's gaze, clearly weighing up how to answer her question.

'I'm not.'

'Oh, I—'

To Abbie's surprise, she saw Allyssa's shoulders slump. Her eyes filled with anxiety and she started to fiddle with the delicate silver bracelet at her wrist. A twist of guilt shot through Abbie, and she wondered whether she should have pushed Allyssa, but she knew she had to do this, had to find out what was going on and the only way to do that was to ask awkward questions. To her relief, a few seconds later, Allyssa spoke, her voice tight, yet determined.

'Oh God, Abbie, it's all just so stressful. I don't think I can keep it to myself any longer.'

'What do you mean?'

'Okay, so I've been a model since I was seventeen, and I've loved every single minute of it; the travel, the clothes, the stylists, the parties, the award ceremonies, the product launches, being a social media influencer, and it's exactly what I've always wanted to do. And I'm lucky, I've always been naturally slender, like mum and Gran and Great Gran, it's our genes, I guess. I can eat what I like – within reason – and I never put on weight. I love working for Pierre, too, because he's always been adamant that his models are a healthy size, and I agree totally with that ethos, but…'

'But what?'

'Well, you won't believe this, I…'

Allyssa paused, her thoughts clearly on a different place, a different time.

'Allyssa?'

'I… I don't actually eat very healthily. I love pizzas and burgers and hot dogs and Thai curry and toasted cinnamon bagels with cream cheese smeared on top, and buttery, flaky croissants, and cream scones, and chocolate eclairs, but my real passion is jam donuts. I actually eat at least two a day – when I can get my hands on them.'

'Well, what's wrong with that?' Abbie smiled. 'They're delicious, especially the custard ones, and the ones with the sprinkles on the top.'

'Nothing's wrong with that at all, unless you've built up a whole Instagram and TikTok following based on your healthy living/healthy eating ethos and you're just about to sign a contract to write a book about it. My agent says that if the publisher finds out I'm a fast-food junkie, the contract will be pulled before I can say "Southern-fried chicken".'

'Ah.'

'Don't get me wrong, it's not me I'm worried about. I make a good living from my modelling and social media exploits, but my sister, Martha, is going to help me compile thc cookery book and she'll have a share of the royalties, and she *does* need the money, so when Brad…'

'When Brad what?'

It was immediately clear to Abbie that Allyssa hadn't meant to say those three words and the look of dismay on her face told Abbie everything she needed to know.

'Allyssa?'

'Brad saw me, in Corfu Town.'

'What do you mean?'

Allyssa sighed, then met Abbie's eyes.

'Since my agent first told me about the book offer, I've been really careful about making sure I only eat what I'm supposed to, but six *whole* weeks without a single grain of sugar passing my lips, well, needless to say it's been tough. So, when we finally finished the shoot and moored up in Corfu Town, I snuck off on the pretext of buying some postcards to send home, and instead headed for the nearest bakery where I spent thirty minutes of pure heaven stuffing my face with honey-soaked baklava, which I think could be my new go-to sugar fix. Only, as I said, Brad saw me.'

'But do you think Brad would say anything?'

'Oh, it's so complicated.' Allyssa paused, her eyes filled with indecision, and for some reason her cheeks flushed, too. 'I'm sorry, Abbie.'

'What for?'

'It's nothing personal, but when we docked in Corfu,

I was absolutely adamant that I had no intention of spending the weekend with everyone at a "rest and relaxation retreat" in the middle of nowhere. I'd just done six weeks of highly stressful modelling, where lots of things didn't go according to plan, where some days we worked for eighteen hours straight just to get the shots before flying off to another gorgeous location that we never got to see. I was desperate to go home, I'd even booked my flight over to Paris for Friday night; I missed Xavier so much. I've only seen him once in the last two months, and for once our schedules aligned this weekend, but Brad told me I had to stay. We had a huge row. I told him I wasn't going to be ordered about, and stormed off the yacht and into Corfu Town.'

Allyssa swallowed down on her rising emotions and met Abbie's gaze.

'Then Brad saw me stuffing my face with pastries and drinking a bottle of Coke. Sacrilege! Anyway, as we all know, Brad's no fool; he turned his lucky break to his advantage and threatened to reveal my secret unless I stayed on in Corfu and came to the Hummingbird Hotel with everyone else. We argued, again, but he wouldn't budge. I tried to appeal to his softer side, that if I didn't see Xavier this weekend, that it would be another month before we could get together, but he told me how important it was that I stayed, something about team building and some new project he was working on that he couldn't tell me about.'

'Oh, Allyssa, I—'

'Anyway, if he tells anyone, the contract will be pulled and I couldn't do that to Martha, so, reluctantly, here I am. Although, Abbie, I am actually having a fabulous time, and Brad was right about one thing, I do feel more relaxed than

I have for a long time, so whatever you're doing here in this little corner of paradise is definitely working. It's just that I wish Xavier was here with me, too, then it would be perfect.'

'Thanks, Allyssa, that means a lot.'

Abbie smiled at the earnestness in Allyssa's eyes, delighted at her compliments of the Hummingbird Hotel's first relaxation retreat, until she realised they'd arrived at the time where she had to ask the question she had been dreading. Her heart began to pound with apprehension, and for a moment she contemplated avoiding the issue, or seeking out Nikos to come and help her to confront Allyssa now she knew she had a very good motive for "getting her own back" on Brad. However, that was what the old Abbie would do, the one who let Dan take all the credit for her designs, the one who slunk away without a murmur of objection when he ditched her, and then fired her by text, not the new, confident, self-assured version of Abbie Coleman.

'So, is that why you wanted to have a bit of fun with Brad?'

'Have a bit of fun?'

She saw the look of abject horror stalked across Allyssa's face and she groaned – that hadn't come out as she had intended.

'Oh, no, I didn't mean… no, God, no, I meant the goat.'

'The goat?'

'Yes, and the smoothie?'

'Smoothie? What smoothie? I'm sorry, Abbie, I have no idea what you're talking about.'

Bewilderment replaced Allyssa's horror and Abbie began to feel lightheaded. Why had she thought she could handle situations like this? She was useless at it; she'd never make a good private investigator – Jessica Fletcher would be safe for the time being. However, Allyssa was still staring at her as though she'd completely lost the plot, so all she could do now was press on, and pray she didn't dig her hole any deeper.

'I—'

'Oh God! You think… you think I spiked Brad's smoothie! That that's the reason he fell asleep in the sun and turned out looking like a scarlet panda?'

Heat flooded Abbie's cheeks. 'Well, I—'

'Brad Goodman is a complete pain in the butt, and he drives me *crazy* with his detailed and inflexible itineraries, his weird corporate mantras, his assumptions we don't have a family or a personal life. I'm annoyed with him for making me stay here when I could be spending the weekend with Xavier, but I get why he did it. Pierre wants us to do a photoshoot for the fashion house tomorrow, and, like Brad, I respect his wishes. I would have flown back over here on Monday, with Pippa, and smiled for the camera, just as I always do. Brad didn't have to threaten me, and I would never stoop so low as to play roulette with anyone's appearance.' Allyssa paused, her earlier indignation morphing into curiosity with a side order of excitement as she sat up straight and narrowed her eyes in thought. 'So, if it wasn't me, who did the dastardly deed?'

'I don't—'

'Josh, it has to be Josh! The two of them are always arguing about something, mainly money.'

'I don't think—'

'Oh, so you're saying you think it's Katie?'

'No, I—'

'You're right, there's definitely something going on between them, that's for sure. I did ask her about it when we were out for dinner last night, and she mentioned something about photographs but I didn't really get to the bottom of it. Have you spoken to either of them?'

'I—'

But Allyssa was on a roll. 'Maybe we should team up, start looking for clues, ask a few questions, twist a few arms…'

'No, please, Allyssa, please don't do that. I think we should just—'

'You know, I always thought I would make a great amateur sleuth. I never forget a face. Oh, yes, actually, that was what I meant to tell you!'

Abbie groaned, regretting the fact that she had even started the conversation with Allyssa and surreptitiously checking her watch to see if it was time for the group's taxi to arrive to take them for their cocktails at the marina.

'Allyssa, I think we should—'

'I knew I'd seen Nikos somewhere before.'

Suddenly, the arrival of the taxi was relegated to the shelf marked "unimportant".

'Really?'

'Yes. It was only when I was watching him present the wine-tasting class that I realised where. He's got his own YouTube channel, and whilst his subscriber numbers are nowhere near the number of mine, he *does* actually have quite a decent following of fans.'

'Oh, yes, I heard—'

'He's so photogenic, isn't he? The camera absolutely adores him, with those gorgeous chocolate-brown eyes framed by those long, long lashes, that sensual half-Greek half-French accent, and his toned, sun-kissed body oozing hot, hot, hot sexy charisma. He's like a male version of Nigella! It's no wonder his subscribers swoon over his asparagus soufflé, drool over his pineapple tarte tatin, and lap up his creamy custard bougatsa, not to mention the fact that he specialises in all-things chocolate – endorphins galore!'

Again, Abbie made a mental note to take a look at Nikos' YouTube channel; it was clearly causing a stir with its viewers and subscribers.

'The videos are all so professionally produced, too, although that's probably got something to do with the fact that his girlfriend's an award-winning TV director so she actually knows what she's doing.'

A blast of shock reverberated through Abbie's chest and all she could do was gape at Allyssa. For a number of reasons, she and Nikos had agreed to be careful not to flaunt their fledgling relationship in front of the hotel's guests, although she knew they hadn't always been successful.

'His… his girlfriend?'

'Yes, Véronique, I think she's called. She's a—'

'Hey, you two! There you are! Time to go! The taxi's here to take us over to the yacht, and that's something we're definitely not going to be late for!' Brad called, his tone inviting no argument. 'Come on!'

Allyssa leaned forward to hug Abbie, totally unaware she'd just dropped a grenade into what had been, up to that point, an enjoyable – if a little disappointing on the mystery-solving front – afternoon.

'Don't worry, I'll keep my eyes and ears peeled tonight for anything unusual and report back tomorrow. Ciao, darling!'

Before Abbie could collect her thoughts, Allyssa had disappeared, leaving behind a cloud of Miss Dior in her wake.

Chapter Sixteen

Taverna Sofia, Ropa Valley, Corfu
Flower: Amaryllis 'Dancing Queen'

Abbie had no idea how long she sat there on the bamboo swing, her emotions churching, Allyssa's words ricocheting through her brain, their meaning shooting off into increasingly bizarre directions until she felt dizzy and disorientated. Her confidence monsters circled, screaming at her to plaster a bright smile on her face and ignore the fact that Nikos, for whatever reason, had chosen not to share the details of his relationship history with her, which, after all, was his prerogative.

'Hey, there you are! So, what did Allyssa say? Has she admitted everything under your steely cross-examination, apologised profusely for the trouble she's caused, and promised to confess all to Brad and beg his forgiveness?'

Nikos grinned, a mischievous glint in his eyes, and despite her despondency, she couldn't help but smile back.

'Not exactly.'

'So, what *did* she say?'

Nikos took a seat next to her on the swing, the to-and-froing motion serving to calm her emotions from canter to trot, enough for her to fill him in on the next exciting episode of the "Let's Target Brad" saga that was unfolding at the Hummingbird Hotel.

'Well, she said that none of the incidents had anything to do with her, and, more worryingly, she's now determined to become the next Poirot.'

'*Och*!'

Abbie went on to tell Nikos, as succinctly as possible, the details of her conversation with Allyssa, leaving out the final few sentences they'd exchanged about Nikos' personal life.

'I've spoken to Katie, Josh and Allyssa now and they all seem to have a reason for wanting to upset Brad in some way, but all of them told me that it's got nothing to do with them and pointed me towards one of the others. We're no further forward than we were when we started asking questions.'

'Okay, so, we can either go back to the hotel and wait until they return from their evening out and then sit them all down and confront them with it, in front of Brad, and hope that one of them confesses, *or* we can park it, go out for dinner and deal with it in the morning.'

'I'd prefer the second option.'

'Great, so where are you taking me?'

'I…'

Now was the time to ask Nikos about what Allyssa had said, to clear the air before they went out for dinner.

She was no actress, and she knew there was no way she could keep up the pretence that nothing was bothering her all night. Nikos would guess that something was going on, and would easily be able to wheedle the reasons for her subdued mood out of her, and so the sensible side of her brain told her that the best thing to do was to take the initiative and simply ask him about it – but not here in the Angelopoulos Garden, a place she adored and didn't want to spoil by associating it with hearing unwelcome news.

'Do you mind if we call in at the taverna for a drink first?'

'Sounds like a plan, and if it's okay with you, I have an idea for dinner.'

Nikos looked a little put out that she didn't ask for details, but Abbie didn't want to think about what the rest of the night might hold. All she could think about was how she was going to broach the subject of Nikos having a girlfriend and asking him why he hadn't mentioned it to her before. She didn't want to admit how upset she was about it. After all, they had only known each other for a short time and whilst they had enjoyed a few romantic interludes, neither of them had promised anything more than friendship and a mutually supportive business partnership.

'Come on, then. Let's head over to Sofia's.'

She took a seat in his rust-blistered old Peugeot, winding down the window in the hope that would make it less like the inside of a sauna – to no avail – whilst Nikos drove to the taverna like Lewis Hamilton's Greek cousin. Fortunately, as it was still relatively early, apart from one large, extended family who had commandeered the biggest table inside the restaurant, the outdoor veranda at the rear was deserted and she was able to take a seat at her usual table.

'Hi there, guys, what can I get you?' asked Sofia, looking stunning in a tasteful turquoise blouse with bat-wing sleeves and ruffles around the collar, paired with her favourite hooped gold earrings. As usual, not a hair was out of place in her neat caramel bob, and her makeup showed no signs of the fact that she had spent all day in and out of the kitchen serving customers with Panos' delicious food.

'I'll have a Coke, please, Sofia,' said Nikos, shaking his car keys as an explanation for not indulging in his usual bottle of Mythos beer.

'Could I just have a sparkling water, please?' Abbie asked.

'Really?' said Nikos, squinting at her in surprise.

Abbie simply nodded; she needed to have her wits about her if she was going to get through the approaching conversation without embarrassing herself or Nikos.

'Okay, coming right up.'

Sofia held Abbie's gaze for a couple of seconds then headed towards the bar to fulfil their order. Abbie knew Nikos had finally cottoned on to the fact that there was something bothering her, but she simply stared at the view, still able to appreciate the beauty of the changing light as the sun slowly descended towards the horizon, sending shards of orange and mauve across the cerulean sky.

'Abbie? Is—'

'Here we are.'

Sofia placed their drinks on the table, pausing again to catch Abbie's eye, sending a silent message of concerned enquiry before retreating back to the bar from where she could watch whatever was about to unfold, and, if necessary, offer her support.

'Is everything okay, Abbie?'

'Can I ask you something?'

Nikos looked at her in surprise. 'Of course.'

Abbie could feel her heart hammering out a rhythm of trepidation, but she pushed on.

'When I was talking to Allyssa earlier, she mentioned that she recognised you from your YouTube channel.'

'Really? She doesn't seem like the sort of person who watches French cookery shows.'

'She must. Erm, she also mentioned your girlfriend, Véronique.'

Nikos' head shot up from where he'd been swirling his Coke around in his glass and his gaze met Abbie's eyes, but she looked away, not able to deal with what she might see there.

'My *ex*-girlfriend,' he said firmly.

Abbie wished she could leave it there, change the subject to something less emotional, like what Nikos had organised for dinner that evening, but she couldn't.

'Allyssa said she's a director?'

'She is, for a French TV company. It was actually Véronique's idea for me to record a few videos showcasing French, and Greek, recipes and to post them on YouTube. I created the dishes and did the presentations – which I loved, I have to admit – and she did all the technical stuff, like the staging, the lighting, the filming, and then the editing and uploading to my YouTube channel. It was just a bit of fun to start with; I had no idea I'd get so many views.'

Abbie could see the familiar passion that appeared in

Nikos' eyes whenever he got the opportunity to talk about his favourite subject – food, in all its guises.

'I enjoyed being at the restaurant in Paris; who wouldn't? I got to work with a Michelin-starred chef on a daily basis, and I learnt a great deal from him, but there was no freedom to do my own thing. I had lots of innovative ideas, dishes that *blended* French and Greek food to create a sensation of tastes and flavours on the tongue – the very best of what both cuisines had to offer on one plate. So, those were the recipes I filmed. I've lost count of how many we did, but every episode attracted more and more subscribers, and the last I heard, which was just before I came back to Corfu, was that the final video had over one hundred thousand views.'

'That's fantastic.'

'Thanks, Abbie, I—'

'So how long were you and Véronique together?' she blurted, causing heat to rush into her cheeks, but this was what she needed to know.

'A couple of years. We were both focused on our careers; Véronique would be away filming most weeks, and I would spend all my time at the restaurant, morning until night, honing my skills, learning about using the best ingredients and cooking techniques to create something exquisite, yet edible at the same time. I've already told you that my family didn't approve of my career choice, or that it took me to a different country, so it was even more important to me to show them that I could succeed as a chef in the culinary capital of the world. I know my father would never agree with me, but being a chef is not so different to being a wine maker, and the end customer is, usually, the same. I just wish I could have talked to him before… before…'

A dark shadow of grief stalked across Nikos' handsome face, and he reached out to take a sip of his Coke, his hand trembling as he lifted the glass to his lips, careful to avoid Abbie's eyes. Guilt washed through her veins; she really hadn't wanted the conversation to stray so far into difficult territory, and she regretted not taking her initial option of brushing Allyssa's news under the carpet, something she was, after all, an expert at doing.

'I'm sorry, Nikos.'

'I wanted him to know that I was good at what I had chosen to do, that in a few years I could be running my own Michelin-starred restaurant, too. I wanted to make him proud.'

'I'm sure he *was* proud of you.'

Nikos nodded, but Abbie could see he didn't agree.

'I'm sorry I didn't talk to you about Véronique. I should have told you about her when you told me about what happened between you and Dan, but I struggle to talk about my life in Paris, and the way it came to such an abrupt end. I think I've come to terms with it and moved on, and then something else happens and the pain rushes back at me like an escaped express train.'

'I understand Nikos, I really do.'

'After the funeral, when I realised that I couldn't go back to my life in Paris, that I had to stay and run the winery, I asked Véronique to come and live with me here in Corfu. She spent so much time flying around the world – filming documentaries, dramas, movies, news items, interviewing actors, directors, producers, models – that it really didn't matter where she was based. But…' Nikos paused to take another gulp of his drink. 'But she refused to leave Paris, in fact, she was horrified that I would even *suggest* she left such a vibrant and cosmopolitan place with its world-famous theatres, galleries, museums, restaurants, clubs, to live in a rustic farmhouse in the middle of nowhere. But then, I suppose Corfu isn't her home; she doesn't see the same beauty, feel the same tug of belonging as I do.'

Nikos finished his Coke, slammed the glass onto the table, jumped from his seat and held out his hand towards Abbie.

'Okay, that's enough talking. Time to have some fun. Come on.'

Ten minutes later, having experienced the most seat-gripping journey since arriving on Corfu, Abbie heaved a sigh of relief when Nikos came to a halt in a car park outside a secluded restaurant surrounded by olive trees, their branches strung with fairy lights and soft bouzouki music rippling through the air around them. Dusk was well into its final act, and lanterns edged the pathway that led through a tunnel of glossy foliage to the beach where an impressive decking area had been built on stilts over the sea.

She wasn't surprised when Nikos guided them towards a table on dry land with a hand-painted "Reserved" sign on it, and as she took in her surroundings, she saw that every other seat was occupied, mostly by local families; three or four generations enjoying a Sunday evening meal together. Conversation flowed, punctuated by the occasional shriek of laughter and the cry of delight as a toddler paddled in the shallow water, supervised closely by a parent or grandparent, and the waft of warm baked bread caused Abbie's stomach to growl.

She stared out at the seemingly endless expanse of gently undulating waves, their crests highlighted by the silvery light from the crescent moon overhead, and the stresses and strains of the day began to fade away to be replaced by a welcome feeling of calm.

'It's really beautiful here.'

'A friend of mine, Stephanos, runs the place with his wife. It's a little off the beaten track, so it's mainly locals and their extended families that come here. Look, here he is now. Hey, Stephanos.'

'Hi, Nikos, good to see you.'

Stephanos greeted him with a friendly fist bump before turning to Abbie, his wide welcoming smile so white it could front a dentist's advertising campaign, causing his dark eyes to crinkle at the corners. His hair was longer than Nikos', worn in a rock-solid quiff, and he clearly belonged to the same school of thought that more is better when it comes to the use of cologne.

'You must be Abbie? It's great to meet you at last. I've heard so much about you.'

'Really?' She smiled, wanting to ask Stephanos exactly what he had heard but, seeing how busy he, and the rest of the waiters at the restaurant were, she didn't want to waylay him.

'How are you finding the hotel trade?' he asked.

'It's been a baptism of fire!'

Stephanos laughed. 'It's an interesting life, that's for sure. There's never two days the same, but that's the beauty of it, don't you think? Who wants to lead a boring life with no surprises? I'll get your drinks.'

'Stephanos and Eleni own a couple of apartments in Dasia that they rent out to visitors,' Nikos explained, leaning back in his seat, his ankle hooked over his thigh, completely relaxed in his surroundings, the difficult issues they'd spoken about earlier already banished to the box marked "past history". 'Which means he knows a thing or two about catering for the weird and wonderful whims of holidaymakers – although if we were to ask him, or Eleni, I don't think either of them have ever had to deal with an underwear-eating goat!'

'Hey, I thought we weren't going to talk about that tonight?'

Nikos held up his hand. 'Sorry, sorry.'

After consuming the most delicious vegetarian moussaka she'd had since arriving in Corfu, Abbie finished her glass of red wine – sourced from the same winery as the final wine on Nikos' wine-tasting session – and relished the feeling of soft mellowness that steeled over her whole body. The moon had disappeared behind a cloud, but had left behind a cascade of bright stars peppering the night sky as far as the eye could see, and, for once, the cicadas had muted their melody as the children fell asleep in their pushchairs or on their parents' laps, whilst the adults lingered over their coffees, ouzos, and brandies.

'Thank you for bringing me here, Nikos. I've had a wonderful evening.'

'Oh, no, it's not over yet. In fact, it's just getting started.'

And, as if to underline the point, the background

music suddenly stopped, and applause erupted from every corner of the restaurant for the arrival of a group of musicians carrying a variety of instruments – a bouzouki being the only one that Abbie recognised – who proceeded to play a selection of upbeat tunes. When the band paused briefly before their next piece of music, the applause resumed, and Abbie joined in enthusiastically.

'Wow! That was—'

However, she got no further because, not only had the band started to play again, a troop of dancers, dressed in their national costume, had appeared from inside the restaurant, one of whom Abbie recognised as the father from the table next to theirs. Now the music ratcheted up several notches, the rhythm becoming faster, with everyone present joining in – tapping their feet, clapping their hands, and in the case of one elderly gentleman, singing at the top of his voice until chastised by his granddaughter.

Abbie stared, mesmerised by the Greek dancing; the men performing a circular dance, the pompoms on their shoes and tassels around their shins bouncing vigorously as they joined hands and moved from left to right, showcasing the occasional high kick and pirouette. Then the women, looking resplendent in their traditional dress, joined the circle briefly, before the dancers split into pairs and continued their rotation around the dance floor, the men with their right arm held aloft, the women with their left hand on their hip, their long, pleated skirts rippling around their ankles.

'This dance is called the *Kalamatianos*,' said Nikos, leaning over to whisper in her ear as the dancers took a bow and prepared for their next exhibition. 'And this one is the *Sirtaki*, a choreographed version of the *Hasapiko*, which I know you'll recognise.'

Abbie listened to the first, slow bars of the next tune, a jangly, bouzouki-laden piece famous for its starring role in the film *Zorba The Greek*. The dancers regrouped, placed their arms across each other's shoulders, and, moving with practised synchronicity, they stepped forwards and backwards, kicking their legs from left to right, occasionally kneeling towards the floor, the music becoming ever faster, their steps quickening to keep up, the dance culminating in a joyous display of arm waving and a magnificent crescendo of sound.

'Okay, now it's our turn.'

'What?'

Abbie's jaw dropped, then her stomach tightened when she saw the whole audience – parents, grandparents, teens and toddlers – launch themselves from their seats and storm onto the makeshift dance floor in front of the bouzouki band, and realised exactly what Nikos meant.

'Oh, no, no, no, no, I'm not a dancer! No, I can't—'

But Nikos was already pulling her up from her chair.

'Come on, you can't say no.'

'Oh, God!'

She took her place between Nikos and Stephanos, her heart pounding to the beat of the Greek music, then tentatively placed her arms over first Nikos' shoulder, then Stephanos' shoulder, feeling awkward and embarrassed. This sort of thing was so far out of her comfort zone she wished she could melt into the background and watch the show from the side-lines. However, it didn't take her long to master the simple steps, left to right, kicking her foot outwards as she went, and after only a few rotations, she got the hang of the rhythm and started to enjoy herself more than she ever thought she would. She couldn't wait to tell Emily that she needed to add a new type of video to her exercise-viewing regime.

When Abbie and Nikos finally stumbled from the restaurant, it was after midnight. She could feel her cheeks glowing with the unexpected exertion, as well as the amount of red wine she'd consumed, and a swathe of contentment suffused her whole body. She linked her arm through Nikos' and together they sauntered back to where he'd left the car, pausing beneath the branches of a lemon tree where Nikos pulled her into his arms and drew her close, so close that the tickle of his breath on her neck caused ripples of desire to roll out to every extremity.

'Have you had fun?' Nikos murmured.

'More fun than I've had for…' She was about to say "years" but realised that made her sound dull and boring. 'For a long time.'

'Good, that was the intention.'

Abbie held his gaze for what felt like an eternity, and then his lips were on hers, soft, gentle, merely a whisper. He reached up to brush the hair from her cheek, snaking his palm around her neck so he could kiss her more urgently, more deeply, his thumb caressing that delicate spot at the nape, sending a surge of electricity pumping through her veins. She kissed him back, savouring every moment of the intense joy that flooded every part of her, filled with gratitude that the evening had ended in such a wonderful way, when it could have been a completely different story.

'Abbie, I—'

Nikos pulled away, his dark gaze scorching her, clearly wanting to say something. However, as she waited, anticipation and curiosity swirling through her mind in equal measure, he seemed to change his mind.

'Nikos?'

'I think we should get back.'

Thankfully, the journey back to the hotel was more sedate than the journey there, the car radio playing soothing tunes which ensured that Abbie, much to her annoyance, fell asleep within moments of the first rev of the engine, and she missed out on appreciating the scenery washed in the ivory glow of moonlight.

Later, after she'd made sure her guests were safely ensconced in their guestrooms, and there was no risk of further incidents befalling any of them, she climbed the stairs to her own room, the events of the day flashing through her mind as though being replayed on a film screen.

Living in Corfu, it was like she was playing a role in a movie; the stunning location, the musical backing track, the handsome love interest, and when she undressed and slid between the cool cotton sheets, she couldn't prevent a smile from tugging her lips as she slipped into the welcoming arms of Hypnos.

Chapter Seventeen

The Veranda at the Hummingbird Hotel
Flower: Checkerbloom 'Party Girl'

Abbie woke extra early the following morning, just as the first blades of daylight sliced through her bedroom shutters. In a couple of hours, her guests would be checking out, ready to head to Corfu Town to meet Pierre and Pippa from the plane and head over for their corporate photoshoot. Time was ticking away if she wanted to uncover the truth about what had been going on with Brad, and a sneaky thought rolled into her mind that maybe she could just avoid it altogether, just let it go and hope that he didn't post a negative review when he got home. But then the intrepid voice on her other shoulder asked her when she got to be so cowardly.

No, she had to do whatever it took to sort this out.

She jumped into the shower, ran an extra dollop of coconut oil through her wayward curls, and pulled on her favourite Capri pants and blue and white striped tee-shirt.

She spent a few minutes searching for her straw sunhat with the pretty white ribbons, but then remembered she'd left it on the garden swing at the Angelopoulos Garden, so she slipped her feet into a pair of sparkly flip-flops, and headed down to the kitchen to make herself a coffee.

'Hi, Abbie, I thought you said you were going to have an early start this morning?' Nikos grinned as he handed her a cup of thick, dark Greek coffee and a warm, buttery croissant fresh from the village bakery. Despite the early hour, he radiated energy and vitality; his hair neatly gelled into spikes, his powder-blue shirt pristine, and of course, a waft of his fresh lemony cologne floated in the air.

'It's seven a.m.'

'The first on the scene catches the worm.'

'That isn't… never mind.'

'Okay so, what's the plan?'

'I really don't have any idea.'

'I vote we get everyone together, show them what you found in the vineyard yesterday, and ask them who it belongs to.'

'Do you think whoever that is will admit it?'

'I…' Nikos paused to reflect more carefully on the question.

'I'm not so sure they will,' said Abbie.

'In that case the only other alternative is to talk to them separately, to put each one of the incidents to them, and ask them if they know anything about it.'

'But I've already done that, and they've all denied it or blamed each other, it's like going round in circles, and anyway there's no time to do that. They're checking out at eleven to head over to the hotel for the photoshoot, and you know, I really don't want to spoil what was meant to be a relaxing retreat weekend by ending it with an interrogation.'

'What if we asked Brad if we can tag along with them to the photoshoot? Maybe, when everyone's mind is on other things, they will let something slip?'

'That's a great idea!' Abbie smiled, a zip of excitement replacing her swirling anxiety. She had never been to a photoshoot before – unless she counted the many weddings she and Dan had attended as florists – *and* it meant she would get to see Pippa again. 'Okay, yes, that's what we'll do. I've always wanted to watch a fashion shoot taking place.'

'It's not a fashion shoot, it's a corporate photography session.'

'With celebrities!'

'Brad? Josh?'

'Well, Pierre's going to be there and he's a celebrity fashion designer, and I'd love to see my friend Pippa and find out how she's getting on. Oh, maybe I could ask her to grab her magnifying glass and deerstalker and help us find out who's been targeting Brad. Perhaps she knows some snippet of insider gossip that will point to one person in particular? Yes, yes, that's perfect. Okay, I'll ask Brad if—'

'Ask Brad what?' the man himself said as he walked into the kitchen.

'Oh, hi Brad, I—'

Abbie couldn't prevent her jaw from dropping when she saw Brad's face without Allyssa's concealer and foundation covering his sunburn. His skin was almost as red as it had been the previous day, and he still sported two incongruous white circles around his eyes, but now his nose and his chin had started to peel. It was definitely not the most attractive look to be captured on film for all eternity on the company's website and promotional literature. For all of his faults, she experienced a sharp nip of sympathy for him and his predicament, which gave her the push she needed to set aside her embarrassment at asking if they could, in effect, gate-crash the private photo session.

'Nikos and I were wondering whether it was possible for us to come to the photoshoot this afternoon? I've never been to one before and I'd really love to see what goes on. It must be so exciting, and I promise that we'll stay on the side-lines and be as quiet and inconspicuous as possible.'

Abbie realised she was gushing and stopped before she made a complete fool of herself.

'I'm sorry, Abbie, I'm not sure that's something I can—'

'Oh Brad, don't be such a bore. Of course you can come, Abbie. We'd love to have you, especially after everything you've done for us this weekend,' Allyssa said as she joined them. She gave Brad a stern, meaningful stare that told him she meant business and that she wouldn't take no for an answer.

'But Allyssa, this is a really important, more important than…. I really don't—'

'If they don't come, I won't come.'

Brad opened his mouth to continue his argument, but then thought better of it. Clearly there would be no photoshoot without its main attraction, which was always going to be Allyssa, as well as Pierre, and he couldn't risk her following through on her threat.

'Okay, okay. Abbie, Nikos, we'd be delighted to have you.'

Brad strode to the coffee machine and fixed himself an espresso, downed it in one, then refilled his cup, after which, to Abbie's surprise, he prepared a latte for Allyssa and handed it to her with a wide smile.

'Thank you, Brad.' Allyssa beamed, selecting a slice of melon from the platter of fruit Abbie had just finished preparing. 'Let's take our breakfast out to the veranda, shall we?'

Without waiting for an answer, she spun on her five-inch heels and headed outside, the blonde highlights in her hair shining in the early morning sun, the hem of her pale lemon, halter-neck sundress whipping up around her knees à la Marilyn Monroe, reaffirming the point, if it were needed, that she was, truly, the star of the show.

'Morning, guys.'

'Oh, hi Josh, can I tempt you with any breakfast?' Abbie asked.

'I could really murder a black coffee. I had a great night last night; the music was good, the food was amazing, and I got lots of stunning photographs of the sunset, but I definitely overindulged in the local brandy. That stuff's lethal.'

'One coffee coming right up.'

'And maybe I'll take a plate of those delicious looking pastries, too.'

'No problem, help yourself.'

As Abbie prepared Josh's coffee, she watched him pile his plate high with croissants, mini pain au chocolat, and several slices of honey-soaked baclava. There was something about him that was different; he'd clearly made an effort for the afternoon's shoot in his plain black tee-shirt and figure-hugging designer jeans, his beard neatly trimmed and sandy quiff immaculately styled, but there was something missing.

'Hey Josh, where's your camera?' Allyssa called from the veranda.

'All packed away in its case. Today is about being in *front* of the lens,' said Josh as he took a seat next to Brad at the table and made a start on his mammoth breakfast, nodding his thanks when Abbie set down his double espresso in front of him.

'Want a few tips?' asked Allyssa.

'I'd *love* a few tips!'

'Brad? How about you?'

'I don't need tips on how to look good in front of a camera.'

'Are you sure?' asked Josh, his lips twitching at the corners.

'What about a little tinted moisturiser?'

'After what you did to me yesterday, Allyssa, there's no way I'm letting you loose on my face again! I looked like a pantomime dame!'

Contrition flooded Allyssa's face, and she reached out to squeeze Brad's hand, which caused him to stare at her in surprise. 'I'm sorry, Brad, I shouldn't have done that, but I couldn't resist after what you… never mind, anyway, I can assure you that I understand how important this shoot is to you, and I give you my word that a smidgeon of tinted moisturiser will cover all your… your blemishes, and enhance your natural good looks. And you don't have to worry, I've worked with Carlton before he's an am-az-ing photographer – but of course, not as good as you, Josh,' she added quickly.

'Thanks, Allyssa,' said Josh, through a mouth crammed full of pastry.

'So he'll definitely be able to bring out that charismatic preppy vibe you've got going on,' Allyssa finished.

Abbie smiled when she saw the genuine delight on Brad's face at Allyssa's unexpectedly generous compliment, but then, after checking his gold Rolex, his expression returned to its more usual efficient-business-manager expression.

'Where on earth is Katie? I told her to be here by nine at the latest so we could all have our breakfast together and do a minute-by-minute run-through of the schedule for the rest of the day, just to make sure everyone is singing from the same song sheet before we check out and head over to the Corfu Palace and our rendezvous with Pierre and Pippa. There's a great deal riding on this, so it's more important than it's ever been that everything, and I mean *everything* goes according to plan, and the last thing we need is for Katie to renege on her timekeeping responsibilities.'

'She's probably dealing with the hangover from hell.' Josh laughed, fiddling with the handle of his coffee cup, clearly missing the comfort provided by his constant companion. 'I reckon she'll need more than a couple of Felix's smoothies before she's ready to face the world this morning.'

'I really wish that just this once she'd….' Brad began, his eyes flashing with irritation.

'Don't worry, I'll go and see if I can chivvy her along while Nikos makes you all some more coffee,' said Abbie, jumping from her chair before anyone else could.

She headed into the kitchen, whipped up a quick mango and banana smoothie, added a splodge of Greek yoghurt, and, after helping Nikos fill a silver tray with cups, saucers and a cafetière, she made her way across the courtyard towards the guest rooms.

As she passed in front of Allyssa's room, she glanced through the French doors, which Allyssa had left open, and performed a double-take; the place looked like a hurricane had hit it, with clothes strewn over every available surface; shoes, sunhats and handbags discarded all over the place, and the dressing table and bedside cabinets cluttered with every lotion, potion, cream, and gel known to the beauty world. She sighed and quickly pulled the glass door shut, although even if a brigade of drunken Greek goats decided to rampage through the room, she probably wouldn't be able to tell the difference.

Maybe they'd been there already?

Next up was Brad's room, and she wasn't surprised to see the patio doors firmly closed, the room beyond immaculately tidy, with his laptop charging and his already-packed suitcase resting on his neatly made-up bed, ready for check-out, and the laminated itinerary card the only item on his dressing table.

As she continued towards Katie's room, she heard a raised voice through the open patio doors and paused, not wanting to barge in and interrupt her conversation. However, within moments, she realised that Katie wasn't just having a chat with one of her friends, but was clearly distressed.

Abbie hesitated, unsure what to do, until she heard the next sentence to float from the room.

'But Mum, I can't afford to engage the services of a lawyer. You've no idea how expensive they are, especially one who specialises in intellectual property. Yes, that's apparently what I need advice on. I know, I know, I *will* speak to Pierre, but what if what Brad told me is true? All those late nights and long weekends, working on my designs until my eyes crossed and my fingers bled, will have been for nothing.'

Katie paused and Abbie heard her blow her nose. She took a step backwards, the smoothie still in her hand, embarrassed that she had inadvertently overheard what was clearly a private conversation, and knowing she should leave before she was discovered loitering, and yet, her interest was piqued. So, against her better judgement, she moved closer to the gap in the French doors, and then nearly jumped out of her skin in shock when someone spoke behind her.

'Abbie? What are you doing?'

'Oh, I… I was… well…' Warmth flooded her cheeks as she whipped around and held Allyssa's gaze, accompanied by a flash of guilt that she had been caught snooping. 'It's just that I think Katie might be distressed, and I didn't want to just—'

'Oh God, Mum, what am I going to do? Pierre is definitely going to fire me; I know he is. I hate Brad, I really do!'

And then Katie burst into loud, rasping sobs.

Chapter Eighteen

Katie's Guestroom at the Hummingbird Hotel
Flower: Weeping Willow

Abbie exchanged a glance with Allyssa and, without saying a word, she pushed open the door into Katie's guestroom where she was shocked to find her slumped on the bed, like a puppet clipped of its strings, shoulders hunched, head lowered, as though her world had come to an end, which clearly she thought it had.

'Sorry, Mum, I've got to go. Allyssa's here. Yes, yes, I'll be fine. I'll call you later, okay? Yes, I promise. I love you.'

As soon as Katie tossed her mobile phone onto her bed, Allyssa stepped forward to take control, scooting down next to her and gathering her friend gently into her arms, stroking her head, muttering consoling words of solace, until she had calmed down enough to speak.

'Katie, darling, what's going on?'

Katie accepted the bunch of tissues Abbie handed to her,

blew her nose and dabbed the tears away from her eyes, then pushed herself to the top of the bed, hugged her knees to her chest, and met their gaze.

'I… Oh, you're going to hate me.'

'No, I am most definitely *not* going to hate you. I—' Allyssa began.

'No, I meant Abbie.'

'Why is Abbie going to hate you?'

'Because…'

And then Abbie knew. 'It was you?'

'What was you? Katie, what did you… Oh.' Understanding dawned on Allyssa's face as she flashed a quick look at Abbie for confirmation. 'You spiked Brad's smoothie.'

Katie nodded mutely.

'And the goat?'

Katie nodded again.

'What about the sunlounger?' asked Abbie.

This time Katie shook her head. 'No, that had nothing to do with me; it has to have been an accident, but I'm not saying I wasn't happy it happened.'

'But why Katie? Why did you do those things?' Allyssa said, completely bewildered.

Katie opened her mouth to say something, then shut it again, clearly searching for the right words to explain her actions, but struggling. Eventually, she inhaled a deep breath and sought Abbie's eyes.

'Because Brad's a complete and total—'

She stopped to swallow down on the flare of anger.

'Pain in the butt?' Allyssa supplied, smiling, hoping to make Katie feel a little better.

'Yes.' She smiled back, but the smile didn't reach her eyes.

'Do you think you can tell us what he's done?'

'I... he... he found out about... about my handbag venture.'

'Your handbag... What do you mean? I didn't think that was a secret.'

'It's not, well, not really, but I haven't told Pierre about it yet. Don't get me wrong, I adore working with Pierre, and I'm learning so much from him, but it's all about his designs, his inspiration, and his ideas – as, of course, it should be. I just wanted to explore my own creativity, and I've always loved handbags, and purses, and wallets, and all kinds of luggage. So, for the last six months, in my spare time, I've been researching, designing, sourcing materials, and loving every minute of it. Mum helped me to make up a few samples and, well, it just went from there, and before I knew it, I had twenty pieces, and I was absolutely thrilled, but I have lots more ideas, too.'

'But what's Brad got to do with it?'

'When we were in Antigua, doing the first shoot six weeks ago, I'd had a few margaritas – remember, at that beach bar in St John's? – and I told him about my dream of one day having my own eponymous line in accessories, like Kate Spade or Rebecca Minkoff. He gave me a twenty minute lecture on how to set up a limited liability company, and how to market and promote my products properly, before he moved on to talk about the co-ordinated stitching on the leather interior of his new Audi. Anyway, I completely forgot that I'd said anything until...'

'Until what?'

'Until Friday, when I told him I had no intention of

staying on in Corfu to do a retreat and a corporate photoshoot. I'd been away from home for six weeks and I was exhausted, although looking back, I have to admit that Brad was right about one thing at least – this weekend at the Hummingbird Hotel has turned out to be exactly what I needed, but I'm not going to tell him that anytime soon. Anyway, he said I *had* to stay, and when I said that he couldn't make me… well, he threatened me.'

'He threatened you?' Allyssa gaped.

'Oh, no, not physically, no, no, nothing like that. He said that if I didn't stay here with you and Josh, then he'd tell Pierre about my accessories business. He said that as I'd created the products whilst employed by the Pierre Fontaine Fashion House, then the designs belonged to the company and not me. I told him that I'd worked on them in my own time, but he was adamant that it didn't matter, that they still owned the intellectual property in them. I have no idea if that's true, but he said that if I didn't stay on in Corfu, like he'd asked, he would tell Pierre what I've done and that Pierre would fire me.'

'Oh, Katie, I'm so sorry.'

'Which means that I had no alternative but to tag along, but I was angry, furious, and I wanted to get my own back on him while I looked into whether what he had said about the legal position was true. So, yes, I let the goat into his room and introduced her to his designer underwear, and when I heard him going on and on about never needing to sleep and how siestas were for wimps, I added a couple of drops of my herbal sleep remedy to his smoothie.'

Katie glanced down at her lap, where she was

shredding the tissues that Abbie had given her, unable to meet either Abbie or Allyssa's eyes after her admission of guilt.

'I had no idea Brad would fall asleep under the full glare of the afternoon sun, and I was truly horrified when I saw his face and realised what had happened. I panicked, I got rid of the bottle, and I was going to come clean straight away, but we were on our way to the wine-tasting event and there didn't seem to be the right opportunity to confess. I promise I'm going to find him, right now, and tell him what I did. I'll apologise profusely, and face the consequences. I'm sorry, Abbie, I really am. If I had known how amazing it is here then I would have jumped at the chance to come.'

Abbie reached out to lace her fingers through Katie's and smiled.

'It's okay, no harm done.'

'Apart from Brad's cherry-red face,' said Allyssa, with a smirk.

'I'm just glad it's all been sorted out,' Abbie continued, the relief seeping through her veins. 'But there's one thing I still don't understand.'

'What's that?'

She cast a sideways look at Allyssa before looking back at Katie.

'Why was Brad taking photographs of Allyssa?'

'Photographs? What photographs?' Allyssa stared at Abbie, completely nonplussed. 'Katie? What's Abbie talking about?'

'I saw Brad, on Friday morning, when we were having drinks at that café on the Liston in Corfu Town. He was hiding behind a potted palm, taking photos of you with his phone, and, when I challenged him, he was horrified that he'd been rumbled.'

'He was taking photographs of me from behind a tree?'

'Yes.'

'But what for?'

'I have no idea, but it's totally unacceptable.'

'Too right!' Allyssa cried in indignation. 'There's no way I'm going to let him get away with that! Pierre would *never* condone that kind of behaviour; it's totally unethical and against the company's Code of Conduct – and Brad knows all about that. Right! Come on! We're going to see what he has to say for himself.' Allyssa jumped up from her perch on Katie's bed, her jaw set, fire flashing in her eyes until something else occurred to her. 'You know, something strange *is* going on, I'm sure of it.'

'What do you mean?'

'Well, now I come to think of it, when I told him I wanted to fly to Paris on Friday to spend the weekend with Xavier, promising faithfully to come back with Pierre and Pippa on Monday, Brad sort of threatened me too.'

'Did he?'

'Yes.' She paused, wrestling with whether to confide in Katie. 'He told me that if I didn't stay, he would drop me in it with my publisher, tell them that I'm a fraud, which would mean I would lose my book deal.'

'A fraud? Why are you a fraud?'

'Because… because he caught me cramming my face with donuts.'

'So?' Katie asked, confused.

'And pizza, and spaghetti, and hot dogs.'

'Again, so?'

'I don't lead a healthy lifestyle. I never have. I adore fish and chips, chicken curry, burgers with melted cheese, Victoria sponge cake, clotted cream scones… Well, you get the picture.'

Katie laughed for the first time that morning. 'I know you do.'

'You do?'

'Yes, I saw you in Antigua guzzling king prawns drenched in garlic butter, gobbling down a bucket of fried chicken in Valetta, and hoovering up a creamy carbonara in Sardinia.'

'Oh God!' Allyssa groaned, dropping her face into her palms. 'I thought I was being careful.'

'Do you think that was why Brad was photographing you?'

'Possibly. The only way we'll find out is by asking him. I vote we go and confront him.'

Before Abbie could stop either of them, they'd marched out of the guest room on a mission.

***

'Hey, guys, where have you been? You've been gone ages,' said Josh, jumping out of his seat when they arrived on the veranda, his expression swiftly changing from anxiety to confusion when he saw the look on Allyssa's face. 'Allyssa? What's wrong?'

'We have something we want to say to Brad.' Allyssa looked at Katie. 'Do you want to go first?'

Katie nodded and took a step forward so she was

standing in front of Brad, who, as usual, had commandeered the chair at the head of the table, enjoying his third cup of coffee as he scrolled through his emails on his phone, totally oblivious to their presence.

'Brad?'

'Mmm?' he said, without looking up.

'I'm sorry,' Katie started.

'Mmm? What for?'

'It was me.'

Something in Katie's tone made Brad finally look up, his forehead wrinkled in enquiry.

'What was you?'

'The smoothie.'

'The smoothie? Sorry, I…'

'And the goat.'

'The goat?' Now Brad's enquiry turned to full-on confusion.

'Yes, that was me, too, I did it.'

It was a couple of seconds before Katie's confession truly sunk in and Brad's jaw dropped in astonishment. If the situation hadn't been so serious, Abbie would have giggled.

'You fed my silk boxer shorts to a goat?'

'Well, I didn't actually feed—'

'But why would you—'

'It's no less than you deserve!' Allyssa interrupted, stepping in front of Katie, her hands on her hips, towering over Brad as she stared down at him in his chair, her expression stony, her eyes boring into his.

'What do you mean?'

'Katie tells me she caught you taking covert

photographs of me from behind a bush.'

'You were photographing Allyssa from behind a bush?' Josh gasped. 'Why would you do that?'

'I wasn't actually—'

'I saw you!'

'Well, yes, I was *photographing* you, but I wasn't... Sorry, I can't go into this right now.'

'But—' Allyssa started.

'Look, Katie,' said Brad, once more taking command of the situation that had been at risk of spiralling out of control. 'I accept your apology. Why you might have wanted to... to do what you did, well, we can talk about that later, but I really wish you hadn't because I'm going to look like a real idiot in my photograph, which is... which is unfortunate in the circumstances. Abbie, please would you extend my sincere apologies to Felix for suspecting his smoothie was sub-par, or in any way to blame for my unscheduled afternoon nap yesterday.'

'Yes, of course, but—'

Brad glanced at his Rolex, his eyes widened, and he vaulted from his chair.

'Okay, now all that's settled we need to check out. The taxi will be here in twenty minutes and whilst I'm packed and ready to go, I doubt you are Allyssa, so please – and I can't stress this enough – this is one thing we *cannot* be late for. I'll see you in the lobby at eleven o'clock *on the dot*, no excuses.'

And with that, Brad strode from the terrace with everyone staring after him.

'Okay, well, that went better than I thought,' said Katie, smoothing her hands down her hips.

'Well, I've not finished with Brad, yet. I want an

explanation about that photograph and I'm still going to report what he did to Pierre, but I'll wait until after the shoot is in the bag because if we engage in a full-blown showdown now, the frosty after-effects will be reflected in the photographs. Come on, let's pack,' Allyssa said.

'Need any help?' asked Katie, a knowing smile playing around her lips.

'I thought you'd never ask!' Allyssa laughed before linking her arm through her friend's and sauntering from the veranda as though they had all the time in the world.

'Hang on, guys, wait for me,' Josh called after them as he scampered in their fragrant wake. 'You promised to give me some tips on how to be a model in a photoshoot.'

As soon as they were out of earshot, Abbie plonked herself down into the seat next to Nikos, who had been reclining in his chair, his ankle hooked nonchalantly over his thigh as he watched the proceedings unfold with calm curiosity, clearly delighted to have nabbed a front row seat at a particularly engrossing theatre production.

'Wow, I know I've said it before, but there's really never a dull moment at the Hummingbird Hotel with Abbie Coleman in charge! You really should sell tickets!'

'Ergh,' Abbie groaned, dropping her chin into her palm as a wave of exhaustion washed over her, making her feel strangely woozy.

'You know, after living amongst the hustle and bustle of Paris for five years, I thought life back home at the winery would be routine, mundane even, but, of course, I hadn't factored in the arrival of a woman with wild corkscrew curls and a talent for attracting chaos and confusion.'

'Mundane and boring would be welcome right now.'

'Really? So does that mean you're *not* joining Allyssa and Katie when the taxi arrives to take everyone to the photoshoot in Corfu Town in…' Nikos glanced at his watch, a smile playing around his lips. 'Ten minutes' time?'

Abbie stared at him for a beat until his words sunk in, and a slice of panic shot through her chest. She scrambled to her feet.

'Oh God! I've got to get changed and do something with my hair!'

Chapter Nineteen

The Corfu Palace Hotel, Corfu Town
Flower: Holly 'Golden King'

Abbie looked up at the impressive triple-arched portico of the five-star Corfu Palace Hotel, and understood immediately why Brad and Pippa had chosen it as the location for their company's corporate photoshoot.

Excitement and nerves swirled through her body in equal measure as she made her way up the marble steps to the majestic entrance of the most luxurious hotel in Corfu Town, before turning round to take in the lush, manicured gardens where no weed or dried leaf would dare to venture. To her left was an attractive swimming pool, its turquoise water glittering beneath the sun's rays, surrounded by sumptuously upholstered sunloungers occupied by a smattering of hotel guests, their identities hidden from view by large floppy hats or the daily newspaper as they enjoyed a brief sojourn from the hustle and bustle of their normal lives.

'Wow, this place is absolutely stunning,' said Abbie as she and Nikos were welcomed into the lobby by a uniformed doorman who, when asked, directed them to the suite where the Pierre Fontaine entourage were gathering prior to the photoshoot. 'Look at that staircase, and those columns, and that chandelier!'

Nikos laughed. 'I have to admit that this is my favourite hotel in Corfu Town – but, of course, not the whole of the island; that spot is reserved for the Hummingbird Hotel! My sister had her wedding reception here and it was a wonderful celebration; the food is exquisite, and wait until you see the view from the gardens!'

Abbie followed Nikos down a bright, airy corridor dotted with expensive furniture, original watercolours of the island, and beautifully arranged potted plants, the ambience cool, tranquil, unhurried and peaceful.

'Here we are.'

Nikos pushed open the door to the suite, and a cacophony of sound immediately assaulted Abbie's ears, coupled with a whirlwind of high-energy activity as the room's occupants rushed around like characters on fast-forward – unpacking camera equipment, unravelling cables, setting up lighting, brandishing clipboards, even manoeuvring a huge electric fan into place – and shouting out instructions, offering suggestions, calling for assistance, chastising errors.

'Want to take a look at the gazebo?' Nikos asked.

'Absolutely.'

Abbie beamed with delight when she saw where the actual photoshoot was going to take place; a raised, white-washed and columned gazebo in the gardens just beyond the terrace. It was the perfect setting; the lawned and gravelled gardens, vibrant geraniums bursting from a plethora of ceramic pots, trees and shrubs strategically placed to offer the maximum shade, set against the heart-stoppingly beautiful backdrop of the sapphire blue Ionian Sea upon which several sleek, white yachts bobbed.

Over to her right, the frenzy of activity continued as the crew put the finishing touches to the gazebo – which included rolling out a red carpet that led all the way to the steps of the terrace upon which Abbie was standing, like a fashion show runway – in the middle of which was the shoot's photographer, Carlton, directing operations with calm authority.

'Wow.'

It was the only word Abbie could think of to say. She felt as though she'd stepped through one of Alice's looking-glasses and entered a completely different world. She'd attended photoshoots before, but none in such spectacularly beautiful surroundings, and certainly not one with a fifteenth century Venetian fort as part of the scenery, or its own jetty on which to moor your one-hundred-and-fifty-foot superyacht.

'Hey Abbie, hey Nikos, over here!'

Abbie glanced over her shoulder, back into the suite, where she saw Allyssa perched on a high bar stool – her hair already styled into an attractive up-do and decorated with several diamanté clips – having her makeup done by a makeup artist. Next to her, also sitting on a high bar stool with a wide smile stretching her lips, was Katie, having her long chestnut locks teased into a cascade of loose curls.

Abbie returned to the suite so she could inspect their transformation more closely.

'Gosh, you both look amazing.'

'Thanks, Abbie,' said Allyssa. 'Wait until you see the clothes Pierre has had sent over for us to wear. Josh is in his element! Look.'

Everyone switched their gaze to the other side of the room, where Josh was standing in front of a silver clothes rack crammed with a variety of menswear; pale linen suits, sports jackets, trousers – long, short and cropped at the ankle; shirts – long-sleeved, short-sleeved, sleeveless and in every colour of the rainbow; and even jauntily patterned waistcoats. His brow was furrowed, clearly overwhelmed with the choice on offer for his important modelling debut.

'And this is what *I'm* wearing,' Katie announced, slipping from the stool to collect a short, flimsy summer dress, fashioned from flower-sprigged fabric, with shoestring shoulder straps and a narrow silver belt at the waist. She held it against her body and performed a theatrical twirl, the hem swinging attractively just above her knee.

'That's absolutely gorgeous, Katie.'

'Thank you, Abbie.'

'Where's Brad?' asked Nikos, looking around the suite.

'Over there, doing what he does best: *strategizing*,' Allyssa said with a roll of her eyes.

Abbie glanced across the room to where Brad was issuing instructions like missiles.

'Guys, guys, not over there! Over here! Zoe, you know that's not what I asked for, and Donna, please take these flower pots out to the gazebo, one on each step, and Jacob, could you move these cables before someone trips over them and sustains an injury? The last thing we want is a Greek law suit on our hands.'

When Brad finally looked up from his notes and saw the group watching him, he handed over a huge white board reflector to the woman Abbie assumed must be Zoe – who staggered slightly under its weight – and made his way towards them. As he drew close, Abbie was relieved to see that he had already taken his turn in the makeup artist's chair, and there was no evidence of the earlier sunburn to spoil his "preppy" good looks. Dressed in a pale grey, two-piece silk suit with lavender tie and matching pocket handkerchief, he looked suave and sophisticated, exactly how she expected a corporate mover-and-shaker to look. However, what she hadn't expected to see was a ginger-haired cameraman following in his wake, and she took a swift step back so that she wasn't standing in the direct path of his lens.

'Hi, guys, great to see you. Let me introduce you to Carlton's talented assistant, Jonti Grainger. He'll be our videographer for the day.'

To Abbie's surprise, she detected an uncharacteristically nervous wobble in his voice as he introduced Jonti to them, and, on closer inspection, she saw that Brad was almost vibrating with nervous energy, unable to keep still, moving from one foot to the other, clenching and unclenching his fists, his eyes continuously flashing around the room, checking everything, and everyone, was in the proper place.

'Hey, everyone.' Jonti grinned, showcasing an immaculate smile.

'Hi, Jonti,' said Nikos, holding out his palm until, at the

last minute, he realised that, as Jonti was sporting a cumbersome camera on his shoulder, he was unable to shake hands, and so performed a forearm bump with him instead.

'Okay, much as I'd like to, I can't stop to chitchat,' said Brad, flashing a quick look at the camera. 'I need to run a few things up the flag pole with Carlton before we start shooting. Catch you later, and Allyssa, please keep an eye on these two. Remember what I said? No beers, no cocktails, no white wine spritzers, nothing apart from sparkling water or soda until the shoot's in the can, okay?'

Without waiting for an answer, he hustled off through the French doors in a cloud of Aramis cologne, with Jonti following behind, jogging along the red carpet to make sure he captured Brad's every move.

'Mind if I disappear for an hour or so?' Nikos whispered in Abbie's ear. 'Photoshoots are really not my thing, and I said I'd grab a quick drink with my friend Loukas while I'm in town.'

'No problem, see you later.'

Abbie saw Nikos hesitate, as though he wanted to kiss her, but thought better of it and gave her a quick hug instead before slipping out of the room without anyone noticing.

'I've never seen Brad so stressed!' Allyssa mused, staring out at the gazebo where he was now directing Zoe in the complicated task of affixing the reflector to one of the columns. 'I don't understand it, he's done almost as many professional photoshoots as I have, and he's usually loitering in the background, "maintaining a helicopter view" of everything that's going on, and not getting involved. Look at him over there; he's like a cat on a hot tin roof!'

'I agree, he does seem overly distracted by all the details,' said Katie, wrinkling her forehead in bafflement at Brad's strange behaviour. 'However, I have to admit, I'm relieved. It stops him from focussing on what happened at the hotel, mulling over his options and coming to the conclusion that the only thing to do is to fire me.'

'What would Pierre do without you, though?'

Allyssa reached out to squeeze Katie's hand, and Katie gave her a weak smile filled with uncertainty, but her despondency didn't last long as her gaze fell on Jonti – who was now pointing his lens at an unsuspecting Josh as he finally made his sartorial selection from the clothes rack – and her eyes narrowed, filling with suspicious.

'Do you know what I'd like to know?' Katie continued.

'What?'

'Why we're being filmed. This is a photoshoot for our company's website, not a movie.'

'Oh, I overheard Brad chatting to Carlton when we arrived, he said something about live streaming,' Allyssa said calmly.

'Live streaming!' Katie gaped at Allyssa. 'Are you sure?'

'Yes, I'm sure. Why?'

'Because I—'

'Hey everyone! Pierre's here!' someone shouted.

If Abbie had thought the room was a whirlwind of activity when she'd arrived, it became a maelstrom of panic now, as everyone rushed to finalise their remaining tasks before their famously fastidious boss arrived to inspect the venue and approve – or critique – their work. Even as an anonymous by-stander, watching from the side-lines, Abbie experienced wriggle of anxiety.

Moments later the doors to the suite were flung open, and Pierre Fontaine strode into the room like a conquering king, his laser-sharp eyes sweeping the room and taking in every detail, then zooming in on Jonti as he filmed the celebrity designer's grand entrance. Abbie saw that, just like Allyssa, Pierre took personal grooming to the highest level; his skin was flawless and sported a rich Mediterranean tan, his eyebrows were professionally shaped, his dark stubble immaculately barbered, and she could already smell his expensive oriental cologne burgeoning through the air. He possessed a rather haughty demeanour, with an almost arrogant tip of the chin, and Abbie wasn't in the least bit surprised to see that he was dressed from head to toe in black, albeit fashioned from the most exquisite of fabrics. However, she *was* surprised that he wasn't as tall as she remembered, that he was actually probably no more than five-foot-three in his stacked heels.

'*Bonjour mes amis*!'

Pierre was immediately engulfed by a welcoming committee, including Brad and Allyssa, and everyone from the photoshoot crew – with Jonti recording every greeting – whilst Katie and Josh hung back and watched the proceedings with interest.

'Oh, look, there's Pippa! Pippa, darling!'

Katie rushed to where Pippa had followed Pierre, completely unnoticed, through the door. She was wrestling with a gigantic suitcase, two overstuffed sports bags, and a huge leather portfolio case, which she handed over to Katie with a sigh of relief.

'Hi, guys!' Pippa tossed her hair over her shoulder, and moved in for hugs with Katie, and then Josh, before turning to Abbie, a warm smile on her face, her hazel eyes softening. 'Hi, Abbie, it's great to see you. How's life as a hotelier in Corfu?'

'It's… interesting.'

'Katie told me you'd be here at the shoot. I'm… I'm sorry about what happened with Dan; the guy's an idiot, if you ask me.'

'Thanks, Pippa.'

'Did you know that Pierre engaged the services of *FlowerEssence* to do the floral decorations for his fiftieth birthday party last month, over at his apartment in Paris?'

'Yes, I did know.' How could she forget? It was a question about the event that Dan had surprised her with when she had thought he was about to propose. 'Why?'

'Well…'

'What?' Abbie experienced a sharp twist of anxiety in her stomach.

'Well, I don't want to speak out of turn, but Pierre wasn't happy with the theme, or the designs, or the freshness of the flowers that were chosen. He said they were *décevant*, underwhelming, absent of the usual flair, and…'

'And what?'

'That his chihuahua could have done a better job.'

A complicated mixture of emotions tumbled through Abbie's body. Whilst she didn't want *FlowerEssence* to disappoint customers, or be associated with substandard workmanship, there was a nip of satisfaction mingled in there that during her time at the boutique she'd been able to add a certain *je ne sais quoi* that resonated with creative gurus such as Pierre Fontaine, and that they had noticed her absence.

'Pippa, darling, there you are! Welcome to the Corfu Palace Hotel!' cried Brad, bursting into their conversation. 'You've certainly outdone yourself this time! Finding and securing this place was a stroke of genius; it's the perfect location to showcase the myriad talented people who spend their working lives at the Pierre Fontaine Fashion House! *And* you've selected the best crew out there to ensure the whole thing runs without a hitch. Thank you.'

Pippa gawped at the unexpected praise falling from Brad's lips, and was even more astonished when he leaned forward to greet her with elaborate cheek kisses, a gesture that was clearly for the benefit of his ever-present shadow, Jonti, who was still filming everything that moved, and if Allyssa was to be believed, live streaming it, too.

'Erm, thanks, Brad.'

Pippa exchanged a surreptitious eyebrow raise with Katie who simply shrugged her shoulders. She had just opened her mouth to ask Pippa what on earth was going on when Pierre climbed onto a discarded camera case, clapped his hands, and called for everyone's attention. Silence fell swiftly and all eyes turned towards him.

'*D'accord,* let's get this photoshoot started!'

Chapter Twenty

The Corfu Palace Hotel, Corfu Town
Flower: Corn Lily 'Spotlight'

A surge of bodies rushed for the French doors, then spilled out onto the terrace and down the red carpet before taking up their places around the gazebo where Pierre was already demanding that Carlton make a number of tweaks to the gold-painted, Louis IX-esque throne – which he'd commissioned specially for that day's shoot – before he was even prepared to sit on it.

Abbie stood with Pippa, Katie, Allyssa and Josh as they waited for their turn to be photographed, whilst Brad continued to run round in circles, making sure everything was on point and on schedule. He was spouting increasingly cringe-worthy gobbledegook about "squaring the circle" and "going back to sharpen our pencils", and at one point Abbie thought she heard him telling one of the crew members who had responded to one of his questions with an innocent "I hope so" that "hope" was not a strategy that led to success, whilst Jonti caught it all on camera.

'So, Pippa, want to tell us why Jonti's here?' asked Katie. 'I thought this was a *photo*shoot, not a *film* shoot, and that guy's certainly enjoying channelling his inner Spielberg; everywhere I look, he's there, pointing his lens at us.'

'To be honest, I have no idea,' said Pippa, scrunching her nose in bafflement as she watched Jonti perform a three-hundred-and-sixty-degree sweep of the hotel's grounds before concentrating his lens back on where Carlton was gently encouraging a flagging Pierre into numerous original poses, incurring Pierre's wrath when he suggested they turn the industrial-sized fan on him for a more windswept look. 'I booked Carlton and his crew, but I didn't have anything to do with booking Jonti, I think that must have been either Pierre or Brad.'

'Don't get me wrong, I've always wanted to star in a movie with a gorgeous male lead, but I'm not sure I'm comfortable about having my every move recorded without knowing where it's going to be uploaded, not to mention the fact that Allyssa says she thinks it's being live streamed.'

'Live streamed? No, no way.'

'Allyssa? Tell Pippa,' said Katie.

'That's what I overheard Brad say to Carlton earlier.'

'Do you think you could have misheard?' said Pippa.

'I don't think so, I definitely—' began Allyssa.

'And why on earth does the shoot have to be in Corfu? Surely it would have made more sense for us to have it at the office? Where we could be photographed actually doing our jobs, *in situ*, so to speak?' Katie continued.

'I agree,' said Pippa. 'And so did Brad to start with, but Pierre was adamant, and when Brad started talking about running the numbers past the accountants, they had this really long pow-wow in the boardroom with one of Pierre's investors, and afterwards Brad had changed his tune and was completely on board with the shoot being here. When I asked him what was going on, he said I just had to just go with it. Okay, I think I'd better go and get—'

But Katie was on a roll.

'And another thing. I totally understand why Pierre and Allyssa are involved in this shoot, why Pierre wants photos of himself and our best model plastered all over the website and in frames around the offices, or maybe as a backdrop for a catwalk show, but why me? Why Brad? Why Josh? And why not Greta? Or Jules? Or Henrietta? I don't get it.'

Pippa sighed as they all watched Pierre, without the merest hint of irony, declare that he'd endured enough discomfort in the name of modelling and photography, and was going in search of a revitalising glass of Pernod. He relinquished his place in the spotlight to an enthusiastic, and clearly very excited, Brad, who proceeded to follow Carlton's shouted instructions to the letter, even agreeing to the "industrial fan" treatment.

'Pip?'

'Look, Katie, all I know is that Pierre wanted to feature someone from every facet of the business. So, of course, there's him as the figurehead of the company, and the driving force behind the brand. Then there's Brad, who represents the commercial side of things – marketing, publicity, all the boring corporate stuff – and me, from the events organising and catwalk-staging side of things. Allyssa was chosen to showcase the workings of the fashion house from a model's perspective, and you, Josh, you were selected as our brilliant and gifted photographer.'

Josh beamed, clearly delighted at Pippa's description of him. 'Thanks, Pip.'

'And last, but by no means least, there's you, Katie, Pierre's talented protégé, who keeps him on his toes with his designs for our younger clientele, as well as helping to extend the Pierre Fontaine fashion brand's product range into handbags, luggage, jewellery, perfume…'

'Perfume? We don't do perfume,' said Katie.

'At the moment.'

'What do you—'

'Okay, Allyssa, your turn!' Brad called, bounding towards them so he could shepherd Allyssa to the gazebo, just in case she got lost on the way, even though it was only twenty metres away and there was a red carpet leading straight to it.

'Right, if you've finished your interrogation, I really need to get changed into my outfit.'

Pippa stooped to unzip one of the pink sports bags she'd brought with her, and started to rummage inside, pulling out a pair of ivory silk stilettos decorated in sequins, and a crammed-to-bursting makeup bag, then she paused and met Katie's eyes.

'If it makes you feel any better, when the shoot's over, we'll ply Pierre with lots of the local ouzo – apparently, it tastes like Pernod – and ask him to tell us what he and Brad are up to, okay?'

'Okay. And I'm going to inform Pierre that I caught

Brad skulking behind bushes in Corfu Town taking photos of Allyssa without her consent. I know he'll go ballistic when he finds out about that.'

'Brad was taking pictures of Allyssa?'

Pippa glanced to where Allyssa was twisting and turning, swishing and swaying, in the shade of the gazebo, completely at ease in front of the camera, striking every pose with the minimum of instruction from Carlton, her peppermint-coloured chiffon dress floating around her ankles in the scant breeze, the diamanté hairclips sparkling in the sunshine.

'But why would Brad do something like that? It doesn't make any sense.'

'Well, I—' Katie started.

'Actually, guys, I think we should shelve this conversation until after the shoot, don't you?' said Josh, pointing to where Allyssa had completed her part in the photoshoot in record time, and was now, for some reason, doing a piece to camera for Jonti, a smile on her face, a colourful cocktail in hand.

'Katie? I think that Carlton is waving at you,' said Abbie.

'Oh, no, there's no way I'm going over there straight after Allyssa. You can go, Josh.'

'Really?'

'Yes, break a leg!'

'And I'm going back to the suite to get changed!' Pippa rushed off towards the terrace before Katie could delay her any further, re-appearing only minutes later, totally transformed in an elegant navy-blue jumpsuit with cropped trousers, the cuffs and neckline edged in a garland of white embroidered daisies, and her previously travel-mussed hair, the colour of a fox's tail, now sleek and glossy, the outfit completed by the addition of the sparkly stilettos.

Abbie watched, along with Pippa and Katie, as Josh worked his way through the photoshoot, his caramel quiff holding up magnificently against the increasing humidity, his face running the gamut of every expression in the modelling manual, from sultry and brooding to perplexed and mystified, from playful and mischievous to full-on Cheshire Cat grin. He had clearly listened to every nugget of advice Allyssa had imparted to him and Katie on the way over, and was studiously putting it into practice to great effect, so well, in fact, that Abbie thought if he ever decided to give up his photography career, he could have a lucrative future on the catwalk.

'Oh God, I'm so nervous,' groaned Katie, pulling at the hem of her dress. 'What do you think the odds are of being able to sneak away without anyone noticing?'

'Nil,' said Pippa, giving her a gentle shove forward onto the red carpet as Josh's star turn came to an end with a jolly fist bump from Carlton. 'You're up; you never know, you might even enjoy it.'

Katie rolled her eyes, forced a smile, and made her way along the carpet and onto the set, her stiff body language screaming anxiety and broadcasting a clear signal that she didn't want to be there. But Carlton was a seasoned expert in dealing with reluctant subjects, and within minutes he had struck up an animated dialogue about the sunshine-shaped handbag she had chosen to accessorize her outfit, and the ice was broken. The creases in her forehead melted away, her frown was replaced by a smile, and it was clear that she was having fun – so much, in fact, that when Carlton declared himself satisfied, she even asked if he would take an extra photograph with her phone so she could send it to her mum.

'Okay, Pippa, last but by no means least!' called Brad, wafting his hand in her direction.

'Good luck.' Abbie smiled.

Pippa performed her poses with poise, and twenty minutes later, after calling Pierre back from the bar for a few more shots of him standing on the terrace with the Old Fort, the marina, and his yacht in the background, and a final shot of everyone together, Carlton declared "it's a wrap". The crew immediately dispersed to start dismantling the equipment so they could make the most of the hotel's pool and other facilities before they flew back to London the following day.

Abbie joined Pippa and the rest of the Pierre Fontaine group at the bar where she caught up with the insider fashion gossip and devoured cocktails, listening to Pierre regale them all with stories from the catwalk until he declared himself exhausted and disappeared to his luxury two-bedroomed suite for a siesta with instructions not to disturb him until dinner.

'How come Brad's still frazzled? Will someone please tell him that the shoot's over, that Carlton's got the photographs he needs and there's no need to pace around the garden like a caged lion? He's making me feel dizzy just watching him!' said Katie.

Abbie looked over to where Brad was circling the gazebo, his phone glued to his ear, nervous energy exuding from his every pore, just as it had been since they'd arrived at the hotel.

'Don't know about dizzy, but it's the perfect time to ask him about what he's planning to do with the photographs he took of me. Then I'll speak to my agent about it. Come on.'

Allyssa slipped from her bar stool, a determined expression on her face, with Katie and Pippa hot on her heels. Abbie exchanged a glance with Josh, and they followed, too, their curiosity too strong to resist. With perfect timing, as they approached the steps of the gazebo, Brad's call came to an end.

'Brad? I need to ask you—'

'Whoop! Whoop! It's a go, guys! We've done it! We've actually done it!'

Brad punched the air and Abbie was shocked to see tears in his eyes.

Chapter Twenty One

The Swimming Pool at The Corfu Palace Hotel
Flower: Rosa 'Champagne Celebration'

'Brad? What's going on? What are you talking about? What have we done?'

'Hang on a minute, I just need to call Pierre.'

Brad dialled Pierre's number, then turned his back on the group and strode towards the swimming pool so they couldn't listen in to his conversation.

'What's going on?' asked Allyssa.

'No idea,' said Pippa, her forehead creased with puzzlement.

'Well, I'm going to find out!' said Katie, jogging off in Brad's wake.

'Come on, guys!' said Josh, 'We don't want to miss this, do we?'

Abbie wasn't sure whether she should join them, but she didn't have to think about it for too long as she exchanged a brief glance with Pippa and Allyssa and joined them in their sprint across the hotel's gardens to where Brad was winding up his conversation with Pierre. After a gleeful "*à tout à l'heure*!", she watched him slide his phone back into the pocket of his trousers, then drop onto one of the sunloungers, his hands shaking as he pushed his glasses back up to the bridge of his nose and combed his fingers through his fringe. However, she was pleased to see that the earlier nervous energy had abated, and had been replaced with the zing of unfettered excitement.

'Brad? Spill!' Katie demanded, coming to a standstill in front of him, her hands on her hips, the jut of her chin informing him that she would entertain no fobbing off, or corporate fudging.

'You might want to sit down.'

'Why?' asked Allyssa, nervously.

'Just do as he says, it'll be faster.' Josh quickly gathered several patio chairs into a circle around where Brad sat, staring across the bay towards the horizon, a slightly dazed expression in his eyes.

'Okay Brad, you have our undivided attention so—'

'Champagne?'

In disbelief, the whole group swung their gaze to a twenty something waiter who could have played a younger version of George Clooney in his biopic – who was holding a silver ice bucket and a tray of crystal Champagne flutes, his eyebrows raised in question, a polite smile on his face. His arrival served to rouse Brad from his fugue and he jumped from the sunlounger to relieve the waiter of the bottle of Louis Roederer Cristal Brut on ice, which Abbie knew cost more than her weekly salary when she worked at *FlowerEssence*.

'Thank you.'

Brad tipped the waiter and then proceeded to pop the cork, pour the Champagne, and hand around the glasses, all the while a wide grin stretching his lips. Finally, he raised his glass high into the air.

'To the Pierre Fontaine Fashion House!'

'Brad! Tell us what's going on. Now!'

'Okay, well, you're not going to believe this, I'm still trying to process what it actually means myself. I mean—'

'Brad!' cried the group in unison.

'Sorry, sorry, okay, so—'

'Hey, guys, I've been looking for you all over. How did the photoshoot—'

'Nikos!' Abbie said.

'No!' Katie shouted.

'Later!' Allyssa pleaded.

Abbie couldn't help but giggle at the shock sprawled across Nikos' face at the onslaught of high-pitched objections to his pleasant, cheery greeting. She pressed her finger against her lips, handed him a glass of Champagne, and then guided him to the sunlounger that Brad had vacated so he could address them standing. She sat with Nikos before whispering 'Brad's got an important announcement to make.'

'Brad, will you just put us all out of our misery?' said Pippa.

'Okay, so I owe you all an apology.'

'An apology?' gaped Katie.

'Shush,' whispered Allyssa, reaching out to lace her fingers through Katie's.

'Yes, an apology. I know how upset you all were when I said you had to stay on in Corfu after the fashion shoot, that you thought I was being unreasonable, encroaching on your private lives, and your time with family and friends, but I had no choice.'

'No choice? What do you mean?'

Brad ignored Pippa's question, inhaled a deep breath and turned to face Katie.

'I'm sorry, Katie, for what I said about your fledgling handbag empire, but it was the only thing I could think of to make sure you didn't fly home on Friday night like you wanted to. We were *all* exhausted after the shoot, short-tempered, irritable with each other, but I knew it was imperative that we enjoyed some time together just relaxing, replenishing our energy levels, and getting some of our natural sparkle back. And the best way to do that was by spending a quiet, carefree weekend at a hotel tucked away from the hustle and bustle of daily life, with as few distractions as possible.'

'So, you're *not* going to report me to Pierre?' said Katie, the relief evident in her voice.

'There's nothing to report; they're your designs to do with as you wish, but I can assure you that if you talked them through with Pierre, he'd be more than happy to invest in your enterprise. He also wants you to get involved in the creation of the Pierre Fontaine perfume and men's cologne project, but we can talk about that later.'

'So, the intellectual property thing that you mentioned—'

'Just a mechanism to keep you here in Corfu. Again, my profuse apologies, Katie. Like I said, I couldn't risk you ignoring my request to stay and jetting off home. I know how stubborn you can be.'

'I'm not—'

'And Josh?'

Brad switched his attention to where Josh was sitting in the shade of a parasol, his empty Champagne glass on the table next to him, watching the unfolding drama with growing astonishment.

'Yes?'

'I want to apologise to you, too. I'm sorry I didn't give your request for support more attention. You caught me at a really frantic time, when I was right in the middle of negotiations that had reached a crucial and delicate point and I just didn't have the bandwidth to think about anything else. I should have helped you out, and I apologise for not doing so, but I hope when I tell you the news that you'll forgive me, and that you'll understand why I was so distracted.'

Brad paused to run his fingers through his hair and drain his glass of Champagne.

'And what about Allyssa?' Katie asked. 'Are you going to apologise to her, too? Has all this got something to do with why you were photographing her?'

'Yes, I'm sorry about that, too. You have to believe me, Allyssa, I feel dreadful about it, but I had to do it, and please allow me to also apologise for threatening you with exposure.'

'Exposure?' Josh gaped. 'What are you talking about?'

'Brad said that if I didn't come to the Hummingbird Hotel with everyone, he would drop me in it with my publishers.'

'Drop you in it?'

Allyssa sighed. 'I—'

'She'll explain later,' Katie snapped. 'Brad, will you get to the point before I explode with frustration!'

'Okay, okay, so, Jonti, the videographer, well, he's from a TV production company and he was live streaming—'

'I told you he was live streaming!' said Allyssa.

'Allyssa!' Katie reprimanded.

'Sorry.'

'Jonti was live streaming the photoshoot back to Zach Mayhew in London.'

'Who's Zach Mayhew?'

'He's only one of the most talented TV directors on the circuit at the moment!' said Josh, now fully invested in the conversation, his gaze focussed completely on Brad. 'He's a documentary maker primarily, but he's done a few successful fly-on-the-wall TV series which… Oh my God! No way!'

Josh's face flooded with colour, and his eyes widened as he gaped at Brad.

'What?' said Allyssa, looking from Josh to Brad and back again.

'Brad? Is it true?' Josh asked.

Abbie saw that Brad was beaming from ear-to-ear and her own curiosity mounted.

'Yes, it's true. That's why I needed all four of us to be on our "A" game today. I wanted us to be revitalised, and upbeat, and filled with vibrant energy so we could flaunt our various personalities without the accompanying exhaustion, which I know from experience can spark irritation and heated arguments. I wanted us all to have renewed our bond over good food, great wine, trips to the beach and the local winery, a few yoga sessions and cookery classes, so that today we would showcase exactly what we could bring to the show.'

'Show? What show?' demanded Allyssa, now completely bewildered.

'I've just had the call from Zach. We've been selected – from a list of *twenty* other companies – to be the stars of his next reality TV show that will follow the exploits of the fashion world.'

'No way!'

'Wow!'

'Oh my God!'

'There will be six episodes in total, each one concentrating on one of the aspects of the business; from the initial brainstorming and creation of the designs, which will, of course, feature Pierre's and Katie's side of things, to the planning and orchestration of our catwalk shows, which are handled by Pippa, and all the corporate marketing and promotion work, which is my field of expertise. Allyssa, you will feature in the episode that focusses on the ins and outs of the modelling industry; Zach is particularly keen to highlight the importance of ensuring there is a diverse range of body shapes on the runway, and also to reflect that the profession is not as glamorous as some people may think. Finally, there will be an episode about the life of a fashion photographer, which is your domain, Josh.'

Silence descended as each person in the group processed the information Brad had just revealed. Abbie looked around at each of their faces; a mixture of shock, disbelief, incredulity, and excitement. Life continued around them; the cicadas still chirped, the birds still flitted from branch to branch, the hotel's guests still launched themselves into the swimming pool a mere three metres away, but it was as though their little group existed in a bubble all of their own.

'And whilst you will get the opportunity to see the contracts before shooting starts next month—'

'Next month!'

'—I can assure you that the fee for each of you is extremely generous – more than any of you, or I, have made in the last two years, for just over three months of work.' Brad paused and seemed to be swallowing down on an upsurge of emotion. 'When Zach first approached Pierre, he made it clear that any on-going discussions were highly confidential, that apart from his business manager, yours truly, he wasn't permitted to communicate even a whiff of the possibility of a show with anyone, otherwise the deal would be off. Pierre and I were charged with the task of selecting the best people in each of their fields of expertise, and we are proud to have each of you here to represent the brand. Whilst you all have every right to be angry with me about insisting you remained on Corfu, and about the secrets I utilised to ensure you stayed, I hope that now you know why I did it, that you will forgive me.'

'Can I just—' Allyssa began.

Brad raised his hand. 'Before I start answering your questions… Katie? Now that this is in the bag, I want you to know that I have no hard feelings about the smoothie and goat incident. Contrary to popular belief, I do have a sense of humour, but I'll admit that it's been somewhat missing-in-action over the last couple of months. I've spent every waking hour preparing, tweaking, and finalising our pitch to Zach, answering every question tossed in my direction by his production team, talking to our lawyers and accountants about privacy, insurance and other technical issues as well as keeping Pierre as calm as possible until the final announcement was made – which I can assure you was the hardest task of all.'

'Kudos for that,' muttered Josh.

'We were informed just last week that the Pierre Fontaine Fashion House had made it into the final three contenders, so it was imperative that nothing, absolutely nothing, went wrong at this photoshoot because I knew that Jonti was flying over to film and live stream as part of the final assessment process. So you can imagine my horror when I saw my sunburnt face in the mirror after falling asleep in the sun. If I was responsible for letting the company down at the last hurdle, well…'

'Oh my God, Brad, I'm so sorry. I really—' began Katie, her hands flying to her mouth as she realised how close her actions had come to potentially wreaking the opportunity of a lifetime.

'It's okay.' Brad laughed, finally starting to relax as he dropped onto one of the pool terrace's chairs and glanced around the group.

'No, it's not. I shouldn't have—' Katie argued.

Brad held up his hand again. 'We've all been under immense pressure, so what do you say we spend the rest of the time we have here at the Corfu Palace Hotel celebrating our good fortune? Because I can assure you that when we get back to London tomorrow the hard work is *really* going to begin.'

'Agreed!' Allyssa cried, leaping from her chair. 'God, I don't think I've ever been so excited! I've got lots of things I want to publicise about life as a runway model. I think this is going to be so much fun. Thanks for doing this for us, Brad.'

Allyssa leaned forward and gave Brad a warm hug. Abbie's heart skipped a beat when she saw how delighted he was at her gesture. Now that the secret he'd been harbouring for so long – a secret that had made him so unpopular with his colleagues – was finally out in the open, he looked more like part of the group, someone who could relax and enjoy his colleagues' company instead of always being switched on, dialled in, and on duty.

'Okay, let's adjourn to the bar. The drinks are on me!'

Brad stepped forward to hook his arm around a still-dazed Josh's shoulder, and the two men meandered back towards the hotel, chatting away about their impending stardom, laughter floating in the air as they disappeared from view.

'Oh my God, I've got to call Xavier! He's going to be so jealous! Oh my God, Katie, Pip! We're all going to be TV stars!' Allyssa exclaimed.

'Wow, just wow,' whispered Pippa, who hadn't spoken once since they'd been told to sit down and listen to Brad's special announcement. 'Will someone please pinch me, and tell me I'm not dreaming.'

'You're not dreaming, darling.'

Katie stood up, held out her hand to pull Pippa to her feet, then linked her one arm through Pippa's and the other through Allyssa's, a smile lighting up her face, the shadow of resentment over Brad's threat to her future lifted and replaced with elation.

'I'm so happy for you all,' said Abbie, reaching out to hug Pippa, and then Allyssa, and finally Katie.

'Thanks, Abbie,' said Allyssa. 'And thanks for making our stay on Corfu the best time I've ever had. You can rest assured that I'll be recommending the Hummingbird Hotel to all my family, friends and fellow models in need of a restful and revitalising break from the frenzy of normal life. In fact, I'm going to make sure I drop a mention of the hotel, and you, into one of my conversations when Zach is filming, and I'm sure you'll be deluged with inquiries.'

'Oh, I'm not sure I—'

Nikos squeezed Abbie's hand and smiled. 'Shh.'

Abbie laughed, her heart soaring at the joy that sparked around the second group of guests that she'd hosted at the Hummingbird Hotel, delighted that, from disastrous beginnings, things had eventually turned out better than she could have ever hoped.

Chapter Twenty Two

The Hummingbird Hotel, Ropa Valley
Flower: Clematis 'Fond Memories'

The next morning, Abbie woke with a fuzzy head and a groan. The celebrations at the Corfu Palace Hotel had continued until well after two in the morning, with Pierre taking centre stage as the most exuberant fashion designer on the planet as he became ever more vociferous in his excitement about the TV deal as the ouzo flowed.

She pushed back the flimsy cotton sheet and padded to the window, flinging back the shutters to let in a fresh burst of morning air, accompanied by a waft of sweet floral scent from the garland of jasmine above the window. The sun had already poked its nose above the horizon, sending shafts of golden light scooting across the valley and her mood skywards. As she stood in the shower, the lukewarm water rinsing away the last remaining cobwebs of sleep, a feeling of accomplishment flooded her veins.

Despite her constant battle with the self-confidence demons, she had achieved something she would never have thought possible two months ago – sent another group of happy guests on their way, their promises to sing the praises of the Hummingbird Hotel giving her a warm feeling inside. With the progress at the vineyard, and Thanos' expert hand on the tiller, the vines were thriving, and there was a better than average chance that that year's grape harvest would be better than the last, and hopefully – Dionysus willing – the final product would be, if not spectacular, then at least more drinkable than the previous year's vintage had been.

She was also inordinately proud of having successfully hosted her first guided tour of the Angelopoulos Garden. Whilst four members of the fashion industry and a couple of friends from the local taverna weren't exactly her target audience, she was still grateful for the lovely compliments she had received. She knew there was still a long way to go with both the hotel enterprise, and the winery and garden projects, but progress had been made and that was worth celebrating.

Something else she wanted to celebrate was the many friendships she'd forged since coming to the island paradise, something she hadn't expected when she'd arrived heartbroken from Dan's rejection and focussed only on selling the hotel as quickly as possible so she could hightail it back to the UK to lick her wounds. Sofia, Felix, Rachel, and Dimitris had all shown her that, as the owner of the Hummingbird Hotel, she was an integral part of the local community, a community that would rally round in times of need, and to her surprise, the feeling of insecurity she had carried with her like a millstone since her mum's passing had abated.

She had started to put down roots there – on Corfu!

Her dream of moving to a little cottage in Devon had faded into the distance. She felt safe here, and it was the perfect place to move on from the past and make a fresh start. She had already formulated a plan to free up a few extra hours every day so she could spend more time at the winery and garden, and she smiled when she envisaged Felix's face when she asked him if he would consider taking on a more expansive role at the hotel in return for a share of the profits. She still had to work out the details, and chat them through with Nikos, but she was excited about the possibility of having Felix on board; it meant that no two days would be the same, which for someone who had avoided sticking her nose above the parapet, was something she never thought she'd look forward to.

However, what really caused her heart to skip a beat was her strengthening relationship with Nikos; not only had he rushed to her rescue when things threatened to spiral out of control at the hotel, he had also supported her and guided her, subtly and respectfully, always ensuring that she was the one who made the final decisions and never once foisting his own views on her.

She appreciated everything he did for her and the hotel, but, most important of all, whenever they were together, he made her senses sing. It was a feeling she couldn't put into words but it was one she relished, especially when she thought about the long, increasingly passionate kisses they'd shared whilst strolling through the gardens of the Corfu Palace Hotel the previous night, which had left her breathless and gasping for more. She had only known him for two months, but she had never felt as close to anyone as she did to Nikos, and, now that she was contemplating a future on Corfu, she realised that it was time to tell him that.

She dressed quickly, slid her feet into her favourite sparkly sandals, and grabbed her satchel. With a spring in her step, she trotted down the driveway to the taverna, her stomach rumbling as she conjured up a picture of one of Panos' breakfast omelettes and, to chase away the final vestiges of her hangover, a cup of rich, dark Greek coffee – something else she would never have believed she would ever enjoy.

'Hey, Abbie, I didn't think I'd see you before lunchtime today,' said Rachel, her habitual smile returned as she handed Abbie her coffee and flopped down into the seat next to her, a strong whiff of Turps floating on the air, which meant she had already found a few moments to spend with her paints, a development that made Abbie's spirits edge even higher. 'I heard you didn't get back from Corfu Town until the early hours of the morning. I take it that means the photoshoot went okay, and there were no more crazy mishaps?'

'More than okay. You wouldn't believe what happened!'

Abbie settled back in her seat and spent the next ten minutes filling Rachel in on Brad's surprise revelation about the TV deal, interspersed with lots of "oohs" and "aahs" and searching questions from Rachel, most of which she couldn't answer.

'Morning, guys, fancy joining me for a tai chi class?'

That morning Felix was channelling his inner ninja, wearing what looked to Abbie like a pair of black pyjamas with a rope belt around his waist. As usual, he was bare-foot, his tousled curls sprung from his head like a frothy blonde halo, and his demeanour was cheerful and composed.

'Tai chi? That's new,' said Abbie.

'Yes, I thought I'd mix it up a bit because my horoscope said I shouldn't be afraid to take on fresh challenges today. It also said something about unexpected visitors from foreign shores, but that happens all the time! *Er…* I *do* run yoga sessions for holidaymakers, and I live in a studio above a taverna!'

'Mmm, perhaps you should think about refreshing your astrological sources?' Abbie laughed, taking a sip of her coffee and enjoying the rush of caffeine it delivered, which made her feel almost human again. 'I'll take a rain-check on your tai chi lesson, Felix, but could you come over to the hotel later on this afternoon? There's something I'd like to chat to you about.'

'Another retreat?'

Abbie loved the way Felix's eyes lit up at the prospect.

'Possibly.'

'Count me in!'

'Great, is around four okay?'

'Perfect.'

'Hey, Abbie, do you have plans for tonight now that your guests have checked out?' asked Rachel.

'No, actually, I don't.'

'Why don't you come with me and Felix to a gig over in Paleokastritsa?'

Abbie's curiosity was piqued when she saw Rachel's

cheeks flush with colour.

'You know, I think this might be the start of something special for you, Rach,' Felix mused. 'I read *your* horoscope this morning, too, and it said that you'd have plenty of opportunity to invest in your artistic side today, but it also said that "music will be the route to a new adventure".'

'Oh, I do hope so!'

'*You're* playing a gig?' Abbie stared at Rachel; she hadn't known her for long, but she'd never heard her mention anything other than her passion for all-things painting related. 'I had no idea you—'

'No, no, no.' Rachel laughed. 'Not me. Dimitris! He's persuaded one of his many cousins – Roxanni, who owns a restaurant over on the west coast – to book his band for the night, and he's invited Felix and me over to support him. I'm sure he'd want to invite you and Nikos, too.'

'Sounds like fun! You can definitely count me in.'

'Oh, I…' Felix hesitated, an awkward expression on his face.

'What?'

'Nothing, it's just…'

'Felix!'

'It's just that your stars didn't feature anything vaguely musical for today, Abbie. In fact, you will be spending the whole day immersed in a frenzy of activity, surrounded by a mountain of paperwork, and culminating in an explosion of surprise.'

'An explosion of surprise? What on earth does that mean?'

'Hey, chill, I'm just the messenger. Catch you later.

Namaste.'

Abbie and Rachel watched Felix unfold his six-foot-four frame from his chair and saunter off to make a start on his tai chi routine in the shade of the olive tree that had presided over the taverna's garden for over a hundred years.

'Ignore him,' said Rachel, also getting to her feet. 'I'll see you tonight.'

'Great, looking forward to it.'

As Abbie lingered over her coffee, running through their conversation, she suddenly made the connection between their talk about Dimitris' gig that night and Rachel's reddened cheeks. She remembered how well the two of them had got on at the wine-tasting session on Sunday afternoon, and she hoped that her friend's horoscope was right, that this could be the start of something new for Rachel after her disappointment over Kostas leaving so abruptly to make a new life on Kefalonia. She and Dimitris would certainly make a great couple; both of them seemed to occupy the more whimsical end of the personality spectrum where timescales and accuracy were of minimal importance when compared to the value of their true passions – music and art.

'*Kalimera*, Abbie. Have your guests left?'

'Hi, Sofia. Yes, they should be at the airport by now.'

'So, what do you have planned for the rest of the day?'

Sofia placed a fresh cup of coffee down in front of Abbie and took the seat recently vacated by Rachel, the sleeves of her voluminous emerald-green kaftan flowing like angel wings in her wake. Abbie met her gaze, sensing a hidden agenda to Sofia's enquiry.

'I thought I would spend some time at Nikos' garden. There's so much to do over there that I—'

'What about at the hotel?'

'Oh, I'm not expecting any more guests until the end of the month, so I've got plenty of time to sort out the rooms, and the swimming pool, and I thought I might tidy up the courtyard and ask Felix to help me clean the fountain.'

'I didn't mean your housekeeping duties.'

Abbie's stomach lurched, and her breath caught in her throat when she realised what Sofia had meant. The familiar reaction of wanting to spin on her heels and dash for the hills invaded her chest, and it took every scrap of her willpower to remain sitting in her chair with a neutral expression on her face.

'Oh, I—'

'Abbie…' Sofia reached out to take her hands into hers, her eyes softening with sympathy, but also with a steely determination. 'It's time.'

'I—'

'The longer you put it off, the larger the horns will grow.'

'Yes, yes, you're right, of course, but I really don't—'

'I've spoken to Panos and Rachel, and they've agreed to cover me here at the taverna, so I've got the rest of the day off. I understand how difficult this is – sorting through a relative's belongings is hard, and sometimes heart-breaking, as we fear what memories we may stumble across, what secrets we might discover. Abbie, you *need* to do this, but you don't have to do it alone. I knew Liz for ten years, and I can assure you that she wouldn't have wanted her personal possessions to fester in her bedroom, gathering dust. She would want them packed away and donated to a worthy cause.'

'I…'

Abbie stopped. How could she admit to Sofia that she was terrified of what she might find hidden amongst her aunt's paperwork? Terrified, and yet at the same time, hopeful that maybe, just maybe, she would stumble across a diary, or a journal, or even just a letter addressed to her that would contain the information she had sought for so long about her past. Sofia had already shared what she knew, but Abbie suspected there was more to tell. Would she discover what that was in her aunt's personal documents?

'I'm… I'm frightened, Sofia…'

'I know, I know, and that's understandable, and quite normal,' said Sofia, her voice soft and sympathetic. 'Without knowledge of the past, our imaginations invent ever-escalating scenarios until we feel disorientated, bewildered, and scared. But our pasts shouldn't control us, Abbie, and especially not *someone else's* past. Once you have completed this task, I know that you will break away from those emotional tethers that are holding you back, and fly freely towards your future. Come on.'

Sofia stood up and held out her hand to Abbie, and her emotions pulled her in different directions; those in the red corner told her to resist, while those in the blue corner told her to just do it, to get it over with, and to simply stitch whatever she found into the fabric of her life and move on to make a fresh start, free of the shackles of her past.

Fortunately, those advocates in the blue corner hollered the loudest, and so she accepted Sofia's hand of friendship and walked with her, out of the taverna and along the driveway towards the Hummingbird Hotel, her aunt's beloved Hummingbird Hotel, her stomach churning, her knees wobbling, her heart pounding in her chest, as she tried to prepare herself for what she was about to uncover.

Chapter Twenty Three

Aunt Liz's Suite at the Hummingbird Hotel
Flower: Rosa 'Times Past'

Abbie pushed open the door to what had been her aunt's personal space, the place she came to escape her many duties as the chatelaine of the Hummingbird Hotel, and paused on the threshold, a deluge of diverse emotions surging through her body. She couldn't get away from the fact that she felt as though she was invading her aunt's privacy.

She surveyed the room in front of her; the rustic white-washed walls and stripped floorboards, the shabby-chic furniture, the hand-embroidered sheets, the bookcase sporting a varied selection of books and ornaments, the French doors leading out to the balcony, which boasted the best view of the whole valley and her aunt's beloved mini-vineyard. Dust particles danced on the shafts of sunlight, and a tangible feeling of melancholy lingered in the air, along with the slight waft of rose petals, and Abbie's heart gave a squeeze of trepidation as she took her first step into the room.

Where on earth was she going to start?

She paused, suddenly ambushed by a wave of grief, and was forced to drop down onto the bed, tears spilling down her cheeks, not for the loss of her aunt – although she was sad about that – but for the loss of her mum. She had faced this same, seemingly unsurmountable task before, after her mum's funeral, and it had been the hardest thing she'd ever had to do in her whole life. Everything she had touched had held a memory; the pictures, the ornaments, the linens, even the kitchen utensils had reminded her of the times she'd stood at her mum's side, laughing and gossiping as they whipped up a batch of fairy cakes that they would go on to decorate with sprinkles.

However, despite the trauma, she had been able to do what needed to be done because she hadn't been alone. Her mum's friends and neighbours had rallied around, and she wasn't alone this time, either. Sofia had hung back and given her space to collect her thoughts, but she now scooted onto the bed next to Abbie, her fingers lacing hers as she waited for her tears to abate.

'Sorry, Sofia.'

'Don't be. It's okay to cry. In fact, it's a good thing. There's no benefit in keeping our emotions bottled up inside. Life has its sorrows and its challenges, and we all have to deal with them in the best way we can. So, shall we make a start and see how we get on? We don't have to do this in one day; small steps will deliver us to the same destination in the end.'

'You're right,' said Abbie, accepting a tissue from Sofia, and feeling a little better now that the initial shock of entering the room had diminished.

'Why don't you empty the bookcase over there, while I bag up Liz's clothes? I know exactly where she wanted them to go.'

'You do?'

'Yes.' Sofia laughed. 'When your aunt first arrived on Corfu, before the hotel was up and running, she wanted to make friends and learn the language, so she joined an amateur dramatic society in Corfu Town. She used to do a little acting when she lived in California, so it was a great idea, really.'

'Acting?' Abbie stared at Sofia, surprised by the revelation.

'Yes, as a support artist – that's what she called it, we would say "extra" – in a long-running mini-series about the loves, lives and losses of the people who called the wine country in northern California their home. She had so much fun, and met some really fascinating people, some of whom even came to stay at the hotel from time to time.'

'Wow.'

Abbie was about to say that she had no idea about that aspect of her aunt's life, but then she realised, why would she? She knew very little about her, and what she did know, she'd gleaned from the snippets given to her by Sofia, which so far had been sparse, a situation that had led her to suspect that Sofia was holding a great deal back.

'Your aunt had a happy life, Abbie.'

Another wave of emotion rolled through Abbie's chest. Of course, she was pleased that her aunt had found happiness, alongside the man she adored, and that, after his passing, she had had the courage to make a fresh start, again, in a different country far away from her childhood home. But she couldn't help but think about her mum, who she knew had been content, with her family life and her wonderful garden. Had she been happy though? Truly happy?

'Anyway, Liz made it clear that she wanted her clothes, shoes, handbags, hats, costume jewellery, that sort of thing, to be offered to the theatre's wardrobe department, and whatever they don't want to go to charity. How are you getting on with the books?'

Abbie looked at the shelves in front of her. To her astonishment, she saw that they were empty, and at her feet were two large cardboard boxes filled with her aunt's books, magazines, and CDs.

'Finished.'

'Great, that's one box ticked.'

The next two hours were spent in companionable silence, interspersed with the occasional reminiscence from Sofia as she came across a particular item of clothing, or ornament, or necklace, that reminded her of an occasion she had shared with Liz. With every detail shared, Abbie felt her Aunt Liz come to life, becoming a real, rounded person with hobbies and favourite authors and books and musicians, rather than a flat sketch on a piece of paper.

As they continued with the task, she found there was something almost cathartic about methodically working through her aunt's belongings, the rhythmic actions of folding, wrapping, and storing in various boxes and containers calming her earlier anxiety. To her immense surprise, she discovered that her aunt had shared some similarities with her mum; their choice of beauty products, for example – they had both loved Estée Lauder – and, of course, their love of birds. There was no doubting that her aunt had adored hummingbirds, their presence was everywhere from the prints on the walls to the ornaments on her dressing table, but Abbie's mum had love birds, too, and had welcomed them into her garden with an ornate bird feeding station, which she replenished frequently.

'Is that your phone buzzing, Abbie?' Sofia asked, jolting Abbie from her thoughts.

'Oh, yes, I think it is.'

She removed her phone from her satchel and squinted at the screen, her heart giving a nip of pleasure as she read Nikos' text. She replied immediately, saying that she would love to accompany him to Dimitris' gig that night and that she would be ready when he came to collect her at six o'clock so they could have a drink together before driving over to Paleokastritsa because there was something he wanted to tell her.

Smiling, she sauntered over to one of the bedside cabinets and picked up what was clearly a favourite photograph, showcased in an ornate silver frame. Her aunt stood next to her husband, Greg, both of them beaming into the camera, dressed for what looked like an important occasion; Liz in a knee-length silver-beaded cocktail dress and clutching a diamanté purse, her hair teased into an elegant chignon, Greg in white tuxedo with a jaunty peacock-green bow tie, his arm resting gently on his wife's shoulder. They made a handsome couple, and they clearly loved each other very much.

'Sofia, do you know much about Greg?' asked Abbie, scrutinising the man in the photograph, who, but for a twist of fate, could have been her mum's husband, which meant she would.... No, she didn't want to go there.

'A little, and only what Liz told me; that he was the love of her life, and she was devastated by his death, which was why she left California to make a new start here.' Sofia paused in her task of zipping up a suitcase to join Abbie on the balcony, taking the picture frame from her, a soft smile on her lips when she surveyed her friend and her husband. 'But that doesn't mean she didn't regret the hurt they caused because they wanted to be together. She spoke many times of her remorse – sitting in this very spot, in fact – as we shared snippets from our life stories.'

Another whoosh of sorrow caught Abbie by surprise. She wished her mum could have found love again, and the fact that she hadn't been able to let go of the trauma of her fiancé leaving her for her younger sister, gave Abbie pause for thought. When Dan had terminated their relationship, she, too, had felt lost, cast adrift, and most of all, determined that romance would never feature in her life again; it was just too painful to risk giving your heart to someone only to have it cracked open by just two little words: "it's over".

And yet, despite her determination to wrap herself in cotton wool to protect herself from further emotional assault, she had somehow found the courage to fly to Corfu, a blissful place where her heart had started to heal. Unlike her mum, who had been alone, *she* had an even more exciting future ahead of her than before, alongside a gorgeous guy with a penchant for citrusy cologne who made her senses zing.

'Liz made several attempts to build bridges with your mum, Abbie, but, as I've already told you, all were rejected and she was left with no choice but to respect her sister's wish to cut all ties. So, she threw herself into her life in America, and into building Greg's family's vineyard and winery.'

'That's what I don't understand, though.'

'What do you mean?' asked Sofia, handing the picture frame back to Abbie.

'Why did Liz leave me the hotel if she and Mum never made up? Why would she give everything she owned to a niece she had never met? She obviously bought the hotel using the money from the sale of Greg's winery, so why didn't she leave it to his family? Surely, he had a sibling, or a cousin, or someone, anyone, who was more deserving of the inheritance than me?'

Sofia pushed herself out of the chair and went to stand at the railing, her back to Abbie as she stared out over the expanse of the Ropa Valley. It was almost four o'clock, but it was still hot, with not a wisp of a breeze, and even the cicadas seemed to have retreated into the shade.

'Sofia?'

'I'm sorry, Abbie, I can't answer your question.'

Once again, Abbie got the distinct impression that her aunt's best friend was hiding something from her, and if ever there was a time to press her, this was it.

'Sofia, if you know something, please share it with me. Is it about my aunt? Did she tell you anything, anything at all, about my mum? Anything else about what happened when she found out about them? There must have been an argument? Words exchanged? And what about later? When she tried to apologise, try to reconnect, did she tell you anything about that?'

Abbie couldn't go on, her throat had constricted and she was having trouble breathing, her heart hammering painfully in her chest as memories crowded in on her. The only person she had spoken to about her past was Emily; confessing during one of their many cookery-show-and-ice-cream marathons that she had struggled to deal with the two huge voids in her life – not just the loss of her mum before her time, but also the fact that she knew nothing about the other part of who she was. Until that missing piece of the jigsaw was found, she knew, no matter how hard she tried, no matter how much support she had from a loving friend or partner, she would never be free of the ghosts of her past. They would always be there, lingering just beneath the surface, agitating at her subconscious; she needed to know who her father was.

'Come on,' said Sofia, turning away from her contemplation of the glorious Greek countryside, her eyes gentle. 'We've almost finished. Do you want to make a start on the bureau? While I wash the windows and sweep the floors?'

'Okay.'

Abbie swallowed down on her rampaging emotions, keen to keep busy so her demons would withdraw to the dark crevices of her mind where they belonged. She followed Sofia back into the bedroom and started to empty her aunt's handsome oak bureau of stationery, address books, and several boxes of photographs, mainly from her time there in Corfu. Finally, on the bottom shelf, she found a box marked "Personal".

Abbie exchanged a glance with Sofia.

'What do you think is in here?'

Her heart was now in her mouth. Was she about to find what she had been hoping for? She peeled off the lid and stared at the contents, tears prickling at the corners of her eyes, her breath coming in spurts.

'It's… it's her diary.'

With trembling fingers, Abbie removed the cream, leather-bound journal and placed it on her lap, smoothing her hand over the cover, tracing her fingertip over the word "Journal" in gold lettering. This was it. Everything seemed to have led to this moment. Was she ready? Could she do this?

'I'll go make us some coffee,' said Sofia, and before Abbie could object, she had left the room, clearly wanting to give her some privacy.

However, as soon as the door had swung shut behind Sofia, Abbie heard a loud banging on the front door of the hotel. She placed the diary back into its box with a sigh of relief, and trotted down the stairs to the lobby, pulling open the front door.

'Hey, Felix, what are you…'

And then she remembered. She had been so caught up in sorting out her aunt's possessions that she had completely forgotten that she had asked Felix to come over to chat about extending his role at the hotel.

'Sorry I'm a few minutes late. I was just finishing up an extra yoga session with a few guests over in Nissaki. Don't suppose you've got an ice-cold beer, have you? I'm parched!' Felix said.

'Sofia's making coffee in the kitchen. Why don't we…'

she said, leading him inside.

Hearing a noise on the lane, Abbie and Felix paused and looked over their shoulders in unison to see a white airport taxi bouncing down the driveway towards them.

'Who's this? Are you expecting any more guests?'

'No, absolutely not!'

'Oh, hello there, Felix. I thought I heard your voice,' said Sofia, appearing by their side. 'Oh, more visitors?'

'No, I can assure you that I'm not expecting anyone.'

The three of them remained on the hotel's marble steps, inadvertently forming a Hummingbird Hotel welcoming committee, waiting for the taxi, which drew to a halt in front of them in a cloud of dust. Abbie pinned on her best hotelier smile, but when the passenger emerged from the back seat and she realised who it was, a firework of shock exploded in her chest and her jaw dropped.

'Oh my God! Dan?!

Chapter Twenty Four

The Veranda of the Hummingbird Hotel
Flower: Penstemon 'Shock Wave'

'Hello, Abbie. It's good to see you.'

'I…'

She scrambled around for something to say but her thoughts had completely frozen, as had her body, and she remained there, standing on the hotel's steps like a marble statue, staring at her ex-boyfriend as though he'd just arrived from outer space.

As usual, his short blonde hair was neatly barbered, he was clean-shaven, and doused in the cologne he sourced from a specialist boutique in Paris. Despite the temperature, he wore a long-sleeved designer shirt with gold cufflinks, polished Gucci loafers, and his chunky silver watch at his wrist made him look as though he was about to attend a board meeting alongside Brad.

He showed no sign of nerves at appearing in the middle

of the Corfu countryside, meeting her for the first time since their break-up two months ago, nor any hint of embarrassment that, despite her best efforts, he'd not seen fit to return any of her calls or inform her of his impending arrival. Now that her initial shock had eased, her brain reconnected to its modem and she was able to ask the question that burnt bright.

'What are you doing here, Dan?'

'I thought I'd come and see how you were getting on. It took me ages to find out where you'd disappeared to. Emily refused to tell me anything, but I saw a photograph of you with Pippa on Instagram, and a little detective work led me here. Although I have to say, Abbie…' She watched Dan take a step back to evaluate the facade of the Hummingbird Hotel, its whitewash pristine but its blue-painted shutters admittedly in need of a little sprucing up. 'I didn't expect you to be staying in a place like this.'

'What do you—'

'Why don't we go inside?' Felix said, reading Abbie's expression and stepping forward with his palm outstretched towards Dan. 'I'm Felix Morgan, by the way, the hotel's fitness instructor and wellbeing guru.'

'What's a wellbeing guru?' Dan smirked, running his gaze over Felix and his bright pink Hawaiian shirt, orange cycling shorts and plastic flip-flops.

'Oh, it's—'

'Never mind,' Sofia interrupted, casting a concerned glance in Abbie's direction. 'Let's get you some cold drinks, shall we, and then Felix and I will leave you to talk.'

Sofia gifted Felix with a stern, no-nonsense look, then ushered everyone through the lobby, into the kitchen, and out to the veranda at the back of the hotel where she indicated the rattan chairs. Abbie followed as though in a trance, unable to quite believe what was happening, while Felix stared at Dan, then Abbie, and then back to Dan again, trying to work out what was going on, clearly wanting to bombard them with questions.

Abbie dropped down into a chair opposite Dan, and the only thought to pop into her head was that he was the first person to sit on the Hummingbird Hotel's veranda and not comment on the spectacular view.

'Here we are.' Sofia set down a tray with a jug of freshly squeezed lemonade and two glasses, then hooked her arm through a disappointed Felix's, and led him – quite forcibly – back towards the kitchen. 'Felix and I will be over on the pool terrace, Abbie, if you need us.'

'Thanks, Sofia.'

Abbie felt as though a concrete block had taken up residence on her chest, pushing the air from her lungs, making her feel lightheaded. As Dan reclined in his chair, she poured them both a drink, handed a glass to Dan, and then took a long satisfying gulp, allowing the cool, tangy elixir to slide down her throat and douse her churning turmoil.

'Dan? You haven't answered my question.'

'I'm here because I miss you, Abbie. I've had time to think, lots of time, and I realised that I made a huge mistake that night at the Sky Garden. I should have handled things differently, but it was just such a shock. I had no idea you were thinking about our future in that way, that you wanted to *get married*, and when all of our friends jumped out like that,

I… well, I panicked. I had no idea what was going on, and I was totally unprepared for it, so what happened afterwards was just a knee-jerk reaction. I was shocked and a little scared, if I'm honest. Getting engaged is a huge commitment, and not something to do on the spur of the moment. I needed to think long and hard about it, which is what I've been doing.'

'Dan, it's really—'

'I'm sorry, Abbie, I didn't act very honourably, did I? I should have arranged to meet you to talk things through. I know how upset and embarrassed you were, Emily's made sure of that, and believe me, she left me in no doubt whatsoever what she thinks of me and the way I treated you. And she's right, I was a coward. I did avoid your calls, but only because I was trying to work through how I felt about what had happened. I needed to get my thoughts straight in my head before I spoke to you, and now I've had time to do that so that's why I'm here. Abbie, I'm ready to talk about the future.'

Abbie almost choked on her lemonade.

'You're here to talk about the future?'

Dan smiled and she saw the man she had fallen in love with; the man who loved spending time at the gym working on his physique and getting a sneaky manicure, who loved driving around town in the yellow Porsche his parents had bought him, who craved a celebrity lifestyle, and adored attending the VIP parties, the product launches, the gallery openings, and the fashion shows, but not the hard work that accompanied those things – the four a.m. starts, the freezing cold flower markets, the quirky demands of the clients, all the things that came with running a successful business.

'Yes, as I said, I made a mistake, and for that I apologise. I hope that you can forgive me because I'm here to offer you a partnership.'

'A partnership? What kind of partnership?'

'A share in the business, in *FlowerEssence*. An equal share. I've already had the papers drawn up, so all you have to do is sign them. I want to make things right between us, Abbie. I didn't realise before how much you did at the boutique.'

Abbie gaped. 'You didn't realise how much I did?'

'No, what I mean is, I didn't realise how invaluable and essential your creativity is to the business – not just the business, but also the individual designs we supply to our customers. You are talented, Abbie. I knew that, of course, but I didn't realise *how* talented. It's true what they say – you don't know what you have until you've lost it. You have *no* idea how hard I've worked these last couple of months, how many hours I've had to put in since you left!'

'You mean since you fired me?'

'I didn't actually fire you, Abbie. I just said that I thought it was better if we didn't work together after what happened.'

'It's the same thing.'

'Anyway, I've been working eighteen-hour days, sometimes longer, just to fulfil our orders. I've hired three different assistants, all of whom were completely useless. No one has your flair, Abbie, or your unique panache. I don't mind telling you that you are a true genius when it comes to floral architecture. Do you remember I told you about the contract *FlowerEssence* landed to supply the flowers for Pierre Fontaine's fiftieth birthday party at his apartment in Paris?'

'Yes, I do, actually and—'

'Well, I pulled out all the stops for him. I spent an absolute fortune on flowers and foliage. I poured every ounce of my own extensive knowledge and skill into providing exactly what he wanted. I stuck to the brief religiously, but do you know what he said after I'd worked flat out until my fingers bled? My fingers actually bled!'

Abbie did know what Pierre had thought of Dan's designs from Pippa, but judging from the way his cheeks had turned a dark shade of pink, she decided it was probably prudent to maintain her own counsel at this point.

'He said the arrangements were subpar! Subpar! I've never, in the whole time since my family bought me the boutique, had a client say that about our flowers, but then last week we lost another prestigious contract. Remember Marcus Pendlebury? He owns that high-end art gallery in Mayfair?'

'I do. He was always very specific about wanting cutting-edge modern design that would enhance his artists' portfolios and the gallery's reputation for avant-garde artwork. I loved working with him.'

'Well, he's cancelled his contract.'

'Oh, I…'

'But that's okay because there's a potential new contract in the pipeline. Oh, Abbie, you're going to be *so* excited. Annika Coolridge's people have approached us to dress her home for her monthly cocktail parties during her run at the National. Annika is *the* hottest actress in the West End at the moment and they want us! Apparently, we came highly recommended by Josie Faversham – remember her? You did the flowers for her wedding to that American singer? Anyway, Annika has specifically asked for you. The contract is worth *tens* of thousands of pounds.'

'Dan, I—'

'And before you say anything, I want you to know that I accept full responsibility for perhaps overstepping the mark sometimes.'

'Overstepping the mark?' Abbie muttered, starting to feel like she was inhabiting some kind of alternate universe, one where the last two months she'd spent in Corfu, at the Hummingbird Hotel, had been a dream and she had now woken up back in her old life, talking to Dan about celebrities and contracts and money. She wanted to press the pause button until she'd had time to gather her thoughts, or at least pinch herself just to make sure it *wasn't* a dream, that she *could* still hear the cicadas chirp, tasty the tang of the lemons in the lemonade, smell the jasmine floating on the scant breeze, but Dan was still talking.

'Yes, by accepting the prizes *FlowerEssence* won for our designs, when I should have allowed you to have your five minutes of fame. It's just that, as the figurehead of the company, I felt it was my duty to represent the business at these awards ceremonies, but I now understand that I should have shared the limelight with you. So, from now on, all accolades, rosettes and trophies will be collected by you, and I hope there'll be a great many of them so you can enjoy all of the glitz and glamour our fresh start is going to bring.'

Abbie's brain now felt like it was stuffed with marshmallows and she swayed in her seat as her light-headedness threatened to overwhelm her.

'I'm sorry, Dan, I really need to—'

'I realise this is a surprise, and a big decision, although I'm sure you don't need *too* long to think about what to do. This is a fabulous opportunity to have the financial security I know you've always wanted, Abbie, and it's the springboard for you to achieve even greater things in the realm of floral design – the world's your botanical oyster. And there's one final thing I want to say.'

For the first time, Abbie heard a slight wobble in Dan's voice, and when she looked up to meet his gaze, she caught a flash of movement in the kitchen just beyond the French doors. She turned her head to see who it was, expecting to see Sofia, come to make sure she was okay, but to her surprise it was Nikos. When she glanced at her watch, she realised he'd come to collect her for their drink before Dimitris' gig that evening.

'Oh, I—'When she turned back to Dan, to her utter astonishment, she saw that he had risen from his seat and was standing in front of her, his eyes fixed on hers, and as she watched on, he produced a black velvet box from his pocket, lowered himself down onto one knee, and flicked open the lid to reveal a diamond ring.

'Abigail Louise Coleman, will you marry me?'

Chapter Twenty Five

The Veranda at the Hummingbird Hotel
Flower: Confused Bridewort

Abbie stared at Dan, completely unable to formulate a response. The world seemed to zoom around her, until her bubble of shock burst, and she tumbled back down to earth with a bump.

'Dan, I'm sorry, I—'

She glanced over her shoulder and her heart sank when she saw that Nikos had disappeared, his departure confirmed moments later when she heard the harsh roar of his dilapidated Peugeot's engine as he raced down the driveway away from the hotel and the scene he'd clearly just witnessed.

'It's fine, it's fine, I can see it's a bit of a shock, me turning up like this, offering you the deal of a lifetime, and then this.' He waved the engagement ring in front of her, a smile on his lips. 'Please, take a little time to think about it – not too long, though. I'll give you some space. I saw a rather rustic taverna at the end of the driveway, so I'll go and grab myself a bite to eat – the aeroplane food is *so* disgusting – and I'll come back later, okay?'

Without waiting for her response, Dan leaned forward to drop a kiss on her cheek, then sauntered from the veranda, completely relaxed, his hands in his pockets, whistling a random tune. Abbie, on the other hand, felt as though a grenade had been tossed into her world.

'Abbie? Is everything okay?' Sofia asked as she appeared on the veranda.

'I… I'm not sure.'

'Why? What's happened?'

Abbie was touched by the concern spread across Sofia's kind face, which served to calm the maelstrom of emotions that swirled through her body and threatened to engulf her after Dan's unexpected proposal.

'Dan, he… he's just asked me to marry him.'

'To *marry* him?'

Abbie watched Sofia drop down into the chair opposite her, her lips twitching into a smile when she saw her friend's expression switch from worry about her wellbeing to complete and utter disbelief.

'Yes, I know, crazy, isn't it?'

'I… I really don't know what…'

'He also offered me a partnership in his business.'

'Back in London?'

'Yes.'

'Where is he now?'

'He went to the taverna to "give me some space" to think about what he said.'

'He's expecting you to decide straight away?'

'It seems so.'

Abbie thought Sofia was going to launch into a monologue of sage advice, but she changed her mind.

'Then I will give you space, too.'

'Hey guys! What's going on? Am I missing something important?' Felix asked, joining them.

'Felix, you're coming with me back to the taverna. Abbie, you know where we are if you need us.'

Sofia pushed herself out of her seat, and before Felix could object, she hooked her arm through his and led him from the veranda. He continued to glance over his shoulder at Abbie, his eyes filled with questions and confusion, but she knew that as soon as they were out of earshot, Sofia would explain the situation to him.

Now that she was finally alone, her thoughts slowed from dash to dawdle, and the aftershock from Dan's bombshell started to abate so she could look at things from a calmer perspective. She poured herself another glass of Sofia's tangy lemonade, took a sip, then sat back in her chair, her eyes trained on the horizon where the sun sank slowly behind the hillside just as it did every day, no matter what kind of turmoil was going on in the world.

What was she going to do?

She couldn't believe Dan had come all the way to Corfu to ask her to marry him. Despite the fact that he had barely let her get a word in edgeways, he had been very clear about how he saw their future together – equal partners at the boutique as well as in life, working together on prestigious contracts with the rich and famous, and sharing in all the razzmatazz and excitement that would bring. She had thoroughly enjoyed working with Marcus Pendlebury, who had always been very complimentary about the floral artistry she created to enhance the exhibitions he curated, which had been a welcome boost to her ego. And to have the chance to work with Annika Coolridge would be exciting, too.

She knew it wouldn't take her long to slide back into her old life in London, and this time – being Dan's business partner, *and* fiancée – she would have the security she had craved since her mum had passed away. Together, she knew they could achieve even greater things at *FlowerEssence*. In fact, she still had a wealth of ideas that she would love to try which, as an equal partner, she could bring to fruition without the risk of Dan shooting them down in flames. There would be no clients complaining of goats eating their underwear, or that their smoothies had made them sick, or their beauty products had turned their hair pink, and all the paperwork would be in a language she understood.

Wasn't this exactly what she had wanted two months ago?

A proposal from Dan?

To turn back the clocks to the night at the Sky Garden and have it end with his ring on her finger, celebrating with Emily and asking her to be her bridesmaid?

But that wasn't what had happened.

And then there was another nagging feeling in her stomach that she couldn't ignore.

Why now?

Okay, so Dan had said that he'd needed time to think, to reflect on what had happened and how he felt about it, but he'd also told her that the boutique was floundering under his sole charge, that contrary to his initial expectations, after he'd fired her – and that was exactly what he'd done, despite his denial – he'd had complaints and lost valuable contracts. Although he hadn't actually admitted it, it had been her talent that had attracted the high-end clients to their boutique, not Dan's, and without her the business was clearly suffering.

Was this why he wanted her back? Because without her floristry skills, *FlowerEssence* was unlikely to win any more of those shiny silver trophies and rosettes that he stored in his specially commissioned glass-and-chrome cabinet?

The more she pondered the question, the more she knew that was exactly why he'd offered her a partnership. With her onboard, the boutique would continue to be at the forefront of floral decorating excellence, catering for the clientele Dan loved to be associated with.

And what about the marriage proposal?

Abbie's stomach gave an uncomfortable lurch. Surely he hadn't asked her to marry him just so she would say "yes" to coming on board at the boutique and saving it from potential financial ruin? No, that would be ridiculous, and not a little offensive, and, more importantly, doomed to fail. But if it *was* true, was she so desperate for someone to be there for her, to provide an emotional safety net, that she would marry him on that basis?

Heat flooded her cheeks. Hadn't that been *exactly* what she'd been doing when she took her seat in front of Dan at the restaurant at the top of the Walkie Talkie building, expected him to propose in front of all of their friends? Craving that elusive feeling of belonging, of being part of a family unit?

No!

The difference between then and now was that two months ago she had loved him, she knew she had. She had wanted to spend the rest of her life with him, and when things hadn't worked out the way she'd hoped, she had been devastated.

But did Dan ever love *her*?

The realisation hit Abbie with unexpected force. Dan had asked her to marry him barely twenty minutes ago, but not once had he told her that he loved her. He'd said he missed her, that he regretted the fact that they had broken up, that he wanted her to come back to London with him, and that he wanted her to be his business partner, but he hadn't said he loved her.

A window of clarity sprang open.

She wasn't the same person who had left the UK heartbroken, lost in a sea of pain and confusion. She had changed. No more would she be steamrollered into situations by Dan, or relegate her own dreams and ambitions to second place just so he could pursue his own. Not once in his grand speech had he shown any interest in how she had ended up on Corfu, or at the Hummingbird Hotel. In fact, he had not asked her a single question about what she was doing there. Did he even know that she owned the hotel?

She finally realised that she didn't need someone to always be by her side, beating the encouragement drum. Since arriving on Corfu, she had steadily built up the self-confidence to know that she could rely on herself to deal with whatever was thrown her way, and for those things she couldn't handle on her own, there were people around her whom she could ask for help.

But more than that; she could offer *her* help to others.

She could be the supportive one.

Hadn't she proved that to herself? Look at what she'd done at the vineyard and winery. Interviewing and engaging the services of Thanos to give the business the best chance of success, planting the Angelopoulos Garden to add an additional stream of income when they started to offer tours, and perhaps, at some future point, growing flowers commercially and supplying them to the local businesses. These plans for the future gave her confidence a huge boost, which in turn inspired her to push even harder to achieve her ambitions, which enhanced her confidence even further – a magical circle.

She was making her own way in the world, and she loved it. Since arriving in Greece, she had achieved more than she had ever thought possible, done everything she wanted, when she wanted, and that felt amazing. She didn't need a share in Dan's business to make her feel good about herself. She was already her own boss, making her own decisions and reaping the rewards of success, but also learning from her mistakes and coming to understand that the fear of failure shouldn't be allowed to jeopardise hope for the future.

As the sun sunk ever further from view, and the cicadas ratcheted up their evening sonata, Abbie's heart filled with affection. She had finally found her place in the world; a place where people loved her for who she was, not what skills she had to offer. She couldn't go backwards, only forwards, for that was the path that led to contentment, to happiness.

Then her affection ballooned into something much deeper.

She knew what her answer to both Dan's questions was going to be because her future did not feature her in the role of "celebrity florist", nor did it feature her as Dan's fiancée or wife. She didn't need to consult one of Felix's astrology charts to know that her role was as a hotelier, a trainee winery manager, a landscape gardener, and best of all, an apprentice sous chef.

But most of all, she hoped her future would feature the most handsome man in the whole of Corfu; the man with the spiky hair and the dark, brooding eyes, the man with a penchant for lemony cologne and honey-soaked baklava, the man who celebrated her successes and laughed at her mistakes, and more importantly, the man who made her soul sing.

She had to talk to Nikos. She had to explain the scene he had just witnessed, make him understand that she had no intention of ditching everything she'd achieved at the Hummingbird Hotel so she could run off back to London to get married.

But first she had to find Dan.

With a whoosh of exhilarating determination, she leapt from her chair and made her way out of the hotel, down the driveway, and towards Sofia's taverna.

Chapter Twenty Six

Sofia's Taverna, Ropa Valley, Corfu
Flower: Dahlia 'Braveheart'

As soon as Abbie stepped onto the balcony at the rear of the taverna, her earlier resolve melted and was replaced by a kaleidoscope of churning anxiety. How was she going to start this conversation? She had always avoided causing waves, preferring to take the route of least resistance, to smooth over any bumps when they appeared just so she didn't have to deal with any more trauma.

She could see Dan, sitting at a table in the shade of an olive tree, his back to the mesmerising view, scrolling through the notifications on his phone, totally oblivious to his surroundings. He was clearly so engrossed in his social media accounts that he hadn't noticed her arrival, so she took the opportunity to inhale a few deep breaths and wait for her emotions, and stomach, to settle, and to plan what she needed to say.

'Hey, Abbie, are you here to talk to Dan?' Felix asked, surprising her as she hadn't heard him approach.

'Yes, I—'

'So does that mean you've made a decision?'

Abbie met Felix's gaze and to her surprise his relaxed demeanour served to calm her nerves and clear her thoughts. He had been faced with a similar decision only a few weeks ago when his ex-fiancée Carlie had contacted him out of the blue to apologise for leaving him standing at the altar "like a discarded possum" and running off with his best man. Carlie had wanted him to give her a second chance and Felix had given the suggestion careful consideration then told her, gently and without any recriminations, that he couldn't go back to his former life in Sydney as a commercial banker, nor could they pick up the pieces of their shattered relationship.

Looking at him now, standing in front of her in a vivid blue shirt, frayed denim shorts and flip-flops, his blonde curls surfer-dude-tousled, ready for his night out with Rachel to watch Dimitris' gig, it was clear for anyone to see that he had made the right decision. He was happier than Abbie had ever seen him, and she took strength and inspiration from that.

'Talking is good,' Felix said, then hesitated. 'Can I give you a piece of advice, from someone who's been there?'

'Of course.'

'Follow your own star.'

Abbie smiled. 'Thanks, Felix.'

'No worries, take a seat and I'll bring you some fresh drinks over.'

She watched as Felix sauntered off to the bar, then

inhaled a deep breath, squashed down the rampaging self-confidence sprites intent on persuading her to run for the hills, and dropped down into the seat opposite Dan who, at last, looked up from perusing his screen.

'Oh, Abbie, hi. I wasn't expecting you so soon. I've just checked into the Corfu Palace Hotel in Corfu Town for the night; it's supposed to be one of the best on the island.'

'Yes, yes, it is.' She could scarcely believe that it had only been yesterday when she'd attended the photoshoot in the gardens there. So much had happened since she'd waved goodbye to Pippa and the rest of the Pierre Fontaine gang. 'I know you'll like it there.'

'Here's your drinks, guys. If I can get you anything else just let me know.'

Felix set a couple of bottles of cold beer down in front of them and left them to it, but not before giving Abbie one of his complicated thumb and finger waves in support. She took a quick sip of her beer, feeling her anxiety start to swirl once more, but clearly Dan wasn't as apprehensive as she was about how their conversation was going to pan out. She wished she had even a modicum of his confidence, of his unwavering certainty that things would go his way just because he wanted them to.

As her breathing quickened and she began to feel a little nauseous, she decided that the best thing to do was to just come out and say the words that had been circulating through her mind since she'd made her decision, to just get the sentence out there, wait for the dust to settle, and then deal with the after-effects as best she could. No more avoiding the issues that were difficult to deal with, no more taking the easy option.

'I'm sorry, Dan, the answer's no, I don't want to marry you.'

'You don't…'

A look of complete astonishment flittered across Dan's face. In a flash of sudden self-insight, she realised that because she had always deferred to Dan's ideas, plans, and ambitions, he had grown accustomed to getting exactly what he wanted without having to even consider an alternative point of view – namely, hers. She recognised that she had to take her share of responsibility for that. It wasn't Dan's fault that she had relied heavily on him for emotional support, perhaps unreasonably so, expecting him to be her rock, her anchor, her place of comfort when she had nowhere else to turn. She had thought that being engaged, making things permanent, would eradicate that need, but she now knew that she was wrong.

'You were right, Dan.'

'Right? What do you mean?'

'When we were sitting at that table at Sky Garden at the end of June, you were right to be shocked that I was expecting you to propose. As a couple we were nowhere near ready for that kind of commitment. I realise that now, and I should thank you.'

'Thank me? What for?'

'For knowing that. Otherwise, I think we would have made a huge mistake.'

'But I—'

'And it's very generous of you and your family to offer me a partnership in *FlowerEssence*, but I'm sorry, I can't accept that either.'

'I don't understand. I thought this was what you wanted: financial and emotional security?'

'I thought so, too, but it's not.'

'But why?'

'For lots of reasons, actually, but mainly because that was an old dream. I'm shooting for new dreams now, brighter dreams, happier dreams – exciting dreams – here on Corfu, at the Hummingbird Hotel.'

'The Hummingbird Hotel? What are you—'

'I own it, the hotel.'

Dan's jaw dropped, and his eyes widened. 'You *own* the hotel?'

'Yes, I inherited it from my aunt.'

'Your aunt? I didn't know you had an aunt. I thought... well, I thought...'

Abbie cringed. Clearly Dan had been about to say the words that had always sent shards of pain slicing through her chest: that she didn't have a family, didn't have any relatives, that she was an... an orphan. She shoved that upsurge of distress away so she could focus on the present, the only thing she had control over.

'It was a shock for me, too, a huge shock. Running a hotel in the Corfu countryside is not exactly what I dreamed of doing with my life, but dreams can change, Dan.'

'But... you don't know anything about being a hotelier.'

'Oh, yes, I know that.' Abbie laughed, her emotions now beginning to calm, her mood swinging upwards as she got her feelings out into the open and the conversation turned to the hotel. 'It's been a baptism of fire, believe me, but it's also been lots of fun, too. I've made loads of new friends here, and you know what?'

'What?'

'If I fail, I'll deal with it. It's better to have tried and failed than to be living someone else's dream, don't you think?'

'I…'

'This is where my future lies, Dan, right here in the Ropa Valley, building on my aunt's legacy, welcoming guests, tending her vineyard, and maybe making a few bottles of delicious Corfu wine from the grapes.'

'You're planning to make wine?'

Dan was now staring at her as though she had gone completely mad; she even saw a dash of fear flit across his eyes, but every word she uttered in support of the choice she'd made, made her feel better and she wanted to continue to press her case so that Dan understood the reasons behind her rejection of his offer.

'Yes, can't you see me as a vintner?'

'Not really. I always thought you wanted to be a florist, or a botanist at Kew Gardens. Are you sure about this, Abbie? I'm offering you the chance of a lifetime; the security I know you've always craved. And when we're back in London, I promise to help you make a start on seeking out the answers to those questions about… about your fath— family.'

Abbie knew what he meant, but she didn't want to go there; not now.

'Family can be anything, Dan, not just blood.'

'I know, but—'

Abbie decided to switch the spotlight away from her. 'Can I ask you something?'

'Sure.'

'Do you really want to be a florist? Is it what you've *always* dreamed of doing? Or are you just doing it because your family bought you the boutique after you dropped out of uni, so you'd have some financial stability and something to do with your time?'

She heard her words and even to her own ears they sounded harsh, and she wasn't surprised when Dan's jaw slackened at her candour. She had never spoken to him so directly. She hadn't meant to criticise what his parents had done for him; they loved him and had been devastated when he dropped out of business school, and they just wanted him to be happy and to have a comfortable lifestyle. However, from everything she'd learned since arriving on Corfu, she realised that sometimes the conveyor belt of life had a way of snatching you up and towing you along without allowing you the time to pause and consider alternative pathways, pathways that might spark more joy.

She realised that Dan was still staring at her as though he'd never seen her before, and she felt the need to expand on what she'd said.

'What I'm trying to say is, are you truly cut out to be a florist? Is there something else out there, something you're more passionate about, that would make your heart sing? Something that would have you leaping out of bed in the morning, excited about what the day has in store? If there is, then you should take a leap of faith and explore the possibility of doing something *you* want, not what makes other people happy.'

Abbie thought she might have pushed Dan a little too far. He was now looking totally bewildered, baffled by what she was trying to say, and his mouth was opening and shutting like a bamboozled goldfish. He was clearly lost for words, which was something she'd never seen happen in the whole time she'd known him.

'Sorry, I shouldn't have said that.'

'Well, yes, maybe…'

'I'm sorry, Dan, I can't go back… I can't go back to London, I can't go back to being an assistant – or even a partner – in a flower shop, and I can't marry you, because… well, because I don't think you love me.'

'Abbie, really, I—'

'And that's okay, because I'm no longer in love with you, either.'

Dan's shoulders drooped and he rubbed his face with his palms before looking up and meeting her gaze, a small smile playing around his lips.

'That's hard to hear, Abbie, but I respect your honesty. You've given me a great deal to think about, and I realise that it was presumptuous of me to swan into your new life and expect you to drop everything to come back to me after how I treated you.' He finished his bottle of beer, deposited a handful of coins on the table, then pushed himself from his chair and came to stand in front of her. 'I truly hope your new enterprise as a hotelier and a wine maker is everything you dream it could be, Abbie, and that you will save me a bottle from your first vintage of Hummingbird Hotel wine.'

'I will, I promise.'

Dan leaned forward to place a kiss on her cheek for what she knew would be the final time. 'Goodbye, Abbie.'

'Goodbye, Dan.'

Abbie watched him saunter from the taverna without

a backward glance. She had no regrets about the decision she had made, and to her surprise, as he disappeared from view, a huge weight lifted from her chest. She felt lighter, more optimistic about the future than she had in a long time, knowing that any remaining loose ends between her and Dan had now been dealt with, and both of them could move on without the spectre of their past relationship stalking them.

And talking of relationships, she now had to find Nikos.

Because there was something she had to tell him, too.

Chapter Twenty Seven

The Garden at the Angelopoulos Vineyard and Winery
Flower: Gladiolus 'That's Love'

'Abbie? Are you okay?'

'Oh, hi, Felix, yes, I'm fine. Better than fine, actually.'

'Where's Dan?'

'He's gone to check in at the Corfu Palace. I don't think the Hummingbird Hotel lives up to his expectations.'

'Then the man has no taste!'

Felix grinned, and stuck his hands into the pockets of his shorts, the vibrant blue shirt he'd chosen to wear to Dimitris' mini-gig at the restaurant in Paleokastritsa reflecting the colour of his eyes. Despite feeling anxious to talk to Nikos, to explain about Dan's unexpected arrival on her doorstep, she realised that Felix must be wondering what she had wanted to say to him that afternoon.

'Felix, I'm sorry I missed our appointment earlier.'

'Well, you were otherwise engaged! Or not?'

'Anyway, we can discuss the details later, but what would you say to expanding your position at the hotel and making it more permanent?'

'What do you mean?'

'As well as being our fabulous wellbeing guru, I'd like you to be the hotel's assistant manager. I want to concentrate on the vineyard over the next couple of months – there's the grape harvest and the wine-making, then the olive harvest – and I know Nikos will be busy building his culinary business, and with you on board I'm sure things will run more smoothly than they have over the last few weeks.'

'You mean Savannah's pink hair incident?'

'Yes, I—'

'And the invasion of underwear-munching goats?'

'Is it an invasion if there's only one goat?'

Despite his teasing, Felix was beaming from ear-to-ear so Abbie knew his answer to her job offer before he reached forward to collect her into a rib-crushing bear hug.

'Assistant manager sounds awesome. You won't regret this, Abbie, and I have lots more ideas for week-long courses and afternoon classes for our future guests. Together we will make the Hummingbird Hotel the go-to destination for the most discerning of holidaymakers. Oh, I can't wait to get started! I'm so excited.'

'Okay, we'll have a brainstorming session later, but first I need you to help me to find Nikos. He's not answering his phone, and the last time I saw him he had just witnessed Dan going down on one knee to propose to me. I need to tell him what happened after—'

'What happened after what?' asked Rachel, appearing on the terrace in a stunning crimson sundress, her auburn hair tied into a glamorous up-do with loose tendrils brushing her cheeks. Her makeup had been carefully applied, with more lashings of mascara and lip gloss than she usually wore; she had clearly made an effort for her evening out watching Dimitris sing.

Abbie's heart softened. She could see the gleam of anticipation in her friend's eyes, and after what had happened with Kostas, she hoped that the spark she'd seen ignite between the two of them at the wine-tasting event would lead to other things.

'Abbie's turned down Dan's proposal.'

Rachel flung her arms around Abbie and pulled her into a warm hug. 'That must have been difficult. Are you okay?'

'Yes, it was the right thing to do. I did love Dan once, very much, but a lot has happened over the last few months, especially since I arrived on Corfu.'

'What did he say? Was he upset?'

'Actually, no, he wasn't, not really.'

Abbie took a moment to think a little more about Rachel's question and her response to it. It was true; Dan hadn't seemed upset when she told him her decision. Disappointed, maybe, but not upset. Surely rejecting a marriage proposal should have caused more of an emotional impact than Dan had exhibited? Did that mean what she thought it meant? That, as she had suspected, he'd only wanted to marry her so she would return to *FlowerEssence* and help him to get the business back on track? Now she *knew* for sure that she had made the right decision, and her spirits edged up a notch further.

'So, Abbie was just asking if we know where Nikos is,' said Felix, the strange emphasis he used when addressing the question to Rachel putting Abbie immediately on her guard, even more so when she saw a meaningful glance pass between the two of them.

'Okay, guys, what's going on?'

'Nothing—' began Felix.

'I think we should tell her.'

'No, Nikos said he wanted it to be a surprise.'

'But that was before Dan dropped a bombshell by proposing!' said Rachel.

'Look, if you know where he is, please tell me. The last time I spoke to him, he said he was taking me for a drink somewhere before we headed off to the restaurant to watch Dimitris' band play.'

'But if we tell you, it won't be a surprise.'

'If you *don't* tell me, it won't be a surprise, either. Please, Felix, I need to talk to him. I need to tell him that there's nothing between me and Dan, nothing at all, and that…' She paused, not wanting to confess her feelings for Nikos to Felix and Rachel before she had spoken to Nikos first. 'And that I'm not going back to the UK.'

'He's over at the winery,' said Rachel, earning herself an eye roll from Felix.

'Okay, so…'

'Come on, we'll drop you off on our way to Roxanni's.'

Abbie climbed into the back of the brand-new Jeep that Sofia and Panos had loaned Felix for the night so that Rachel didn't turn up at Roxanni's restaurant looking like she'd been dragged through a hedge after spending twenty minutes on his bumblebee Vespa. Her thoughts swirled as she tried to formulate exactly what she was going to say to Nikos.

Earlier, when she had walked onto the terrace at the taverna, she had known precisely what she was going to tell Dan; the reasons for her decision crystal-clear in her mind. Conversely, with Nikos, she was now finding it difficult to pin down the right words or the order to deliver them in. She had realised she had feelings for Nikos from the reaction she'd had when Allyssa had mentioned he had a girlfriend in Paris, but, as usual, her internal voice of reason had warned her to keep her feelings to herself in case she spoilt their friendship. Yet, there was a great deal more than friendship at stake now – there was her battered heart.

But now that she had cut the final ties with her former life and made a firm commitment to her new life, surely that should include making a fresh start on how she dealt with challenging situations? Now was the time to move forward with her eyes on the horizon instead of over her shoulder, chasing new dreams, with new friends, with people who loved her.

Felix drew to a stop next to the marble fountain in front of the Angelopoulos winery and twisted round in his seat. 'Do you want us to come with you?'

The old Abbie would have responded with a resounding "yes please", but the new Abbie inhaled a breath, squared her shoulders, and smiled at Felix.

'No, thanks. I've got this.'

'Sure?' asked Rachel.

'Sure.'

'Okay, we'll see you at the restaurant later,' Felix said.

'Great.'

Abbie hooked her arm through her satchel and scooted from the back seat, waiting in the courtyard until the Jeep disappeared from view before going off in search of Nikos. It was almost seven o'clock, and dusk was well into its final act, sending streamers of tangerine and dusty pink floating across the darkening sky and the cicadas into a frenzy of song. The scorching heat of the day had diminished and a light breeze toyed with her curls, delivering a waft of perfume from the lilies in the fountain's pond.

With her heartbeat increasing, she knocked on the front door but there was no response, so she walked to the other side of the courtyard and stuck her head around the door of the winery, but it was obvious Nikos wasn't there either. After a brief detour into the vineyard, she returned to the fountain and perched on the wall, pulling out her phone to try Nikos' number again, unsurprised when her call still elicited no response. She made a quick call to Rachel to ask if Nikos had turned up at the restaurant, but she was told he hadn't.

She slipped the phone back into her pocket, and inhaled a long, steadying breath. So much had happened since she'd woken up that morning expecting the day to be filled with housekeeping duties and, if she was lucky, a stint in the garden, that she didn't know what to think about first. But sitting there, surrounded by nature in all its forms, was a welcome reminder that emotional trauma was transitory, that it was pointless to wallow in the past, dissecting the rights and wrongs of events that could not be changed. The way to move forward was by focussing on the present because that was the only thing you had any control over.

A sense of calm descended, and Abbie closed her eyes briefly, until she detected a very faint tinkle of music floating on the wisp of a breeze, coming from the direction of the garden. She hooked her satchel over her shoulder and picked her way along the gravel footpath to the back of the house, surprised when she saw the first of the arched, honeysuckle-bedecked pergolas had been decorated with a garland of white fairy lights.

'What…?'

She paused, then took another step forward, and discovered there were more twinkling lights twisted through the branches of the magnolia tree and the foliage of a large rhododendron bush, and also the second pergola, this one draped with a violet-coloured clematis. With the soft, other-earthly ripple of music and the lengthening rays of the sun casting long shadows, the whole place had the aura of a magical fairy glade, and she wouldn't have been surprised to see a coterie of elves and pixies dancing a jig between the geraniums and the hollyhocks, with the fireflies joining in the party.

As she stepped into the clearing, relief rolled through her body when she saw Nikos sitting on the sun-bleached bench, completely oblivious to her presence. However, when she realised what he was staring at, her heart bounced hard against her ribcage.

'Oh my God!'

Her exclamation burst Nikos' contemplation bubble.

'Nikos! How… What… Wow!'

Abbie feasted her eyes on the stunning pink butterfly

orchid in the blue ceramic pot in the middle of the patio, in full and vibrant flower. It was the plant that reminded her so much of her mum, and the memory caused tears to rush to her eyes. She knelt down to inspect it more closely, taking in every detail; its tall, straight stem, the linear, lance-shaped leaves clustered around the base, the sepals that looked like pointed helmets, the delicate, silk-like petals with dark pink stripes.

'Do you like it?' Nikos asked.

'I love it, but… where did you get it?'

'Andreas and I have spent hours on the internet, made dozens of phone calls, and pulled in several favours to try to find the perfect specimen for you, and it was finally delivered this morning. I've spent the whole day setting all this up – something as special as a pink butterfly orchid deserves a beautiful backdrop, don't you think?'

'I do. Thank you, Nikos.'

Abbie saw Nikos smile, but it didn't reach his eyes, and she knew it was time to talk.

'Nikos, I—'

'It's okay, Abbie, you don't have to… to…'

She watched him glance down at her left hand and enjoyed seeing the spark of hope in his dark eyes when he looked back up and met her gaze, a question lingering there.

'Nikos, I had no idea Dan would turn up like that. It was a complete surprise, especially as he hasn't had the decency to answer my calls, or respond to any of my messages since I arrived here over two months ago. *And* I can assure you that there was no one more shocked than me when he proposed. But I've turned him down; it's over between us. I don't want to marry him, or to be a partner in the business, because…'

She stopped, her heart pounding so violently that her breath had caught in her throat. Nikos pushed himself from the bench and came to stand in front of her, taking her hands in his, so tantalisingly close, the waft of his lemony cologne igniting her senses and giving her that last push to say the words she wanted, no *needed*, to say.

'Because—'

But before she could continue, Nikos' lips were on hers, his hand slipping around her waist to pull her into his arms. She relished the feel of his muscular chest through the flimsy fabric of her sundress, and gasped as his fingers caressed her cheek, her neck, that delicate place at her hair-line, a whoosh of desire sparkling through her veins and out to her extremities. Everything around her faded from existence as she kissed him back, her passion mounting as she tried to communicate through their embrace how much he meant to her, until she grew breathless and finally, regretfully, they broke apart.

'Nikos, I—'

Nikos placed his finger on her lips.

'Me first,' he whispered. His dark mahogany gaze scorched hers, her stomach performing a somersault when she saw the emotion that lay deep within his eyes. 'I've been wanting to say this for a while, but I needed to find the right moment. Life with you in it, Abbie, is like being at the centre of a whirlwind, tossed from triumph to disaster and back again, but every day is filled with laughter and joy, and not a little comedy. Meeting you has added sparkle to what I had come to accept would be a mundane life after having spent five years in Paris. I love having you on board at the vineyard and the winery, I love what you've done to create this amazing garden, I love exploring my culinary creativity at the hotel, and… what I'm trying to say is, I love *you*, Abbie.'

Abbie's heart soared, and suddenly it was the easiest thing in the world to share her own feelings with him. She laced her fingers through his, stood on her tiptoes and whispered softly in his ear. 'I love you, too, Nikos, and I'm just as excited as you are to see where our relationship leads us.'

'Well, as long as your next guests aren't members of an axe-throwing club, we should be okay.'

Abbie laughed, then stopped abruptly as her eyes caught on a tiny movement amongst the bushes over Nikos' right shoulder. She squinted to try and see what it was, and then gasped.

'Oh my God! No way! I wondered where my sunhat had disappeared to!'

Abbie couldn't help but giggle at the weird and wonderful sight of the Hummingbird Hotel's resident goat munching on her favourite straw sunhat. She was about to dash down the pathway to rescue it, but Nikos' pulled her back, snaking his arm round her shoulders, his warm breath tickling at the tip of her earlobe, before his lips were suddenly mere millimetres from hers.

She enjoyed each and every one of the sensations that tumbled through her body, savoured every one of Nikos' increasingly ardent kisses until the sun finally bade farewell to the most extraordinary of days. A day that had contained a kaleidoscope of emotions, from anxiety and apprehension while sorting through her aunt's paperwork, to the alarm and astonishment of Dan's sudden and unexpected arrival, from the challenging conversation she'd had to have to tie up the loose ends of the past, to the much more pleasant discussion with Felix about a new future at the Hummingbird Hotel, all culminating in the most wonderful way possible – a stunningly beautiful sunset and a wonderful declaration of love.

Chapter Twenty Eight

Roxanni's Restaurant, Paleokastritsa, Corfu
Flower: Aster Alpinus 'Happy End'

'Hey, you two! Where have you been? Dimitris will be on in ten minutes,' Rachel called from the table right in front of an elevated stage on the restaurant's veranda, her cheeks pink with excitement for that evening's entertainment, and probably too many glasses of wine. 'Come on, we've saved you a seat.'

Abbie followed Nikos as he wove his way through the maze of tables, stopping frequently to shake hands and exchange a few words with their fellow diners, introducing her to everyone as his girlfriend, before he went to collect a round of drinks from the bar. As she stepped onto the wooden veranda, she paused to take in the panorama in front of her – this had to be one of the most spectacular views in the whole of Corfu.

Beyond the narrow, sandy beach, colourfully painted

fishing boats and elegant yachts alike bobbed rhythmically on the waves, the whole scene watched over by a midnight-blue sky, its wide expanse dotted with tiny stars and lit by an ivory moon. To her left was a shadowy hillside, decorated in olive groves, orange and lemon trees, and the ubiquitous cypress trees. To her right was a handsome white hotel, its windows winking in the darkness. It was so picturesque; a travel photographer's paradise.

'One glass of white wine,' said Nikos, dropping a kiss onto Abbie's lips. 'Come on, let's grab our seats. I can see Dimitris lingering in the wings.'

They joined an animated Felix and Rachel, and several other friends, and the next hour passed by in a flash, every minute filled with loud, life-affirming music, and Dimitris' surprisingly rich, melodic voice. The band had started their gig with several cover versions before moving on to songs they had written themselves, every band member sporting a wide smile, clearly having the time of their lives, especially Dimitris, whose floppy brown curls and boyish grin gave him the air – to Abbie's mind, anyway – of a boy band hero.

When the band finished their first set, Dimitris joined them at the table for a well-deserved beer, his delight at their compliments oozing from every pore, his smile broadening, if that were possible.

'Thanks, guys.'

Abbie smiled when, minutes later, he drained his bottle of beer, stood up, and left them so he could hoover up the praise and accolades from the rest of his family and friends, clearly enjoying the sprinkle of stardust the evening had delivered. As she followed his progress around the room, she had to laugh when she caught sight of a glint of silver dangling on a chain around his neck. Despite this being a night of good food, good company, and great music, Dimitris had still felt the need to bring his beloved penknife along with him, which she suspected was more of a good luck charm.

'Felix, did you—'

Abbie stopped as her phone buzzed in her pocket, her heart giving a nip of pleasure when she saw the caller's name flash onto the screen. She quickly excused herself and left her seat to find a quieter spot to take the call.

'Hi, Emily.'

'Oh my God, Abbie, I'm just so excited! Guess what?'

'What?' Abbie smiled.

'Jacques' teenage niece, Sylvie, has just agreed to come over to the pâtisserie next month to spend some quality time with her extremely talented uncle before she starts her degree in medicine at La Sorbonne!'

Abbie scrunched her nose. 'Okay?'

'Which means he's agreed to let me have two weeks off, and, as I'm officially "resting" from my theatrical career until the beginning of November, it means that – if the offer's still open – I'll be landing on your doorstep ready to sample every Greek cocktail going!'

'Oh, Emily, that's amazing, of course the offer's still open. I can't wait to see you. In fact, you've just added the cherry to the top of a fantastic day!'

'Great, I've got lots to tell you, but I'll wait until I see you. *Ciao*, darling, or should I say *yassou*?'

'*Yassou*, Em,' said Abbie, then returned her phone to her

pocket, her spirits soaring at the news she would be seeing her best friend so soon.

Before returning to the table, where she could see Nikos and Rachel laughing at something Felix had just said, she paused to glance around the room. Every seat was taken up with not only Dimitris, and his band's, extended family and friends and their many children, but also a smattering of holidaymakers. The whole restaurant thrummed with a warm, happy vibe and she took a moment to send up a missive of gratitude to the director in charge of her destiny for leading her here, to this place, and this gorgeous Greek island where every day was filled with sunshine and laughter. She could truly say that she had never been happier.

And that was because of one person.

Nikos Angelopoulos; the man with the dark, smouldering eyes, the spiky mahogany hair and the mischievous grin, the man who had taught her that when the opportunity arises to step out of your comfort zone, you should just grab it and hold on for the ride, dealing with the lumps and bumps only when they arose, because you never know what the next day will bring. Life is a rollercoaster, and if there was one thing she had learned from her short time on Corfu, it was that happiness was not a distant destination you had to get to by whatever means, it was found on the journey, and in the people you met along the way.

And from now on, she would relish every step.

The End

Acknowledgements

First and foremost, I'd like to say a huge thank you to my amazing editor, Laura McCallen, whose skilful guidance and eagle eye has made Abbie and Nikos' story all the more vibrant and polished. I'd also like to thank Berni Stevens for the gorgeous, summery cover – I love all my covers, but I think this has to be one of my favourites.

The romance writing community continues to be a source of inspiration and support for me, and I thank each and every one of them – authors, bloggers, designers, social media gurus – for their kind words and encouragement. In particular, I'd like to thank Catherine Ferguson for her constant cheerleading and our brainstorming coffee mornings (with my favourite pineapple and coconut scones!) currently taking place outside.

And finally, a massive thank you to all my amazing readers! I have you in my mind and in my heart all the time I'm sitting at my keyboard, immersed in all-things Greek, trying to write the best story I can, hoping that I'm doing you proud.

Also by Daisy James

The Hummingbird Hotel series

Escape to the Hummingbird Hotel

Summer at the Hummingbird Hotel

Snowflakes at the Hummingbird Hotel

Spring Blooms at the Hummingbird Hotel

The Cornish Confetti Agency series

The Cornish Confetti Agency – *Caribbean Dreams*

Summertime at the Cornish Confetti Agency – *Festival Fiasco*

Christmas at the Cornish Confetti Agency – *Mistletoe Mayhem*

Tropical Skies at the Cornish Confetti Agency – *Caribbean Chaos*

Tuscan Dreams at the Cornish Confetti Agency – *Idyllic Italy*

A Summer Wedding at the Cornish Confetti Agency – *Seaside Surprises*

The Tuscan Dreams series

Wedding Bells at Villa Limoncello

Summer Dreams at Villa Limoncello

Christmas Secrets at Villa Limoncello

The Paradise Cookery School series

Sunshine & Secrets

Confetti & Confusion

Mistletoe & Mystery

Standalones:

The Summerhouse of Happiness

Christmas at the Dancing Duck

Sunshine After the Rain

There's Something About Cornwall

Lucie's Vintage Cupcake Company

If The Dress Fits

The Runaway Bridesmaid